THE FAMILY NEXT DOOR

CHARLOTTE STEVENSON

BLOODHOUND
— B O O K S —

For Hannah

"Believe nothing you hear, and only half that you see."

–Edgar Allan Poe

CHAPTER ONE

Viola scrambles around inside her handbag for her keys. Where did she put them? She is sure they were in her hand just a minute ago. Viola checks the floor and her pockets before making her way back outside. She must have dropped them on her way up the garden path. But then, how did she get into the house? Viola shakes her head at her own foolishness, before spotting her keys sticking out of the lock in the front door. Horrified at her unusual lack of care, she grabs them and promptly goes back inside to hang them on their usual hook. Her mind is all over the place at the moment. No particular reason, just the very fact of being on the wrong side of seventy and having to do and remember everything herself.

Viola chuckles at the thought of what her dear departed husband would say about her leaving the keys in the door. Martin has been gone for years, but she still carries him everywhere and will until her dying day.

The removal vans that were clogging up the street this morning have, thankfully, disappeared. Viola sneaks a glance out of the window at the house next door, hoping to catch sight of her new neighbours. She'll miss the lovely young couple who recently moved out and hopes the new arrivals will be just as friendly. She doesn't want to have to deal with tricky people now she's on her own. That sort of thing was always left to Martin.

Viola's feet are aching after a lovely but tiring afternoon shopping with her friends. She eases herself onto the sofa, rests her feet on the coffee table, closes her eyes, and wiggles her toes. She'll definitely sleep well tonight.

Viola hears voices outside. It sounds like a man and a woman. Curiosity wants her to get up and go to the window, but exhaustion and the comfiness of her sofa win. She can't make out any words, but their conversation sounds pleasant enough, and she will pop over later and say hello. Maybe even take them a little something. It never hurts to start out on the right foot with new neighbours.

Viola loves the peace and tranquillity of her home, and she could quite happily sit here for the rest of the evening. But the sun is starting to descend, and she would prefer not to introduce herself to the people next door after dark. It seems impolite somehow.

She forces herself up from the sofa and finds an unopened tin of shortbread in one of the kitchen cupboards. She checks the best before date and polishes the lid with the sleeve of her jumper. She squeezes her tired and swollen feet back into her sandals, then examines her appearance in the hallway mirror. Thankfully, she looks a lot less tired than she feels. Presentable and friendly. Perfect.

Viola knocks politely on the door of number 33. The couple who recently moved out – Kevin and Leo – had one of those awful camera doorbells. It always made her feel self-conscious, and she's glad to see they took it with them when they moved. There's the sound of footsteps followed by scraping and shuffling noises before the door opens, and a frazzled woman's face peers through. Her fair hair is pulled back in a messy bun, and her forehead is pricked with beads of sweat.

"Sorry." Her head disappears briefly, and Viola hears her grunting. Trying and failing to move whatever is preventing the door from opening fully. Eventually, she reappears, her cheeks pinker and face sweatier than before. "Sorry, I can't move these boxes." She gestures behind her, but the aforementioned boxes can't be seen through the small gap. Viola realises she probably should have left visiting until tomorrow. What was she thinking? Obviously, they will be up to their eyeballs on moving day.

"No, no, please don't worry. I just wanted to pop over and say hello. I'm Viola, I live next door."

The woman's eyes widen, and she gives a broad, welcoming smile before performing an impressive manoeuvre that involves sliding her slim body out through the tiny space in the doorway. She wipes her hands on her dusty jeans and mops her brow with her forearm.

"I'm not usually this sweaty and chaotic, I promise." She gives a small laugh and Viola manages to smile back at her, feeling worse by the second for intruding when they are clearly so busy. "It's lovely to meet you, Viola. I'm Wendy and my husband, Rhys, is somewhere in there, behind the millions of boxes." She puffs out air and playfully rolls her eyes. "I'm sure he'd love to meet you, but..."

"Oh, please don't worry. I just wanted to drop off a small gift to welcome you to the street." Viola holds out the shortbread, and Wendy looks genuinely touched by the gesture.

"Thank you so much. That's very kind. You should come over tomorrow for a cup of tea and a proper chat?" Wendy raises her eyebrows, turning the statement into a question.

"That sounds lovely, but only when you're settled and have

3

the time. I don't want to intrude. I know how much hard work moving house can be."

Wendy crosses her arms and leans against the door-frame. "Isn't it just! We've never moved house before, and I can't believe how much stuff we've got. But, anyway, definitely do come over tomorrow afternoon if you're free. I could use a break, and I'll be in on my own. Maybe you could tell me a bit about what the area's like. We haven't had a chance to look around yet and don't know anyone."

Viola's apprehension calms. Wendy seems completely genuine and an afternoon cuppa and a chat sounds nice. "In that case, I'd love to. I've lived here for over forty years, so I do know a thing or two, and I'd be more than happy to tell you all about our lovely village."

Wendy's eyes widen. "Wow, forty years. You must like it here. It's a date. Say twoish?"

Viola is about to agree when a loud crashing sound emanates from inside the house, followed by a few choice curse words in a deep voice.

Wendy grimaces comically and points over her shoulder. "I better go see what Rhys has broken."

Viola takes a step back and waves Wendy away. "Yes, absolutely. I hope he's okay and it's nothing too disastrous."

Wendy squeezes her way back into the house, wincing. "Yikes, I thought I was going to get stuck then. Bye, Viola. So nice to meet you, and thanks again for the welcome gift. Really lovely of you."

Wendy gives a final smile before closing the door, and Viola steps back and looks up at the house. Most of the rooms are lit up, and the windows are bare. She's sure she's got some spare curtains somewhere that could be of use. She'll try to dig them out tomorrow morning before meeting Wendy. Their house is a carbon copy of hers, so they should be the right size. Viola scans the windows quickly before her eyes stop on the one at the top right of the house. The smaller of the two bedrooms.

A small figure is standing there, watching her intently. They are barely moving, and their face is pressed up so close to the glass that a small fog appears with each breath they take. A faint light illuminates the room behind Viola's observer, and it appears to be a little girl of maybe seven or eight years old.

Viola remembers Wendy mentioning her husband. What was his name? Something Welsh sounding, she thinks. But she's sure Wendy didn't mention they had a daughter. That seems like a strange omission to make, particularly when she referenced her husband without being asked. Rhys. That was it.

She looks up at the window again, and the girl hasn't moved an inch. Something about her stillness and the fact she's occupying the darkest room in the house makes Viola feel uncomfortable. She folds her arms around herself to ward off the sudden chill that makes her body shudder unpleasantly.

Trying to shake off the peculiar trepidation she feels, Viola turns to walk back home. Wendy was preoccupied with unpacking and probably forgot to tell her about their daughter. Viola is sure she'll mention it tomorrow. In fact, the girl may even be in the house given it's the school summer holidays. She's just overthinking it.

Viola takes a quick look over her shoulder to check for the girl one last time. As she does, the child seems to jerk sharply before retreating slowly backwards. Viola is mesmerised by the girl's unusual movements, staccato and robotic, and not at all childlike.

Suddenly, the girl runs back towards the window, planting both her palms forcibly against the glass. Viola gasps and is jolted backwards by the abruptness and ferocity of the movement.

Viola's heart is in her mouth and her chest tightens, making her feel a little light-headed. She needs to get home and sit down. This sort of thing isn't good for her high blood pressure. Yet she finds herself unable to look away, and she watches, mesmerised, as the girl moves away from the window again.

Viola watches for a few more seconds, an eerie sensation crawling across her skin, but there is no further sign of the girl.

She ambles slowly back to her front door, grateful that Wendy and Rhys haven't seen her loitering outside their house longer than would be deemed polite. This time, she makes sure to lock and double-check the door. She can feel her nerves beginning to calm.

Sitting comfortably on her sofa, with the curtains closed and a cup of warm tea in her hand, Viola replays in her mind what she has just seen.

Viola and Martin agreed that having children wasn't something they wanted, but even so, Viola has always felt a fierce inner desire to protect and celebrate them. She followed this calling into a career in children's social care. After decades of working with families in need, she thought nothing could surprise her, yet here she sits, shaken and perturbed. Sipping her tea, she resolves to try and put it out of her mind. To be a neighbour. After all, she's not a social worker anymore, and she doesn't know anything about this new family. She mustn't judge. And she needs to keep her professional curiosity to herself. She's very aware that years of dealing with children and families who need support has skewed her view of the world.

Perhaps the little girl isn't happy about moving. Children don't often like change, and maybe she's just upset about having to leave her old home and her friends. Kids lash out when they're angry – she's seen that first-hand on many occasions. That could easily have been a one-off display of defiance. It's probably nothing.

As she drinks her tea, Viola attempts to quieten the gnawing uneasiness building in her chest. She needs to try and put it out of her mind. So Wendy didn't say she had a daughter. They only spoke for a few minutes, so there's no reason she should have mentioned the girl. But add to that the bizarre behaviour at the window – and it all seems a bit too peculiar to ignore. Plus, even from a distance, Viola felt something was not quite right about the girl. Something perturbing about her movements and the way she stared straight through her. Almost sinister.

Viola internally chastises herself for feeling that way about a young child. It's completely out of character for her. If anything, she's always fallen on the side of giving children too much leeway. She's sure that all of this will be sorted out after she visits Wendy tomorrow.

They are probably just a nice, normal family.

Viola most likely has too much time on her hands, is conjuring up old memories from previous cases, and is making up non-existent problems. She's taking two plus two and coming up with twenty-seven.

She sighs. It's times like this she misses Martin the most. He was her sounding board, the sensible one. He'd have talked her down in a minute, stopped her doing anything unwise, and halted the turning cogs in her overactive brain. She inhales deeply and tries to summon up Martin's calming energy. She has nothing to worry about. Tomorrow night, she'll be sitting here laughing to herself at how silly she was to think anything was amiss.

She's sure of it.

Almost sure, at least.

CHAPTER TWO

Viola isn't sure what to wear for her visit to Wendy's. She doesn't want to appear too formal and is aware that Wendy will likely be in attire best suited to unpacking boxes. She settles on a floral maxi dress and a thin cardigan. It's a beautiful day, and Viola loves anything with a bright, bold print.

She wishes they'd arranged to meet this morning. Time seems to be moving backwards, and she's done little more than wait. With two hours left, she decides she needs to get out of the house. She'll take a stroll to the shop, get some steps in, and soak up some much-needed vitamin D.

Viola grabs her sunglasses and makes sure she has her keys in her handbag. She leaves the house, taking a moment on her doorstep to appreciate the sunlight on her face. The smell of freshly cut grass is in the air, and she risks a quick glance over to Wendy's front garden.

The little girl from the window is sitting cross-legged on the grass, her back to Viola and her head bowed, her long blonde curls falling around her shoulders. If Viola had been introduced to her yesterday, she would go over and say hello, but given that she hasn't been made aware of the child's existence and Wendy is nowhere to be seen, she thinks it best to leave her be.

Viola walks quietly down her garden path. Something inside her doesn't want to alert the girl to her presence and, for a moment, she considers going back inside and exchanging her walk for sitting in her garden. Viola rolls her eyes at herself. She's being ridiculous. Too much time living alone with only her own needs to attend to. There is no need to avoid a little girl. She ignores the churning in her stomach and carries on walking.

Viola's heart drops and she stops in her tracks as the girl suddenly sits up straight. Viola stares, unmoving, as the girl begins to turn her head. The movement is slow and measured, at odds with the sudden jerky movements she observed last night. The girl's head continues to turn, until her body looks almost deformed. It shouldn't be humanly possible to turn one's head that far around. Viola gasps and continues to watch with morbid fascination. The girl's body still hasn't moved, and she peers at Viola through one eye, the other completely covered by her hair. Viola is frozen to the spot. Paralysed by the girl's eerie movements and penetrating stare. Her mouth is dry, and she desperately wants to run back inside.

The girl puts her hands on the ground and swivels her body around to join her head. One swift movement. She slowly pulls the hair back from her face, as though opening curtains. Viola doesn't think she has seen the girl blink yet. Abruptly, the girl's face becomes a huge, beaming smile. The smile didn't grow in size. It simply appeared – like turning on a light switch. Viola forces herself to smile back, grateful for the sunglasses hiding her eyes. Martin always told her that one look at her eyes showed the world exactly what she was thinking, and what she's thinking right now should definitely be kept to herself.

Viola walks reluctantly towards the girl, the only reasonable course of action she can think of, wishing she could turn on her heels and get as far away as possible instead.

"Hi, I'm Viola. I live next door." Viola points unnecessarily at her house.

The girl puts her hand to her face to shield her eyes from the sun and looks up at Viola's home. "Is that your bedroom?" Her voice is tinkly and light, almost sing-songy, and Viola's heart thuds faster as the girl points at what is indeed her bedroom.

"Er, yes. It is." She doesn't know what else to say.

"Oh, good. I'll remember that."

Viola is taken aback by the unusual, bordering on ominous, response, but the girl's demeanour remains airy and soft. The big smile still taking up most of her face.

Viola tries to change the subject. "How do you like your new home? I met your mummy yesterday." The girl's face instantly drops, and she mumbles something under her breath that Viola can't make out. "I'm sorry, dear, I didn't catch that." She takes a few steps forward, edging into their garden.

"My name is Mirabelle. Do you think that's a nice name?"

Initially taken aback by the bluntness of the question, Viola eventually manages to smile, grateful that she can answer honestly. "I think that's a beautiful name."

"Thank you. I like your name too. Viola." She says the name wistfully and stares off into the distance before returning to the moment and reaching behind her to pick something up. "Our garden has all of these yellow flowers. I like them. I think I'm going to put some in my room." Viola looks up to the window that Mirabelle crashed into the previous evening. "I'm sorry for banging at you. I like my windows open, and they were being mean." Mirabelle gestures aggressively towards the house, and a couple of buttercups fly out of her hand. She leaps up and grabs them, pulling them close to her.

Once again, Viola is convinced this child is behaving

unusually. Not least because she just referred to her parents as 'they' and in an overtly dismissive tone. She clears her throat and wrings her hands, trying to calm the unease she feels by simply being in Mirabelle's presence.

"That's okay, Mirabelle. It gave me a little shock, but not to worry." Viola laughs nervously, and Mirabelle gives no discernible reaction. "I'm coming to meet your mummy later. When I popped over yesterday, your mummy and daddy were very busy, so she invited me over today for a proper chat and a cup of tea." The feeling that she needs to justify herself to this small girl is strange – but present, nonetheless. The intimate, unblinking eye contact is making her squirm and she has to look away. As she looks down at her shoes, she spots something lying in the grass, and on closer examination, she sees that it's a very sharp pair of secateurs. These are definitely not the sort of thing a young girl should be left with unsupervised.

Viola bends down slowly to pick them up, her knees and back creaking and protesting. Before she can reach the handle, Mirabelle grabs them and flings them violently towards the house, grunting as she does so. The secateurs hit the front door with a thud and crash onto the front step, thankfully missing the small pane of glass towards the top of the door.

Viola is utterly astonished. Everything she has seen Mirabelle do so far completely baffles and alarms her.

Mirabelle looks up with wide, innocent eyes. "You can't have those. They're mine."

Viola struggles to regain her composure before finally constructing a sentence. "Oh, I don't want them. But they are very sharp, you know. Does your mummy know you have them?"

Mirabelle shrugs and flicks her hair in a way that makes her look disturbingly older than she appears. "She doesn't need to know because they're mine." Mirabelle smiles as though this is perfectly normal, and Viola is simply being silly and making a fuss about nothing.

Viola is beyond grateful to see Wendy open the front door. She has no idea how to respond to what Mirabelle has just said and doesn't want to spend any more time alone with her for fear of what she might do or say next. This tiny, cherubic-looking child is tying her up in knots and making her feel rather foolish.

Wendy looks down at the doorstep and picks up the secateurs, looking first at Mirabelle and then placing them on the outside window ledge. Her expression is unreadable. She checks her watch and looks questioningly at Viola, and before Wendy can ask why she is here so early, Viola speaks.

"I'm just popping to the shops. Can I get you anything?"

Wendy looks relieved. "Actually, some milk would be amazing. Thank you so much. I panicked when I saw you then. I thought time had completely run away from me."

Viola gives Wendy a sympathetic smile. "Beautiful day, isn't it? I thought I'd take a quick walk out before I come over."

Wendy mops her brow and looks up at the sky. There is not a cloud to be seen. "It definitely is a lovely day and I'm really looking forward to catching up later. Though I must warn you, the house is in total chaos."

Viola smiles and bats away Wendy's concerns. She can feel Mirabelle's gaze upon her, and not once has she turned towards or acknowledged her mother. Also, nothing has been mentioned about the secateurs, neither that they're clearly a dangerous implement for a child to have nor that they had been flung at the door. The dynamic is so odd, and the tension between mother and daughter hangs in the air like an unpleasant fog. Perhaps it's just that Wendy would prefer to talk to Mirabelle about it in private. Lots of people don't like disciplining their children in public these days.

"Mirabelle was just showing me the beautiful buttercups

she has found in your garden." Viola looks down at Mirabelle and sees that her fists are clenched tightly. The girl lifts up her right hand and slowly uncurls her fingers, revealing the squashed remnants of the buttercups before casually turning her hand over and letting them fall to the grass. A wave of embarrassment overcomes Viola, and she smiles apologetically at Wendy, although she's not sure what she has to feel embarrassed or sorry for.

Wendy's face is blank, there's not a shred of visible emotion. Viola wants to leave. Right this instant. Whatever this is, she doesn't want to be around it. Something about Mirabelle and her interactions, or lack of them, with her mother feels menacing, and Wendy's apathy is no less unnerving.

Viola does her best to appear relaxed. "Anyway, I best get going. I won't forget that milk." She waves at Wendy, who waves back, a small smile now on her face, before looking down at Mirabelle, who is still staring at her intensely. "I'll leave you with your mummy now. It was nice to meet you." Viola turns and walks away, her heart bouncing inside her ribcage. A gentle tap on her forearm gives her a start, and she almost yelps in surprise. Mirabelle is standing right next to her. This girl is going to be the death of her. How had she moved so silently?

Mirabelle is holding out a single buttercup, twirling it gently between her thumb and forefinger. Viola accepts the offering and looks back at Wendy, who is now smiling warmly at Viola.

"That's beautiful. Thank you, Mirabelle. Very kind." Mirabelle says nothing and continues to stand there as though waiting for Viola to do or say something else. She feels unkind for turning her back on the little girl, but after several excruciating seconds, Mirabelle still shows no signs of moving or looking away. "Well, I'll see you both later. Take care."

Viola makes to walk away, hoping there'll be no more interruptions to her attempts to leave. But just as she is about to take her first step, she hears a tiny whisper from Mirabelle. It is so quiet and soft there is no way Wendy would be able to hear the words.

"She's not my mummy."

Viola's blood freezes in her veins, but she forces herself to take a step and then another, pretending she hasn't heard. Thankfully, no more whispers or tugs on her arm materialise, and she walks for a few seconds before she risks a quick glimpse behind her. The garden of number 33 is now completely empty, and the door to the house is closed.

Wendy and Mirabelle are gone.

And so are the secateurs.

CHAPTER THREE

Viola walks along the road in a complete daze. Her head is swimming with thoughts of Mirabelle and what the girl has just revealed.

"She's not my mummy."

There was no mistaking what she had said. Yes, her voice was barely a whisper, but it was as clear as day. There is a small wooden bench around the corner, overlooking the playground. Viola only needs to make it fifty yards or so until she can sit out of sight of number 33 and attempt to digest it all. Her feet are heavy, and the previously pleasant sunlight feels oppressive. Sweat trickles down her back, and her dress is sticking to her skin uncomfortably. If it wasn't for Wendy's request for milk, Viola would undoubtedly loop back around and sneak into her house.

When Viola makes it to the bench, her head is foggy, and a headache is blooming at the base of her skull. She places her handbag on the bench, her hands trembling, praying nobody will sit beside her and attempt small talk. Normally, she would welcome the opportunity to sit and shoot the breeze with a friendly stranger, but she's not sure she could have a normal conversation just now.

Viola sits and plays the events back in her mind. Is she making too much of this? Her whole life, and despite what she did for a living, she has been told by friends and family that because she doesn't have children of her own, she doesn't understand. And while she has never attempted to offer advice or comment on her loved one's children or how they are raised, they have made it abundantly clear that it would be most unwelcome if she did. In a way, she feels that stance is entirely justified. Instead, she has always offered support and been a sympathetic ear to the frazzled and frustrated parents she has known, which has always been gratefully accepted. But this feels different. There's something not right here, and it's different to anything she has ever seen before. Viola feels it deep down in her soul.

She can hear Martin's voice inside her head. "*Leave it alone, Viola.*" She knows that's precisely what she should do.

Still, there is something niggling at Viola. A partially formed thought that keeps trying to get her attention. It's not simply what Mirabelle said or even the unusual way she behaved. It's not just that Wendy didn't mention her daughter yesterday evening, either. It's not even that all of these occurrences together feel greater than the sum of their parts. There's something else about the whole set-up that's completely off-kilter. Viola closes her eyes and takes a deep breath. She empties her head of conscious thought and focuses on the present moment. She listens to the cars and footsteps and breathes deeply and purposefully. A dog barks in the distance, and she hears a jogger's feet pounding the pavement on the other side of the street. She absorbs the feeling of the here and now. Forcing any nagging questions away as soon as they try to enter her mind. She sits like this for a few minutes and feels her body begin to relax. Her burgeoning headache starts to wane, and her mind becomes calmer and clearer.

And then it comes to her. It doesn't hit her like a lightning bolt, but rather a gradual sense of realisation. Not once did either Wendy or Mirabelle acknowledge each other. They didn't speak, and they didn't exchange smiles or gestures of any kind. They only existed in the same space. Wouldn't it be normal for Wendy to have spoken to Mirabelle when she opened the door? Shouldn't she have questioned Mirabelle about the bang on the door that alerted her? She didn't even seem bothered that Mirabelle had been playing with a sharp garden tool, never mind that she had flung it at the house. Those individual occurrences are definitely unsettling, but the fact that they didn't behave like mother and daughter or act like they even saw each other chills Viola to the bone.

"She's not my mummy."

Milk in hand, Viola knocks on Wendy's door. She has given herself a stern talking-to on the journey back from the shop. This will be the last invitation she will accept from Wendy, and she doubts that Rhys will offer more than a perfunctory hello if their paths cross. She will have a quick cup of tea, make her excuses, and go home. All she needs to do is be polite. She won't ask any unnecessary questions, and then she'll simply leave them to get on with their lives. How they choose to do that is none of her business. Mirabelle is clearly a healthy, thriving little girl. Viola prides herself on her non-judgemental attitude, and this situation should be no different.

Wendy opens the door and steps back to let Viola inside. "Keep your shoes on, Viola. It's dusty, and there are bits and pieces everywhere." Viola nods and follows Wendy through to the kitchen.

Viola is surprised and impressed by the lack of clutter and chaos. They've barely been here a day and it's already looking like they've finished unpacking.

"Wow, Wendy. You've done a lot in such a short space of time."

Wendy beams. "If I don't get on with it right away, then I'll lose the will. I wanted to get the downstairs feeling somewhat normal as soon as possible." Wendy yawns. "Sorry, I didn't get much sleep last night."

Viola senses an opportunity. "I can imagine. Well, don't worry. I certainly won't keep you long."

Wendy pulls out a dining chair for Viola and then another for herself. "No, please do. I'm desperate for a break and someone to talk to."

Viola smiles, internally disappointed at the failure of her attempt at an early escape. The house is very quiet, and she has to hold herself back from asking where Mirabelle is. She needs to stick to the plan and keep her curiosity under wraps. No unneeded questions.

The dining chair is made of shiny white plastic. It doesn't have legs like a regular chair. It's a weird Z-shape and doesn't look entirely structurally sound. Viola sits tentatively and is surprised at how sturdy it actually is. The tempered glass tabletop is set with white marble placemats, and both a tea and coffee pot are set up with sleek white china cups and saucers.

Viola takes a moment to scan the room. Everything is highly stylised, and the whole room has a cold, clinical feel. This does not look like an environment conducive to a child.

"Tea? Coffee?"

Viola is pulled back into the moment. "Oh yes, tea, please. Just milk. Sorry, I was just looking around. It's all very impressive." Viola tries to sound light and breezy, but her underlying nerves are making her behave as though she's in a job interview.

Wendy starts to pour. "Thank you. Almost all of our furniture is new. We wanted to make this house our own. Rhys and I are lucky that we have very similar tastes."

Viola nods and takes a biscuit off the plate offered up by Wendy and places it on her saucer.

"This table is really something." Viola traces her finger along the metal edge surrounding the perfect glass.

"Oh, I know, I love it. It's a bit of an indulgence but we couldn't help ourselves."

Viola watches Wendy's face carefully as she speaks. It's easy to scrutinise her without being noticed as she barely makes eye contact. In fact, she looks everywhere in the room except at Viola. Viola considers herself to be a pretty good judge of character and it is painfully obvious that Wendy is uncomfortable. It's as though she's trying too hard to convince Viola of her happiness, but her words come across as insincere, and it is painfully obvious she is not at home in this environment.

Despite her promises to herself, now she's actually sitting here, Viola can't continue to have a conversation with this woman who hasn't yet acknowledged her child. It's beyond weird, and if Viola plans to distance herself from this family after today, she needs to put her mind at rest. Plus, in Viola's experience, parents can't help themselves when it comes to telling stories about their children. They're usually falling over themselves to tell all about little Jonny's latest achievement or share a humorous anecdote that really isn't funny at all.

Viola continues to try to keep her tone light and breezy. "This glass won't look like this for long with Mirabelle around. I imagine it will be covered in scratches and pen marks before you know it." Viola hopes her comment sounds light-hearted and jovial, but she sees Wendy tense up immediately. Her body language becoming closed and defensive.

For the first time since they sat down together, the two women lock eyes. It is brief and fleeting, but something passes between them. Viola sits back in her seat and crosses her legs. What was that? She continues to study Wendy's face. The woman is clearly trying to convey something silently. But why? There's nobody else here. What possible reason could there be for Wendy refusing to speak? Viola can't decipher the look Wendy's giving her. Is she trying to warn her off? Or is it more like a plea? A plea to stop asking about Mirabelle. To change the subject.

They've been sitting in silence for a bizarre amount of time now and the atmosphere is becoming increasingly uncomfortable. If Wendy didn't want Viola to ask questions about their family life, why would she have invited her over so readily? Viola refuses to fill the silence. She needs to see what Wendy will say to her comment about the table. Eventually, Wendy readjusts her position, leaning back and thankfully appearing more welcoming. It feels forced, and Viola is no fool, but she can at least appreciate the effort.

"She chose that name, you know. Mirabelle." Viola scrunches her eyebrows together but waits for Wendy to elaborate further. "When she was born, I called her Isabelle. But now she insists on Mirabelle." Wendy shrugs her shoulders. "I tried to make a compromise and call her Belle, but that didn't go down well."

Viola knows it's not unheard of for children to create alternative names for themselves, and she is relieved Wendy said something to break the tension.

"Oh, okay. Both beautiful names in any case." What else is there to say to that?

Viola watches as Wendy moves to pick up her cup. Her hand trembles so violently that she immediately puts it down, removes a cloth napkin from a silver ring, and wipes her hands.

"Anyway, you said you had some good insider info on the local area. I'd love to hear all about it." It's as though a switch has been flicked in Wendy. She has snapped back into conversation mode, all the nervousness and unease immediately lifting from the woman's face. The wall is back down and Viola is looking at the same woman who met her at the door yesterday evening. Affable, friendly, an outwardly perfect neighbour. Viola takes a sip of her tea, happy that Wendy has at least recognised Mirabelle's existence, even if it was only to unnecessarily explain her name. There is a lot more Viola would like to know, but she suspects it would be like getting blood out of a stone.

"Yes, of course. Have you managed to go out for a walk or anything yet?"

Wendy exhales with relief at the accepted change in conversation. "No, not yet. I haven't left the house since we arrived." She tries for a small laugh, and Viola smiles back at her.

"Well, in that case, I'll–" Viola is cut off by the abrupt, silent intrusion of Mirabelle. She is suddenly standing right next to Viola's left shoulder. Her posture is straight as an arrow, with her hands behind her back, like a soldier standing to attention. Viola turns her head to greet her. Mirabelle certainly does not have her mother's apparent issues with eye contact. She is staring right into Viola's eyes. Not a hint of discomfort at their close proximity. Viola shifts in her chair, turning her body towards the small girl and simultaneously pushing her chair back to create space between them. Instantly, Mirabelle takes a step forward, filling the space Viola had made, her legs almost touching Viola's knees. It feels horribly awkward, but if she were to move back again, the girl may take offence or, more likely, take another step towards her.

Viola stays where she is and gives Mirabelle a warm smile. "Well, hello, dear." She doesn't want to get into any confusion around names, so she sticks to a term of endearment instead. "It's lovely to see you again. How are you?"

Mirabelle doesn't answer. Instead, she extracts one of her hands from behind her back and places it only a couple of inches from Viola's face. Her hand is wrapped in what must be an entire roll of toilet paper. It is secured messily with several pieces of Sellotape and looks like a white boxing glove. Viola flinches and turns to Wendy, fully expecting her to intervene and find out what on earth the girl has been doing. Instead, Wendy is scowling at Mirabelle, her eyes burning ferociously into her daughter. As soon as Wendy notices Viola's attention is on her and no longer on her daughter, she quickly rearranges her facial expression, and an air of calm and concerned parent appears on her face. Mirabelle's gaze never leaves Viola, and she waves the home-made boxing glove back and forth in front of her face like a pendulum.

Viola needs to figure out what to do or say. This may be the strangest situation she has ever found herself in, and that's saying something.

Thankfully, Wendy finally breaks the silence and asks the obvious question. "What have you done to your hand?"

Mirabelle ignores her and continues to swing her hand, all the while staring at Viola. An unsettling grin now on her face.

The mounting pressure and an insatiable need to know what on earth is going on forces Viola to speak. "What's this, sweetheart?" Viola reaches out her hand towards the girl and almost touches the surface of the toilet-paper glove before Mirabelle whips it away and puts both hands behind her back again. The little girl's eyes move slowly and decisively towards

Wendy, the hideous grin still plastered onto her otherwise cherubic face. Wendy's mouth is fixed into a straight, tight line, her cheek muscles visibly twitching. Viola can't decide if it's a face of anger, fear, or embarrassment. Perhaps all three.

Mirabelle walks behind Viola's chair towards Wendy. Viola twists her head and follows the girl's every movement. Her steps are small and silent. Viola can only see Mirabelle's face in profile now and she's holding her breath, waiting to see what the girl will do next. She has no idea what to expect. Nothing that has happened in the brief time she has known Mirabelle has been predictable. The suspense is killing her.

Mirabelle provides the answer in her usual tinkling, childlike tone. "My finger got cut off. So, I stuck it back on and wrapped it up. Look, all fixed."

She brandishes her wrapped hand first in front of Wendy and then swings it towards Viola. All of the blood drains out of Wendy's face, and she leaps to her feet. Viola feels utterly frozen to the spot, still trying to comprehend what Mirabelle has just said. Surely, this is just a prank. But what if it isn't? Viola detests the sight of blood and can't bear the thought of seeing Mirabelle's possibly amputated finger. She knows she has to help, but the very idea is making her horribly nauseated. A cold sweat breaks out on her forehead. Wouldn't the girl be crying in pain if any of this were true? And wouldn't there be blood seeping through the toilet paper? Viola's stomach flips, and a more intense surge of nausea hits her.

Before Wendy can reach Mirabelle, the girl sprints out of the room and starts running up the stairs, singing as she goes. Viola recognises the song – a nursery rhyme, she thinks, and her blood runs cold.

"Mummy finger, Mummy finger, where are you? Here I am, here I am. How do you do?"

Viola turns, her mouth agape, her voice lost, and stares at

Wendy. Tears are pricking the horrified woman's eyes. Wendy wipes her face with her sleeve and chokes on her words as she speaks.

"Could you see yourself out? I'll sort everything. Please don't worry."

Don't worry! What else is there to do in such a situation other than worry? Viola is dumbfounded. Shouldn't one of them be calling an ambulance or something? Wendy staggers out of the room and throws the front door open before bounding up the stairs. Viola sits, momentarily stunned, feeling that if she stands up right away, she'll almost certainly faint. She grabs a spoon, dumps two large sugars into her tea, stirs it, and gulps it down, grateful that it has cooled enough to prevent her mouth from burning. After a few deep breaths, Viola gets slowly to her feet. She takes one last look around the sparse and unwelcoming kitchen and makes her way towards the front door.

Upstairs is eerily quiet. Not a sound. No sign of any frantic phone calls to the hospital, no noises to suggest that Wendy is checking on Mirabelle. Not a word. Not a footstep. Not a single indication of movement of any kind. Viola knows that she shouldn't just leave. This is an emergency. She should stay and make sure Mirabelle is okay, that Wendy is okay too, and is taking all the necessary steps to ensure Mirabelle's hand is taken care of. But Viola longs for her home. She longs to sit in her living room and switch off from all this madness. It is all far, far too much for her to contend with. She has no role to play here. She left all of that behind a long time ago. She is just their neighbour – nothing more. She doesn't know these people, and from what she's seen so far, she'd like to keep things that way.

And so, she walks out of the door, closes it behind her, and presses on towards home.

She doesn't look back.

CHAPTER FOUR

Viola walks straight into the kitchen and grabs the first glass she can find in the cupboard. She pours a very generous measure of bourbon, not caring when she sloshes some on the kitchen worktop. She rarely drinks and knows this will knock her out. Her mind is too critical and questioning when awake, and she has always benefited from the old adage of 'sleep on it' when sorting out problems and straightening out her thoughts.

Wearily, she takes the tumbler of liquor up to her bedroom and closes the curtains, noticing that there is still no discernible movement or sound from next door. This is not her problem. She needs to separate herself from whatever issues there are in that family. It won't be good for her to get involved. Viola flings her dress onto the floor and pulls on her pyjamas before propping herself up in bed and taking a long sip of her drink. The fiery sensation in her throat provides a welcome hit of relaxation that envelops her. She sips slowly until the entire glass is empty, relishing the woozy feeling the alcohol brings. Finally, she pulls on her silk hair wrap and burrows into the covers, blocking out the world, banishing this hideous afternoon, and falling into a hazy dream world.

When Viola wakes up, her mouth is dry. It takes her a few moments to orient herself and remember why she is in bed at this time of day. She gives her creaking joints time to lubricate, stretching out each limb slowly and edging herself carefully up the bed. As always, sleep has performed its magic, lined up her thoughts, and banished the irrationality. There is nothing for her to be concerned or apprehensive about. She was simply an observer. If anyone should be feeling uncomfortable about what occurred, it should be Wendy, not her. And while she hopes that Wendy doesn't feel that way, it is not her business one way or the other.

There is still a hint of sunlight sneaking through the curtains, and Viola surmises it must be early in the evening. Sleep will be difficult tonight after a long afternoon nap, but at least her night won't be filled with anxiety. She reaches out for her robe from the back of the door and wraps it around herself. She won't be going out again today, and getting dressed seems pointless. She sniffs and makes her way to the window. The room needs airing to get rid of the lingering smell of alcohol. When she opens the curtains, she is greeted by Mirabelle standing outside, still as a statue, looking up at the window in anticipation. Viola does a double take. How long has she been standing there? And why haven't Wendy or Rhys noticed their daughter is standing on her lawn?

Mirabelle raises her arm up in the air. The makeshift bandage remains on her hand, but the Sellotape appears to have been removed, and a short length of toilet paper is now dangling down, swinging softly in the summer breeze. Mirabelle takes her other hand and begins to unwind the bandage. Viola's hand flies up to her mouth, and she wills herself to move away from the window, but her feet remain rooted to the spot. The girl continues to unwind it, a puddle of toilet paper forming at her feet, which Viola now notices are bare. Not one part of her wants to see what horror lies beneath the toilet paper, but she can't make herself look away. She continues to gawp with morbid fascination, her heart rate escalating as the layers covering the girl's hand fall away.

Viola feels the bourbon threatening to make its way back up her throat, and she clamps both hands to her mouth, fighting down the waves of panic and nausea crashing through her. She imagines the poor girl's bloody, disfigured hand, and tears prick her eyes. Finally, the last of the toilet paper falls to the ground, and Mirabelle holds both of her hands up to Viola, palms facing forwards. Viola almost sinks to the floor with relief to see the girl wriggle ten perfectly intact digits. She stares in amazement and confusion as Mirabelle jumps up and down giddily, waving both her hands in the air. In a final flourish, she gives an exaggerated bow, as though she had just been the star of a Broadway show, and runs back towards her house. Before entering, she turns back to face Viola and sticks her tongue out.

Viola remains standing – stunned, lost for words, and unable to comprehend why the girl would do something so cruel and unusual. Conflicting emotions whirl around inside her. None of this makes any sense.

She pulls the curtains closed, sits down on her bed, and lets the tears come.

CHAPTER FIVE

MIRABELLE

I hope the lady next door doesn't feel bad. I only did what I did to embarrass Wendy, and I thought it was funny. The lady seems nice, and I like her name. Viola is a much prettier name than Wendy. I could see how much Wendy wanted to impress Viola, so I thought I'd just do a little joke, but I'm not sure Viola found it funny. Even when I showed her I was actually fine and did a little performance for her, she didn't look happy. I feel a bit bad about that. I'll pick her some more of those pretty yellow flowers tomorrow and maybe draw her a nice picture. She'll like that.

I probably shouldn't have told Viola that Wendy wasn't my mummy. I reckon Daddy'll get really mad at me about that. But Viola won't tell anyone. I can see she likes me, and once I apologise for the cutting-off-my-finger joke, I think we'll be good friends.

I hate this new house. It's way too small and I want to go home. Daddy says we'll be home before I know it, but that makes no sense. I know it now, and I'm still here. Plus, waiting is boring and I miss my friends.

Daddy promised me that if I'm good and I'm nice to Wendy, we'll be able to go home a lot quicker. Can't he see I'm trying? But she's not nice to me, so why should I be nice to her?

Everything would be so much better if she wasn't here.

CHAPTER SIX

Viola finally managed to fall asleep with the help of another large measure of bourbon, but that will be the last time she relies on alcohol before bed. She knows these things become habits, and she won't go down that road.

She's groggy when she wakes but is resolved to move on from yesterday's events. There are plenty of neighbours with whom she has little to no contact. Their lives are none of her business. Wendy, Rhys, and Mirabelle will be just another family in the street. They can get on with their lives and nothing else needs to be said. They owe her no explanations. Viola refuses to feel uncomfortable in her own house and won't hide from them. This area was her home long before they arrived.

Although she'd give anything to have Martin back with her, she loves her life. She has friends that she meets regularly and has always enjoyed her own company: happy to spend hours alone reading or crocheting. This morning is her fortnightly brunch meeting with her old work colleagues from the council. Viola hasn't worked there for years, but their friendships have stood the test of time. The nature of the work they did bonded them, and the ladies were a huge source of support when

THE FAMILY NEXT DOOR

Martin died. Her routine matters to her, and she won't have it disrupted by whatever issues are happening with the family next door.

Viola takes her time getting ready. She carefully applies make-up to hide the dark circles under her eyes and highlights her best features. Once ready, she sees she has about twenty minutes before needing to take the short walk to the café and pulls out her crochet bag from behind the living-room sofa. She reckons she's got enough time to complete another granny square for her blanket.

A knock at the door startles and surprises her. An unsolicited knock is a rarity, and Viola knows this is likely to be Wendy, Mirabelle or, even worse, both.

Her first thought is to ignore them and continue with her crocheting. But she promised herself that she would not hide away. She can handle this, and perhaps it's actually an opportune moment to set out her stall and show them she's not interested in having a relationship with them. She injects confidence into her stride and walks towards the door, a welcoming, but not too welcoming, smile on her face. As expected, Wendy stands on her front step, a small bouquet of flowers in her hand. Her eyes are full of sorrow, and the last thing Viola wants to get into is a lengthy, drawn-out apology or explanation.

"Good morning, Wendy. How are you?" Although her tone is polite and genial she doesn't move to let her in. "I was just on my way out to meet friends, so I'm afraid I can't talk for long."

Wendy surreptitiously looks over Viola's shoulder at her crocheting, a suspicious and almost cross look falling across her face. Viola opens her mouth to explain but thinks better of it. Why should she? Instead, she gives her a thin smile. Wendy twists her face back into the doleful expression that greeted

Viola when she opened the door. It's creepy to watch and only increases her distrust of this woman.

"Er, I just wanted to give you these." Wendy thrusts the bouquet rather too forcefully, and they flatten against Viola's chest. "Oh, sorry. I'm a little nervous about seeing you after... well, yesterday."

Viola takes the flowers and brushes down the front of her blouse. "It's no problem. And you didn't have to do this." Viola looks down at the flowers and back to Wendy with a smile. She doesn't want to add anything further or invite her to elaborate. Wendy's coldness towards her own child has irked her. Even when behaving badly, in fact, especially when behaving badly, children need love and acknowledgement from their parents.

Viola takes a step back. "Well, as I said, I've got to be going. The flowers are lovely, and it's very kind of—"

Wendy interrupts Viola's attempt to end the conversation. "Belle's hand wasn't actually hurt. She was just playing a game. I know that seems weird, but kids always do things like that."

Wendy's eyes are pleading, and Viola knows she should throw the woman a bone and agree with her, insisting that it's not a problem and she completely understands. But Viola is nobody's fool and is, quite frankly, insulted by Wendy's attempts to brush this under the carpet as normal child behaviour. Children do not *always* do things like that.

"Yes, I know she wasn't hurt." Wendy's eyes widen. "I know because she stood on my lawn yesterday evening and unwrapped her hand while staring through my window."

"She did?" To her credit, Wendy looks shocked and appalled.

"Yes, she did. Perhaps it might be a good idea to keep a closer eye on her." This is a challenging and potentially insulting statement, but still, she feels it is fair and perhaps this might be an alternative way to separate herself from Wendy and her family.

Wendy looks taken aback. "Look, I'm sorry she did that. But we do keep an eye on her. We knew she was playing in the garden and were just about to call her back inside for supper. So please don't think that–"

Viola holds up her hand. She has lots that she would like to say. For a start, Mirabelle was not playing in their garden, she was in Viola's garden. Plus, it's not the first time the girl has been left unsupervised, and they've barely been here a couple of days. But she has had enough. She wants Wendy to go away so she can head out and enjoy some time with her friends.

"Look, Wendy, you don't need to explain. It's fine. But really, I need to be getting on." Viola reaches for the door with her free hand, the flowers now dangling unceremoniously from the other. She's not sure she could make it any clearer that their conversation is over.

Wendy's shoulders drop, and she gives a resigned look. "Okay, well, perhaps you could come over again sometime, and we could finish our chat? Hopefully, next time we won't be interrupted."

Wendy attempts to laugh, but Viola is not in the mood. "Thanks for the offer, but I'm quite busy at the moment, and I'm sure you've got lots to do getting the house sorted." She gives Wendy a pinched smile and watches her closely. She seems to shrink in front of her. First seeming embarrassed and then sadder and more desperate.

"Okay, I understand. But can I just say one more thing? Then I'll go, I promise."

"Of course."

Wendy swallows uncomfortably, and tears fill her eyes. Viola's heart softens a little.

"It's just that... Belle isn't like other girls. She's... different."

33

A look of guilt and anguish falls over Wendy's face. "And I don't mean that in a negative way. It's just that... what I'm trying to say is..." Wendy is rambling now, but Viola can sense the sincerity in her garbled attempts at an explanation. She finally takes a deep breath and settles herself. "It's not easy for me, and I'm trying my best with the hand I've been dealt." Wendy's eyes fill, and a lump forms in Viola's throat, watching the vulnerability before her.

Despite her better judgement, Viola yields, reconciling that she is perhaps being too harsh. Wendy is clearly struggling, and if Mirabelle's behaviour was upsetting to Viola, she can only imagine how it must feel for Wendy as her mother. Viola steps forward and places her hand on Wendy's shoulder.

"Okay. I can see you could do with a friendly ear. Tomorrow, perhaps?"

Wendy's face lights up. "Great. That would be great." Wendy turns to leave, a different woman than she was mere seconds ago. "Anyway, I must get back and check on Belle. I hope you have a lovely morning and thank you for understanding."

Viola waves Wendy off and closes her door, irritated with herself for not sticking to her guns, but also feeling like she has made the right call. Wendy clearly needs some support and just because she is retired, that doesn't mean Viola no longer cares about families and their well-being. Ignoring a very obvious cry for help and support is not very neighbourly. She'll give Wendy another chance. It's the right thing to do. Plus, she's barely seen hide nor hair of Rhys, and it would be good to see what he's like.

When Kevin and Leo lived next door, they would occasionally help Viola with the odd DIY task. She considers herself relatively self-sufficient, but it doesn't hurt to have the option of help if she needs it.

She takes one last look in the mirror and heads out of the

door. Her stomach is grumbling and if she walks quickly, she'll only be a few minutes late. She glances at number 33 as she walks down her path. It's easy to see through the curtainless living-room window. Wendy is sitting on the sofa, her head in her hands.

What this woman needs is support, not judgement.

And Viola will do her best to help.

CHAPTER SEVEN

Viola returns from brunch full of food and mirth. Her friends never fail to brighten her spirits and, as usual, they shared stories and laughed until their sides ached and tears fell. Getting older doesn't mean you have to act older, and Viola will always be grateful for the many meaningful connections she has in her life. Long may it continue.

As she turns the corner into her street she notices two cars on the drive of Wendy and Rhys's house. One is the large blue car she saw on the evening they moved in. The other is one she doesn't recognise. It's more a jeep than a car, a Land Rover perhaps. It is army green in colour and looks more suited to driving across rough terrain than suburban streets. Viola can just make out two figures sitting in the front seats, their heads turned towards one another in intimate discussion. As she gets closer, she sees that the man in the passenger seat is the same age as Wendy and she assumes this must be the elusive Rhys. Viola slows her pace and pulls out her phone, stopping and scrolling for a few minutes, hoping she'll time things right to meet Rhys as he exits the car.

The other man looks considerably older, more Viola's age.

She is about to give up and simply walk towards her house when the two men exit the car in unison. They are dressed in impeccable black suits and have an air of importance and wealth. The man she assumes to be Rhys looks at her briefly, then quickly returns his eyes to the other man before Viola can raise a hand in greeting. The older man walks towards Wendy's front door and knocks while the younger man walks around the car to open both rear doors before standing to attention at the back of the vehicle. His movements are very formal and precise. Perhaps not Rhys then, maybe a driver. Although it's definitely an odd choice of vehicle for a private hire.

Viola can't drag out her entrance to her house any longer, so she quickly unlocks her door, enters and climbs up her stairs as briskly as possible. The small bedroom at the front provides the perfect vantage point to watch without being seen, and she tucks in behind the curtain, out of sight but still with a clear, unobstructed view. The door to number 33 is open now, and the older man continues to wait. Mirabelle suddenly flies out of the house and crashes into his legs, wrapping her arms around him tightly. She is dressed in a very formal black long-sleeved dress and her hair is pulled back neatly into a bun. Despite her enthusiasm for her visitor, her appearance is uncharacteristically sombre, and she looks much older than usual, almost improperly so.

Wendy soon follows Mirabelle out of the house. Her outfit and hairstyle are identical to her daughter's and her head is bowed. The whole scene makes Viola's flesh crawl. Neither of the men communicate with Wendy, and she slips into the back of the car before the younger man closes the door and returns to the passenger seat. If that is Rhys, his perfunctory attitude and lack of warmth toward his wife are weird, to say the least. Mirabelle is chatting away with the older gentleman, and they hold hands as he leads her to the open rear door. He lifts her gently in, fastens her seat belt, then takes his own seat behind the wheel. He's very limber for his age and Viola can't help but admire him. He's undoubtedly a handsome man. Viola watches as they drive away.

While nothing was overtly wrong with what she has just witnessed, the whole thing leaves her feeling discomfited. There's just something not quite right, something Viola can't quite put her finger on. Of course, she understands that many families have dynamics that others might find unrelatable – she's not entirely out of touch. But this is more than that. Something is going on here, and although she wishes she could just leave it all alone and stop being so bloody nosy, she knows she can't. There is an air of danger about that family and that house, and Viola can't help feeling worried about Mirabelle. She is only a little girl, so she won't necessarily be aware of behaviour in her family that is unacceptable, especially if that's all she's ever experienced. Viola sits on her bed and tries to devise some reassuring explanations to assuage her uncomfortable feelings.

The older man was clearly very dear to Mirabelle, so it's likely that he is her grandfather. If the other man is Rhys, then it would make sense that he and his own father came by to pick up Wendy and Mirabelle for a family outing of some kind. An outing where they all have to dress very demurely and dark. What on earth could that be?

Ah – a funeral, of course. That must be it. Viola feels a little silly for not realising right away. They were all dressed in black, and Wendy in particular looked very doleful. Maybe one of her family members or close friends has died. But then, don't funerals take several days or even a week to organise? So that would mean the person died before they moved in and that definitely doesn't fit with Wendy's behaviour during their previous conversations.

Viola's wildly overthinking things again. She knows all too well that you can't judge a person's behaviour after someone they love has died. Everyone reacts differently, and if Wendy lost someone dear to her at the time they had planned a house move, she can imagine how stressful and traumatic that would be. She'll definitely go over and see Wendy tomorrow. Not to be nosy. No, just to offer a friendly ear and the opportunity to open up if she wants to. Plus, they'd already made an informal agreement to get together, which works perfectly.

Viola spends the rest of the afternoon tending to her front garden. Not because that will allow her to be there if they return. Not at all. The front garden is in desperate need of some TLC, that's all. Viola looks down at her lawn, and as she does, she notices something out of the corner of her eye. A little jolt of excitement bubbles within her. Wendy and Rhys's front door is open. They must have forgotten to lock it. Now this is something Viola can't ignore. It's her duty as a good citizen to ensure her neighbour's house remains secure. Anyone could waltz right in and take whatever they want. Viola won't let that happen. She'll go and close it, and if it's a door that needs a key rather than one that locks when you pull it shut, she'll wait in her garden until they return.

Viola definitely won't go inside. She mustn't.

Even if this is the perfect opportunity to find out exactly what is going on at number 33.

No, that would be wrong.

CHAPTER EIGHT

Cautiously, Viola scans the street before she leaves her garden. Some kids are playing at the bottom of the road, but they are engrossed in their game of football. And in any case, once you hit a certain age, you somehow become invisible to the younger generation.

Viola walks next door, trying to maintain a casual air despite the anxiety she is actually feeling. The door is still open, and the absence of a handle means it is indeed the kind that will lock itself if pulled. A stab of disappointment hits her, and she finds herself delaying closing it. She waits for a moment, contemplating her options. The only sensible action is to shut the door and return to her house. Perhaps push a note through the letter box, letting the family know what happened. After all, leaving the front door unlocked is exceptionally careless.

Viola has a sudden, unnerving thought. What if they did this on purpose? Could they be testing her to see if she's trustworthy? She dismisses it immediately. What a ridiculous, self-important thing to think. Obviously, they were just distracted. Nobody would leave their door ajar on purpose. But what if they did close it and the latch isn't working properly?

That's certainly possible, and if that's the case, then Viola should probably go inside and check. The last thing she wants is to think she's left the house safe and secure only for there to be a fault with the latch. What if someone broke in? She'd feel terrible. Yes, she'll quickly pop in. Close it from the inside and ensure that all is well, then she'll leave and shut the door as planned.

The door closes and locks itself without issue, yet Viola finds herself lingering again. It can't hurt to take a little look around the ground floor. Maybe in their haste, they left the keys behind. Viola doesn't want to lock the house up if the only set of keys is inside. They'd need to call a locksmith, and they don't need extra stress when they've just moved in.

She hears Martin's voice chiding her. *"Just admit you want to be nosy. Stop making up all these daft excuses."* Viola knows he is correct. She is exquisitely curious about this family. She bats Martin away and walks toward the kitchen.

If Viola didn't know better, she wouldn't believe they had just moved into the house. In fact, she would think no one lived here. There's a sense of order and a feeling that everything has its place. No partially unpacked or empty boxes are visible, and every surface is sparkling clean. There is a mild hint of bleach in the air.

Viola ambles around the kitchen island, searching the worktop for any sign of the keys. They are not here. There's virtually nothing here. It's a show home. She watches her reflection in the sleek white kitchen cabinets. She should go home. She has no right to be here.

She peers around the corner into the living room as she makes her way toward the front door. It is more of the same. Two white fabric sofas face each other with a glass-topped coffee table between them. A modern ceramic vase sits precisely in the middle of the table. But there are no flowers. A colourful bouquet would be the perfect thing to brighten up this cold room. Perhaps Viola will bring flowers with her tomorrow. Just like the kitchen, the living room is uncomfortably sparse and clinical. A shiver prickles across Viola's scalp. Where is the warmth? Where is the love?

Viola doesn't even try to kid herself this time. She knows she's going to go upstairs and look around. What is the point in pretending? There's nobody here, they will never know, and she doesn't feel remotely guilty about it. She climbs the stairs, which still have the same plush charcoal carpet that Kevin and Leo laid. Viola suspects it will soon be replaced with something less comfortable.

There are three rooms on the first floor in the same formation as Viola's house. She enters what she knows to be the larger of the two bedrooms. Inside are two twin beds rather than the double she was expecting. Viola muses that beds say a lot about the state of a marriage. She furrows her brow and shakes her head – while the beds are identical, one is dressed entirely in blue bedding and the other in pink. There are no cushions or other adornments atop either. Just plain cotton bedclothes and they are immaculately made. Two simple white bedside tables bookend the beds. But that's it. There are no books, no lamps, absolutely nothing. Viola thinks of her own bedside cabinet crammed with all sorts, inside and out. She knows people are different and she has several super neat friends who don't like superfluous clutter, but this is another level.

A large chest of drawers sits across from the beds, and it has a small white charging station and a speaker on top. Purely functional items. She can't see anything in this room that is here simply because they love it. No art, no photographs, no mess, no boxes. Are these people robots? Viola appreciates that houses may look a little sparse when people move in, but this is different. It's obviously purposeful. The prison-like appearance of the room makes Viola uncomfortable even without the weird 'one for a boy' and 'one for a girl' beds. She had hoped to find some answers to her concerns about her new neighbours, but she falls further down the rabbit hole with every new thing she sees. She will not open any drawers or cupboards, though. She's already gone way too far with her intrusions and can't justify snooping any further. She tiptoes silently to what she assumes must be Mirabelle's bedroom and notices something she didn't see earlier. There is a lock on the outside of the door, and it looks to be newly installed. She tries the handle and the door doesn't budge.

Viola whispers aloud, "Curiouser and curiouser." She bends slowly, her knees crackling like bubble wrap, and peers through the keyhole. Through the tiny aperture, her view of the room is severely restricted. She can see a double bed, taking up most of the room, with white covers. The bed is unmade – the covers are askew, lumpy, and messy. The first less-than-perfect sign she has seen in the house.

Viola tries to crane her neck to see more of the room beyond the door, but as she does, something flashes past the keyhole, blocking her view for the briefest of moments. Viola pulls her face away and gives her head a shake. No sound is coming from the room, so there can't be anyone in there. If someone had moved, she would have heard footsteps, wouldn't she? She must have just blinked or something. Her heart is beating wildly. She leans forward again, closing one eye, determined to get a better look. But this time, she can't see anything at all. It's as though someone has put something over the keyhole. Her knees are screaming at her, and her mouth is dry. She has already taken this snooping mission way too far, and now, more than ever, she knows she should turn around and go back to the comfort and safety of her own home.

She'll definitely leave in a minute, but first she listens

intently for any signs of life in the room while trying to quiet her own panting breaths and thumping heart. She can't hear a thing.

"Hello." Her voice is croaky and tremulous, and she finds herself praying that no one will answer her. What on earth would she do if they did? She thinks she hears a small intake of breath but can't be sure. Her imagination is running wild at what could be behind the door. All her instincts are screaming at her to leave. Why on earth does she have to be so bloody stubborn. Nothing good can come from this.

Viola straightens up. She wishes she hadn't come here. She was hoping for answers but instead is more confused and concerned than she had been before. But she knows she can't ignore the fact that someone might be locked inside this room. She can't just turn her back if there is even the slightest possibility that someone needs her help. Viola knows it can't be Mirabelle in there. She saw her leave in the four-by-four with Wendy and the two men. Of that, she is one hundred per cent certain.

So who on earth could be locked in this room? They must have no access to a toilet, food, or water, and who knows how long they will be left alone. Viola has to try again – she can't leave without at least attempting to communicate one more time.

"Hello, is anyone in there?" Her words are filled with fear and trepidation. Not a sound emerges. Viola taps gently on the door with her knuckles, and this time she is sure she hears a slight rustling from inside the room. She rechecks the keyhole, but whatever is blocking her view is still there. What is she supposed to do? If it wasn't for her bloody-minded curiosity, she wouldn't be in this utter mess. But that's neither here nor there. She's here now, and her conscience won't let her leave. The thought that someone vulnerable, possibly a child, could be behind the door keeps Viola's feet rooted to the spot.

"I'm..." Viola stops herself before giving out her name. "I just need to know you're okay. The front door was open. I was..." Viola's words die in her throat as a harsh, raspy, nigh on inhuman voice spits back at her.

"Go away!"

Viola feels faint. The realisation that there is indeed a person locked in here almost knocks her off her feet. She finds herself babbling, unable to form even a single intelligible word, never mind a sentence.

"I said go away."

Viola's heart is galloping uncontrollably and her chest begins to feel tight. What should she do? Whoever is in there is refusing to open the door and obviously wants her to leave. Plus, she's not supposed to be in the house in the first place. Should she call the police? Surely this is illegal. It's imprisonment.

She'll go home, where she's safe, and then make the call.

Forming a plan of action calms Viola, and her legs feel more sturdy and able to descend the stairs. She doesn't look back at the door, and no further noises or voices emerge as she carefully takes each step towards freedom and away from the awfulness of that house.

She pulls the front door closed behind her, the very thing she should have done as soon as she approached the house. All thoughts of keys and whether Wendy and Rhys may be locked out seem insignificant after what she's discovered. She fumbles for her own keys, and only when she is in her doorway with the front door open does she risk a look behind her at the window of the locked bedroom. There is a dark blind pulled all the way down, a new addition since yesterday, blocking any view into the room. The same room that Mirabelle threw herself against and banged her hands on the day they arrived. The blind shifts slightly and the glare from the sun is reflected in the window, making it impossible to see anything clearly. Viola squints and watches, horrified, as pale thin fingers slowly appear and fold around the corner of the blind, edging it open a crack before letting it fall back to its previous position and disappearing altogether. Viola lets out an involuntary yelp and virtually falls into her house. Her chest is heaving and her breath is coming in thick, ragged gasps.

She closes her living-room curtains and collapses onto the sofa. She wishes she could rewind time and unsee everything that has just happened.

What has she unleashed?

Tears prick at Viola's eyes. She no longer only fears for Mirabelle, but for herself. She may also be in danger after what she has just done.

From what, she doesn't yet know, and this makes it all the more terrifying.

CHAPTER NINE

After a shower and a change of clothes, Viola feels slightly more human. She makes herself a pot of camomile tea and sits down at the kitchen table, notepad and pen at the ready. She has some big decisions to make, and she needs to clear her mind first.

Her thoughts are swimming and swirling around her head. Writing them down will create order and help her figure out what to do next. Viola taps the pen on the table, trying to figure out what to write first. It's all far too much. She takes a sip of the hot tea and starts by writing a single word on the page.

Mirabelle.

Underneath, she lists everything that has worried or concerned her since they moved in.

Playing with secateurs.

Banging on the window.

"Not my mummy."

Bandaged hand.

Viola shivers as she remembers the look in the girl's eyes as she unwound the toilet-paper bandage. Next, she starts on a list for Wendy.

Doesn't acknowledge her daughter.

Upset – "trying my best with the hand I've been dealt."
Possibly attended a funeral.

When it comes to Rhys, Viola realises she has little to add. So, settles on:

Absent.
Possibly attended a funeral.

Viola stares at the page before her, irritated that it does not adequately capture the magnitude of her anxiety about the family at number 33. Once again, this forces her to consider whether she is overreacting.

No, she's not. She won't convince herself that this is within the parameters of normal behaviour. She adds a final heading to her list.

The house:
Clinical and sparse.
Master bedroom with weird twin bed set-up.
The front door was left open.

And then the final and most disturbing discovery:

Someone locked in the second bedroom – "go away." Who is it? Why are they there?

Viola reads through everything again. There is a lot, but the only thing that could warrant calling the police is the person locked in the bedroom. She felt so sure about making the call when she was inside number 33. But now, back in the comfort of her own home, she's lost her sense of conviction. What would she be reporting? And what if there is a perfectly innocent reason? Although what that could possibly be, she doesn't know.

Viola closes the notebook in exasperation and rubs her temples. Her head is aching, and thinking is becoming more of a chore by the second. Exhaustion is taking over, but she refuses to give in to the overwhelming urge to sleep.

She has already decided that calling the police is out of the question, but should she speak to someone? Her lovely friend

Nina was her manager for most of her working years. She was an absolute pleasure to work for and undoubtedly the most caring yet sensible and fair person Viola has ever met. Nina would know precisely what to do. So what is stopping her from making the call? Honestly, Viola isn't sure. But something is telling her to hold off, to get more information first. Viola knows that as soon as she tells someone else, she loses all control of the situation, and if this is a weird misunderstanding, she'll feel terribly guilty about jumping the gun.

Desperately needing something to occupy her mind and stop her thoughts spinning out of control, she decides to crochet. It always helps her to switch off, and it was her salvation when Martin died and she didn't have the concentration to read or watch anything on TV. Somehow, it allows her to be at peace with the world.

Viola stands and makes her way to the sofa but instantly freezes when she hears the unmistakable sound of tyres on gravel as a car pulls up outside. Her living-room curtains are too thick to see through, but it can't be anyone else but the family next door returning. She listens intently, her heart in her mouth, as she hears four car doors open in turn and the sound of footsteps crunching across the gravel. She hears them open their front door and breathes a sigh of relief that she won't have to deal with the unlocked door issue. They need never know she was there. Unless...

There is one person who knows she was there. The occupant of the locked room.

She was hopeful that whoever was inside that room wouldn't be able to identify her through the keyhole, but after the appearance of the long eerie fingers at the window, she knows that they will have seen her and will know where she lives. Viola feels like screaming. How could she have been so stupid? She's gotten herself into an almighty mess, and for what? She's felt nothing but worry and anxiety since she started poking around in their business.

Flopping down onto the sofa, Viola lets out a resigned sigh. She's in limbo, and she can't do anything about it. What's done is done, and she'll have to face the consequences. Everything, well, almost everything she has done, has come from a good place. She's not a terrible person. None of this is to benefit her. She shrugs her shoulders and does something she very rarely does. She swears.

"Fuck it." It feels good, and she laughs. "Fuck the lot of it." Viola sits quietly until, eventually, her mood lifts a little, and she manages to stop catastrophising. But the respite is short-lived, and fear comes crashing back down upon her as she hears a loud, insistent knocking at the front door. She sits, frozen, not wanting to alert the visitor to her presence. She desperately doesn't want to deal with whoever this is just now. But if it is someone from number 33, and let's face it, who else would it be, not answering will only make things worse and fuel her already intrusive thoughts. She groans and forces herself to move towards the door.

"I can do this," she whispers to herself almost silently before straightening her shoulders and opening the door with a smile.

Her visitor does not reciprocate her smile, and Viola feels her own swiftly evaporate. It is the younger of the two men from the car, whom she assumes to be Rhys. He has changed out of the black suit and into equally black jeans and a polo neck jumper. His appearance is very severe, and the look he gives her makes her feel two inches tall.

"Hello. Rhys, is it?" She does her best to exude confidence and appear pleased to be making his acquaintance.

"Yes. Hello, Viola. It's *nice* to meet you." The word nice is spoken in such a way as to make it very clear that it is not, in fact, nice to meet her.

Viola feels her hackles rise. "Likewise." She gives him a pinched smile. "What can I do for you?"

He rubs his hands together before tenting his fingers and pressing them to his lips. He has very fine, elegant fingers for a man.

"I just wanted to come and let you know we have a camera in our master bedroom."

Viola feels as though the floor suddenly falls away. The little white speaker. Was it a camera? Viola quickly thinks through what she did in that room and is relieved to realise she did nothing. She simply stood there, scanned the room, and left. Yes, she shouldn't have been there, but she certainly didn't do anything wrong.

Rhys watches her closely, his dark brown eyes glistening. She already knows she doesn't like this man. His dark smugness is a complete turn-off.

Viola stands tall and attempts an air of calm. "When you left earlier, your front door was wide open. I saw it and quickly checked around the house to make sure nobody had gotten in before closing the door. I was about to come over and tell you."

Rhys raises a sculpted eyebrow at her. "I see." He licks his lips, and Viola feels distaste crawl over her. She crosses her arms and waits to see what he says next. They stare at each other. A stand-off. A battle of wills.

Eventually, he gives her a crooked, leering smile and caves in. "In that case, Viola, we must thank you. Why don't you come over tomorrow evening for dinner? It seems I'm the *only one* in the family yet to have the pleasure of your company."

Is it Viola's imagination, or does he emphasise the words 'only one' far too much? Viola can think of a million things she'd prefer to do than go back into that house, and she has no desire to spend any of her time socialising with this obtrusive and horrible man.

"Actually, I'm..." Viola's ability to talk diminishes as Rhys's eyes darken, and her sentence drifts off.

"I insist. Shall we say six thirty pm? I'm sure Mirabelle would love to see you again before she goes to sleep." Somehow, his tone is both friendly and menacing, and there is an undercurrent of threat when he mentions Mirabelle. Not for the first time, Viola worries for the girl's safety. Rhys flashes her a wide, charming smile that doesn't reach his eyes. He is clearly satisfied with himself.

Viola clears her throat and, once again, agrees to something she knows is a terrible idea. In the brief time she has known this family, she has vowed to stay away from them too often, yet something keeps drawing her back.

"Okay. Yes, six thirty is good for me. I'll see you then." Viola steps back and reaches for the door, wanting to end the conversation quickly. Rhys holds his palm out to stop her. He doesn't touch her but comes uncomfortably close. Viola gasps before indignance takes over. She has never allowed a man to make her feel threatened and vulnerable. And she certainly won't be starting now. Viola glares at his hand before raising her eyebrows and crossing her arms again. She fixes him with her best 'don't fuck with me' stare.

Rhys seems to assess her briefly before relenting and taking a step back. He lowers his hand and places both behind his back.

"Forgive me, Viola. That was a little rude of me. I simply wanted to thank you again for looking out for our home today and to say that there is no need to bring anything with you tomorrow evening."

Viola appreciates the apology, even if she doubts its

sincerity, but she's not ready to yield just yet. She needs to set out her stall with this man. His domineering, arrogant behaviour is not welcome, and she will not tolerate it.

"Apology accepted. I'm sure it was an unintentional lapse in judgement on your part." Rhys looks relieved and also impressed with Viola for standing her ground. Wendy strikes Viola as a more submissive woman, and perhaps he's used to behaving exactly how he pleases without anyone checking him. That's definitely not a good life lesson for Mirabelle.

"Indeed. We look forward to seeing you tomorrow." Rhys turns and begins to walk down the garden path.

Viola can't help herself, and the words are out of her mouth before she even considers their effect. "Will it be four of us for dinner?"

Rhys turns around sharply, his eyes on fire, and Viola has to resist the urge to shrink back. Her heart is pounding against her chest, but somehow, she manages to tilt her head and smile as though simply asking an innocent and very reasonable question.

Rhys takes a moment to gather himself. "No, just the three of us. Mirabelle usually eats earlier than us. She doesn't sleep well if she eats late."

Viola doesn't push it any further. Of course, "No, I meant the person you have locked away upstairs" would not go down well. She has rattled him, and that is enough for now.

"Okay. Bye, Rhys."

"Goodbye, Viola. Nice to meet you."

Viola observes his movements as he turns again and walks away, his hands balled into fists and his back ramrod straight. She returns to the sofa to crochet, determined not to lose the rest of her day to obsessing.

That could certainly have gone a lot worse. Rhys didn't push the issue of her being in their home and seemed to instantly accept her explanation about the door. She also noticed he happily and naturally referred to his daughter as Mirabelle, throwing Wendy's explanation about the girl's name into question. He was obviously perturbed when she mentioned the number of guests for dinner but recovered quickly. That was a risky move. Viola is sure he knows she was alluding to another person in their house. After all, she openly admitted to him she checked all the rooms after discovering the door was open.

A shocking thought suddenly springs into Viola's head. Something she thought about at the time but for a completely different reason. That somebody left the door open on purpose. What if, rather than testing her honesty, somebody wanted her to enter that house and find that room locked. Discover someone was being held prisoner. But who? And why?

She tries to drag her brain back into the moment, but all the crocheting in the world can't keep her mind from wandering. She needs answers and knows she'll need to think very carefully about what she's going to do and say before tomorrow evening. No emotional outbursts. No off-the-cuff remarks. Yes, she wants to know what is happening with the family at number 33, but she needs to be more careful. She needs assurances that Mirabelle is safe and, most pressingly, who was locked in that room today.

An unwelcome chill runs up her spine and spreads across her scalp, and she reaches for a blanket and pulls it over her legs. Viola has always felt as though she has a sixth sense. Before Martin died, there was an air of impending doom that followed her around for months. A dark, ominous presence that wouldn't shift and kept trying to get her attention. Somehow, she knew that tragedy was afoot. Martin, a lifelong non-smoker, was diagnosed with and died from lung cancer within six weeks. He went from being so full of life and vitality to shrivelling up and disappearing before she even had the chance to comprehend what was happening. The suddenness and unfairness of it all haunts Viola to this day, but she tries not to dwell on it and focuses on the positives. She will always be grateful that Martin planned for an early retirement and at least got to enjoy some of those carefree years before the cancer cruelly took hold. Martin worked as a letting agent for a local company. He made good money and never had to work evenings or weekends, and for him, that was the perfect combination. He was a 'work to live' person and never had a career calling like Viola did. Tears spring to her eyes, and she sniffs and rubs them away.

The same sense of foreboding she felt in the weeks before Martin's diagnosis lives with her now. That same menacing presence encircles her.

Someone is in danger.

A life is at risk.

She has to find out whose before it's too late.

CHAPTER TEN

Viola sleeps late and has a lazy morning. She has earned a bit of relaxation. Usually, she'd go to the library today, but she doesn't want to run the risk of bumping into Rhys, Wendy, or even Mirabelle before this evening. Plus, she hasn't been reading nearly as much this week, so there is no need to exchange books. Her head is too all over the place to focus.

It's another bright and sunny day, so she decides to spend most of it weeding the back garden. Martin always complained about the direction their rear garden faced, but today Viola is thankful for the fact that it faces away from number 33 and is protected from view by a substantial fence and thick greenery, even if the sun does disappear after 2pm.

Viola relishes the physical effort of gardening and the satisfaction of a job well done. As she works, she can't help but listen out for any sounds from next door. But all is suspiciously quiet. No loud voices, nobody entering or leaving – nothing at all. Her apprehension about this evening builds as the afternoon wears on.

She's had a tricky start with Wendy and isn't sure what to make of her. Rhys is less complicated. Viola disliked him instantly. He strikes her as a very controlling man. His behaviour is oppressive, and he carries an aura of darkness. She doesn't trust him one bit. Her best chance of getting any information about the family circumstances is through Mirabelle directly. However, how much she can trust anything the girl might say is debatable. Getting Mirabelle alone might be difficult, and she's already seen that Mirabelle is partial to fantasy.

Wendy and Rhys will be expecting her in an hour, so she jumps in the shower and starts to get herself ready. Viola has always believed that clothes can transform how you feel about yourself and elevate your mood and confidence. As such, she has never been shy about wearing the bright colours she loves. Martin always adored how Viola dressed and forever complimented her whenever they went out together. She always felt his pride at having her beside him. One thing they always had as a couple was an absolute acceptance of who they were. They never tried to change anything about each other, which made for an extremely happy and loving marriage.

Viola knocks on the door of number 33 shortly after 6.30pm. She has followed Rhys's wishes and come empty-handed. It makes her feel uncomfortable, and her mother would be horrified if she were alive. Rhys opens the door, a broad and welcoming smile on his face. He is dressed in a crisp black shirt and dark grey trousers. Does this man have anything with colour in his wardrobe? He looks down at her hands and smiles with a hint of smugness. The tips of Viola's cheeks flush, although she's not sure why. He specifically asked her not to bring anything. Rhys is clearly a fan of mind games.

He steps backwards into the house and swishes his arm to

invite Viola inside. She follows him, already irritated with his pomposity and hating the way he somehow manages to make her feel inferior. He leans in to kiss her on the cheek. Viola stiffens slightly but doesn't object, and she kisses the air close to Rhys's ear, breathing in a surprisingly light and pleasant cologne as she does so.

Rhys stands back and slowly looks Viola up and down, appraising her, again making her feel small and insignificant. Viola pulls her shoulders back and gives herself an internal shake. There is nothing special about Rhys, and she won't let him get under her skin like this. Viola can hear sizzling noises and the sounds of pots and pans clanking from the kitchen. Neither she nor Rhys have said a word yet, and it's beginning to feel weird. Whatever game he is playing, she wants no part of it.

"Good to see you, Rhys. Shall I take my shoes off?"

He shakes his head and seems to click into host mode. "No. No need for that. Come on through. Wendy is just finishing dinner, and Mirabelle is colouring at the table. I believe she's drawing a special picture for you." An amused look crosses his face before he turns and strolls towards the kitchen. Viola balls her fists and screws up her face behind his back. Good God, this man is an utter arsehole. She'd love to take off her shoe and throw it at his stupid head. Instead, she gives his back a two-finger salute, mouths 'fuck off', and follows him.

Wendy looks red-faced and flustered, racing around the kitchen and attending to various things cooking on the stove. When she sees Viola, her eyes light up. It appears completely genuine, and Viola is taken aback when Wendy comes over and envelops her in a warm hug.

"I'm so sorry about the chaos. I'm a little behind." Wendy rolls her eyes at herself. "Take a seat at the table, and I'll get you a drink sorted."

"Don't worry about me, Wendy." Viola looks at the table

where Mirabelle is seated, head down, immersed in her drawing. "I'll sit with Mirabelle. A drink can wait." Wendy gives Viola a grateful smile and returns to the stove.

All the while, Rhys is just standing there. Watching. Martin would never have behaved like this. Marriage is a team sport. Rhys is well put together and looks completely relaxed, while Wendy is running around like a chicken with no head. How completely unfair.

"Actually, Wendy, can I help? That looks like a lot for one person to do." Viola looks pointedly at Rhys as she says this, and she notices the muscles in his jaw clench, but still he completely ignores her.

Wendy looks over her shoulder. "No, honestly. Take a seat. Please." There is a hint of pleading from her, and Viola turns to check Rhys's reaction to their exchange.

Viola starts when she sees that Rhys is glowering at her. She watches as he saunters towards Wendy and places a hand gently on her back before whispering something in her ear. Viola doesn't catch a word of what he is saying, but she sees Wendy alternate between nodding and shaking her head. Rhys kisses his wife softly on the cheek, and Viola is sure she sees her wince. He taps Wendy on the bottom, and she jumps a little before he turns and winks at Viola. Viola is completely mesmerised by the whole performance.

Rhys strides towards the fridge before opening it and yanking out a bottle of champagne.

"I'll pour us all a glass."

Viola nods, wholly dumbfounded by what she has just witnessed and thinking that a glass of something is just what she needs to settle her jangling nerves. Rhys reaches into the cupboard and takes out three champagne flutes effortlessly using one hand.

"Do sit down. Mirabelle has been looking forward to

showing you all her hard work. Haven't you, darling? I'll bring your drink over."

Mirabelle hasn't looked up from her drawing. In the absence of any better options, Viola decides to sit next to her. The table has been set beautifully. White china plates and perfectly ordered cutlery. It looks like something you'd expect in a fine-dining restaurant. All except where Mirabelle is sitting. She has pushed the place setting away into the middle of the table to make space for her books and colouring pencils. The previously pristine glass is covered with finger smudges and pencil shavings. Viola is glad to see her behaving like a child in such an adult-centric environment. She sits down gently beside the girl and leans in to see what she is drawing.

"Hi, Mirabelle." Viola speaks softly, not wanting to startle the girl, who is engrossed in her activity.

Mirabelle looks up and beams at Viola before springing up from her chair and holding up a finger. "Wait here," she instructs and sprints out of the room.

Viola laughs to herself and rests back in the uncomfortable chair. Sitting here all night is going to play havoc with her back. She feels Rhys's dark presence loom over her before she hears his voice. He has such a dark, insidious energy. He reaches around her, uncomfortably close, and places a glass of champagne on the table in front of her. Viola's skin prickles and she looks up.

He is holding his own glass, tilting it towards her. "What shall we drink to?"

Viola reaches for her glass, trying to stop her fingers from trembling. He'd love to know he's making her nervous, and she can't have that.

"Don't you think we should wait for Wendy?"

Rhys's face becomes stony, and he takes a step back.

"Wendy, Viola wants you to come over here and drink a toast with us."

Wendy is still clearly busy and looks flustered, and Viola hates how he makes her sound so demanding.

"That's not what I said." She glares at Rhys, but he doesn't look at her. Instead, he calls for Wendy again.

"Come on, dear. Let's not keep our lovely new neighbour waiting."

Viola stands up and reaches out for Rhys's arm. "She's obviously busy. I said wait for her. Not ask her to come over."

"Oh." Rhys puts his hand to his chest and raises his eyebrows, pretending it is a simple misunderstanding.

Viola leans in. "You know full well–"

She's interrupted by Wendy rushing over, a glass of champagne in her hand. "Here I am. Sorry, Viola. Anyway, I'm almost finished now."

Rhys is wearing a disgusting, gushing smile and pulls Wendy towards him. Viola is about to explain, but Rhys butts in first, and she has to use every ounce of restraint she has not to throw the drink in his face and storm out right there and then.

"How lucky am I to spend the evening with two such beautiful ladies." Wendy flushes and chuckles in a self-deprecating way that Viola knows Rhys will love. Viola focuses on Wendy and manages to smile despite wanting to throw up. Rhys is in his element holding court, and Viola wonders what has been taking Mirabelle so long. This moment could most definitely do with being interrupted.

"Let's raise our glasses," Rhys instructs. Wendy raises hers with gusto, and Viola follows her with as much enthusiasm as she can muster. Rhys focuses intensely on Viola as he delivers the toast. Wendy seems utterly oblivious to his dark demeanour. How can she be so blind to his poorly disguised malevolence? "There is always room in our house for one more friend."

Viola feels Rhys's eyes on her, and her blood runs cold. Is he making a veiled reference to their visitor upstairs? Is he threatening her that she'll be next? She hears Rhys's voice again. He sounds far away somehow.

"To new friends!"

Viola finds herself dazedly clinking glasses with her two hosts and gulping down the glass of champagne. The toast would seem celebratory and welcoming to anyone else, but Viola feels the deliberate threat hidden within. The room is out of focus and noisy: an assault on her addled senses. She feels a hand press down on her shoulder and an uncomfortably hard squeeze followed by a sharp shooting pain in her arm. Viola pulls away, dropping her empty champagne flute in the process. It falls to the floor and shatters into what seems like a thousand tiny pieces.

Viola looks down and notices a minuscule cut on the top of her foot. She watches a small drop of red blood begin to form and make a tiny puddle on her skin. In her peripheral vision, she sees Wendy dash away and return with a cordless hoover. Viola needs to sit down, and she finds herself being guided back to her chair. It must be Rhys, but she doesn't care. She doesn't feel well at all. In an attempt to steady herself, she takes several long, deep breaths and closes her eyes. Focusing all of her energy inward. A barrage of emotions is coursing through her, none of them pleasant. Fear, anger, embarrassment, and confusion, all taking their turn to be centre stage in her mind.

A small, soft hand taps Viola gently on the forearm, and she opens her eyes slowly, reorienting herself and taking in the sight of Mirabelle smiling and holding out a piece of paper. The little girl doesn't appear concerned about what has just happened or by Viola's current state. She simply smiles and waits for Viola to take the gift she is offering.

Rhys appears behind them, and Viola worries momentarily

that he'll ask the girl to leave. Viola desperately wants her to stay. Somehow, Mirabelle feels like a safety net at this moment in time – an anchor in the chaos. Instead, Rhys surprises her.

"Sweetheart, why don't you sit with Viola and show her your picture. I'll help Mummy finish dinner."

Mirabelle grins and jumps into the chair next to Viola, her eyes giddy with excitement. Viola looks up to thank Rhys, shocked but appreciative of his offer to leave her alone with Mirabelle, but he's already walked away. She was sure that, given her discomfort, he would continue to twist the knife, try and unsettle her further. Viola can't keep up with this family. One minute, they appear sinister and somewhat disturbing, and the next, they are being thoughtful. It's exhausting, not to mention confusing, and it makes her wary of trusting her own instincts. Is that the whole point, or is she being far too suspicious?

Viola is shaken from her musings by Mirabelle tapping impatiently on the drawing she has placed on the table in front of her. Viola is grateful she's starting to feel a little better and certainly calmer. Drinking the champagne in one go was undoubtedly an error of judgement.

She smiles at Mirabelle. "Wow. Did you draw this?"

Mirabelle sits up straight and tall and crosses her arms. "Yep."

"Well, I think you're very talented."

The compliment has the desired effect, and Mirabelle gives Viola a wide, toothy smile. Viola looks down at the picture. It is indeed very accomplished for a girl of Mirabelle's age, and it's clear that much time and care has been taken over it.

Mirabelle points at a figure in the drawing. "That's you. I think it looks just like you. Do you? Do you like it?"

Viola senses Mirabelle's need for approval and responds

quickly. "I love it. I knew straight away it was me. It looks just like me. Absolutely brilliant."

Mirabelle squirms with excitement. "I did your skin dark brown and made your dress all colourful. You always look so pretty and bright." Mirabelle's face falls a little, and Viola wonders what negative thought has just popped into her brain. The sadness is fleeting, though, and Mirabelle goes on to describe the rest of the figures in the photo.

The drawing depicts a relatively accurate portrayal of this house. Viola and Mirabelle are at the forefront of the picture, wearing bright dresses, large smiles, and holding a bunch of yellow flowers each.

Viola points at them. "What kind of flowers are these?"

"Buttercups. Remember, from the garden. And in this picture world, I picked them all and made two big bunches of flowers. One for me and one for you."

Viola can't help but feel warmed by the girl's innocent descriptions and way of expressing herself, entirely at odds with the ominous child who stood outside her window merely days ago.

Mirabelle puts her forearm next to Viola's as though comparing or checking something. "I like your brown skin. It's beautiful. I wish mine was like that."

Viola places her hand gently on Mirabelle's arm. "Thank you, that's a very lovely thing to say. And I think your skin is beautiful too. In fact, I think any colour of skin is beautiful, don't you?"

This wasn't a conversation Viola expected to have and she finds the simplicity of their exchange refreshing. If only all adults could see things the same way. As a Black woman married to a white man in the north of England, she's had her fair share of disparaging looks and unkind comments, particularly during the early years of their relationship.

Mirabelle looks up and momentarily ponders Viola's question before her face becomes mischievous. "Even crusty, smelly skin with green boils that have spiders inside?"

Viola throws her head back and laughs heartily. Mirabelle joins in, appearing thrilled that Viola found her comment funny.

Viola dabs her eyes and points at the two smaller figures standing to the side of the house. "And who are these two?"

Mirabelle cocks her head in the direction of the kitchen in an oddly grown-up gesture to indicate that the pair of figures is Wendy and Rhys.

Viola studies the drawings. Although taller than his wife in real life, in the picture Rhys is more than double the size of Wendy. He is carefully drawn and is smiling. Wendy, on the other hand, is tiny and the pencil work is slapdash compared to the rest of the picture. On closer inspection, Viola discovers there aren't even any features on her face. They say a picture speaks a thousand words, and if that's true, then Viola's heart breaks for Wendy and she hopes Mirabelle doesn't show her the picture.

Viola is about to question Mirabelle on why the figures have been drawn that way when Rhys appears behind them.

"Dinner is ready. Are you okay, Viola?"

Viola had been so focused on her conversation with Mirabelle that she hadn't noticed that all the glass had been tidied away, and the kitchen was now quiet and calm. She glances over Rhys's shoulder and spots Wendy plating up, thankfully looking much more serene and relaxed.

"Yes, I'm fine, thank you. I'm so sorry about that. I'll be sure to replace the glass. I'm not usually so clumsy." Viola feels her cheeks warming and looks to Mirabelle, who is watching her with quiet interest.

"It's no problem at all. And there is no need to replace it.

We have plenty, and we've broken quite a few ourselves, so please, there's no need to worry. As long as you're okay, that's all that matters to us."

Rhys's snide and inflammatory behaviour has disappeared. He appears genuinely pleasant and concerned for her welfare. It's as though he's a different person, and while Viola is happy to see the back of his unpleasant manner, the change itself is unsettling.

"That's very kind of you. Thank you, Rhys."

He smiles and turns to his daughter. "Sweetheart, could you please go and do your drawing upstairs while the grown-ups eat?"

"Noooooo," Mirabelle answers in a whiny, petulant voice, drawing out the word excessively. Rhys looks at her sternly and crouches down to her level. Mirabelle sticks her bottom lip out comically and looks at her father with sad, pleading eyes. "Daddy, I want to see Viola."

Rhys pulls Mirabelle in for a hug. Viola was expecting admonishment and raised voices and is pleasantly surprised by Rhys's caring approach to Mirabelle's defiance.

"I know you do. And we'll let you stay up a little later so you can come and say goodnight after we've eaten. Then I'll read you a story and put you to bed. How does that sound?"

Mirabelle pops her lip back in and brightens instantly. "Okay, Daddy. Call me as soon as you're done, okay?"

Rhys draws a cross shape on his chest. "I promise."

Mirabelle leans into Viola and whispers, "Eat fast," before grabbing her drawing things and running upstairs.

CHAPTER ELEVEN

Viola feels considerably more settled. She doesn't often meet new people these days, and making a bad first impression is so easy. Perhaps she needs to wipe the slate clean and try to get to know Wendy and Rhys this evening.

Wendy puts three plates down in front of them. Rhys opens a bottle of chilled white wine and pours three small glasses. They must have finished the champagne or decided that Viola can't be trusted with another flute.

Viola had been expecting a bland, unexciting meal and she chastises herself for making unkind assumptions. The food on her plate looks and smells delicious. Wendy has cooked a red Thai prawn curry bursting with colourful vegetables and served it with perfectly cooked rice. In the centre of the table are a large bowl of Thai salad and a plate piled generously high with flatbreads that look handmade.

Viola is very impressed, and her mouth is watering. "Wow. This all looks fantastic. Did you make the bread?"

Wendy flushes. "I did. Thai is our favourite cuisine, and I love to cook it for people."

Rhys reaches for the plate of flatbreads and offers them to Viola. She takes one gratefully.

"Thank you."

"Right, let's dig in, shall we?" Rhys adds.

They all smile and pick up their cutlery. Viola is astonished to find that she is having a really lovely time. The food is devoured by all and, if possible, it tastes even better than it looks. One glass of wine turns into two, and the atmosphere around the table is easy and natural.

The conversation is light and mostly related to the local area and things to do, and when asked, Viola tells them what happened to Martin. They are both very kind and offer condolences. Viola can't help but notice that the conversation remains focused on her and her life, even when she asks them a direct question. But they do seem genuinely keen to get to know her.

Feeling wonderfully satiated, Viola places her cutlery down and dabs her mouth politely with her napkin. "That's the nicest food I have eaten in a long time. Honestly, you're a wonderful cook, thank you."

Wendy smiles coyly. "Well, I don't know about that, but I'm pleased you enjoyed it."

Rhys divides the remainder of the wine bottle between the three glasses, misjudging it so that he ends up with only a few drops. They all laugh.

"I've probably had enough anyway. Big day at work tomorrow."

Viola considers asking about his work, but another thought occurs to her. The evening has been lovely, and she now feels much more comfortable with these people. Could this be an opportunity to address the elephant in the room and ask about the locked bedroom and the person inside? Or would that destroy all the good ground they've made? Viola knows this is probably the wine talking, but either way, she's sure Rhys knows she saw the secured door and perhaps that she tried to speak to whoever was behind it. Waiting for him to bring it up doesn't feel like a good idea. If there is a reasonable explanation, she could put her mind at ease and continue getting to know her new neighbours. Or she could ruin the whole evening and return home anxious and fearful.

"Can I say something?"

Both Wendy and Rhys fall silent and focus on Viola. There's no backing out now.

"Of course you can." Wendy's response is a little high-pitched, and she takes a glug of her wine.

Rhys simply leans back in his chair and smiles. "Sure. Go ahead, Viola."

"You already know I was in your house yesterday." Viola stops suddenly as the surprised look on Wendy's face reveals she did not, in fact, know this. Viola throws Rhys an apologetic glance, but he doesn't seem put out at all.

He rests an arm around Wendy's shoulder. "I'd been meaning to tell you, honey. We somehow left our front door open when we left for Helen's funeral." Rhys turns to Viola. "Helen was an old friend of both our families."

Wendy's hand flies up to her mouth. "Oh my. That must have been my fault. I'm so sorry." Her eyes flit between Viola and her husband, and Viola can't tell who she is apologising to.

Rhys pulls her in closer. "It's nobody's fault, and anyway, Viola spotted the open door, checked everything was okay in the house, and pulled it closed for us. No harm done."

Wendy appears only mildly reassured, and Viola would like to add that she watched them all get in the car. It most certainly wasn't Wendy who left the house unlocked. But she doesn't. That would make her look far too nosy, bordering on stalker-ish. Wendy appears placated, and Viola's nerves peak as she opens her mouth to ask the question she knows could create an explosion.

She directs her words at Rhys and tries her best to sound concerned rather than accusatory. "The thing is..." She trails off and decides to insert a white lie. "Once I'd checked downstairs was okay, I thought I heard a noise coming from upstairs."

Rhys's face is entirely emotionless. He lifts his wine glass slowly and takes a sip. Viola watches his Adam's apple bob up and down.

"So, I went upstairs and tried to check the bedrooms." Rhys maintains a calm demeanour, but when Viola flits her eyes to Wendy, she sees a face filled with pure terror. Her eyes are wide and glassy, and the muscles on her ashen face are twitching wildly. Viola desperately wants to reach out and soothe her, but Rhys interrupts.

"And?"

Viola turns to him, expecting anger or menace, but he looks curious more than anything else. "And I couldn't open the second bedroom door, but I saw someone inside. Someone *locked* inside."

Viola stops and looks down at her hands. Her last words hang in the air. Rhys leans back and takes a large gulp of wine. He rubs his hands across his chin and takes a deep breath before puffing out his cheeks and exhaling noisily.

"I'm so sorry, Viola."

Viola risks a look at Wendy, who appears to have calmed down a little. It feels odd to her that Wendy seems more of a spectator in this discussion. In Rhys's presence, it's as though she becomes childlike, or at least not on his level. It's a strange dynamic. After his apology, Rhys doesn't continue talking, and the silence starts to feel uncomfortable.

"Sorry for what, Rhys?" Viola feels her lips trembling as she speaks, and she wishes he would just spit out whatever explanation he's planning to give her.

"I know we've only just met, but I can already see that you're not going to accept anything other than a full disclosure here, and I'm not going to do that. I will say that although I appreciate you looking out for our home, we don't actually owe you an explanation for a door in our home being locked."

He stops briefly and Viola considers what he's just said. An awful lot of words but nothing of any substance. Despite feeling irked and flat-out disagreeing with his opinion that he shouldn't have to explain having someone imprisoned in a room in their house, Viola decides to proceed with caution.

"Okay. I hear what you're saying. But think of it from my perspective. Someone was locked inside a room in your house. I know that for a fact. They even spoke to me."

Immediately, Viola wishes she hadn't revealed that final part as she watches Rhys's neck flush scarlet and a venomous look appear in his eyes. Wendy reaches out a shaking hand and places it on top of Rhys's. A show of solidarity, perhaps, or a warning? Viola isn't sure.

"But you're right. It isn't my business. I just felt I should tell you and hoped you would put my mind at ease. I mean, it's not really okay to lock someone in a room, is it?" This conversation is taking ten times longer than Viola was hoping, and emboldened by the glasses of wine, she is starting to feel as though she's simply on a different planet from these people. Why can't they see that this is both concerning and absolutely not normal?

Rhys leans forward and rests his elbows on the table, his hands cupped together. "Okay. I can assure you there is a completely rational and acceptable explanation for this, but clearly, that's not going to suffice." Viola nods at him. He's right – that won't suffice. Rhys rolls his eyes and continues. "It was my mother inside that room." For a split second, Viola is sure she sees Wendy's face crumple in confusion, but it's gone in an instant. "My mother is in the early stages of dementia. She lives with my father and doesn't need much care at the moment." His face falls and his shoulders drop, but it all seems far too scripted. "We were all going to go to the funeral together. After all, Helen was probably closer to my parents than any of us. But when Mother arrived here, she became really confused." Rhys looks up as though checking whether Viola is listening but really seems to be assessing whether the story is landing. Viola gives nothing away and hides the fact that Rhys referring to his mum as 'Mother' has unnerved her. Far too Norman Bates-esque.

"We didn't want to miss the funeral, and Father said the best thing to do was to let her sleep. She gets tired when she's confused, you see." Rhys checks in on Viola again and this time she nods briefly, encouraging him to continue. "When we left, she was asleep, and we thought she'd remain that way until we got back, but your entrance to the house must have woken her up." Rhys leans back and crosses his arms, seemingly finished with his story. But there's one essential part of the story that he hasn't yet addressed. The only part that Viola is really interested in.

"And the door was locked because?"

Rhys huffs and throws his hands out to the side as though Viola is being completely stupid for not understanding. "For her safety, of course. If she woke up while we were gone, she would be frightened and might fall or hurt herself."

Viola squints. That certainly makes a degree of sense, but still, isn't it negligent to leave a vulnerable woman alone in a locked room? Surely, the same logic applies. She could hurt herself inside the room, and worse, she would be unable to get any help.

"Look, you asked a question and I explained it, even though

I shouldn't have to. Was it an ideal situation? No. Is this something we'd do regularly? No. But, in a difficult situation, we did our best, and I can assure you that Mother's doctor completely agreed with our course of action. Unless you'd like to check in with him, too? You seem to feel like you have the right to every aspect of my mother's condition, so why not?" Rhys is breathless now, and the tension between them is rising. He stands up suddenly and wipes his face with a napkin before throwing it onto the floor. "Excuse me. Mirabelle would like to see you before you leave. I'll go and call her down."

Viola watches as he leaves the room, muttering under his breath. He calls Mirabelle's name, then stomps up the stairs when he gets no response. This is a new string to his erratic emotional bow – the petulant child. Viola reaches for her wine and drinks the remainder of the glass before reaching out to Wendy with both hands. Wendy's hands are icy cold despite the relative warmth of the kitchen.

"I'm sorry, Wendy. Dinner was lovely. Really. But I had to ask. I hope you understand." A pang of guilt stabs Viola in the chest as she sees that Wendy doesn't look angry, she simply looks sad. She radiates a tragic sorrow that hurts Viola's heart to see.

"I'm sorry too. I'm just... sorry." Viola watches as Wendy appears to fold in on herself, crumpling inwards and shrinking before her eyes. They sit like that for a moment. Viola knows that sometimes it's important to just let sadness be. Chasing it away only means it will come back stronger at a later date, so she simply sits and tries to hold the emotion with her.

The quiet is punctured by Rhys re-entering the room, but Mirabelle is nowhere to be seen. He doesn't make eye contact.

"Mirabelle is tired and wants to stay upstairs. She asked me to give you this." He drops a folded piece of paper onto the table before Viola. The sheet is thin enough that she can see through it and make out it's the picture Mirabelle was showing her earlier.

Viola turns and gives Rhys a perfunctory smile. "Thank you. And please thank Mirabelle for me."

Rhys nods, irritation still evident in his movements and strained face. "If you'll excuse me, I'm a little out of sorts. I'm going to go for a run. Wendy, will you see Viola out?"

"Of course." Wendy stands, but before she can reach Rhys, he leaves the room and closes the door behind him without even saying goodbye.

Viola picks up the picture and slides it into her handbag. "I'll see myself out. And again, I'm..."

Wendy is halfway across the kitchen and returns with another bottle of wine. Rosé this time, and she has it open before Viola can say another word.

"Let's have one more, shall we? Rhys won't be back for at least half an hour, and after that, I think we both need it."

Viola has already hit her limit for what she likes to drink in an evening, but this seems like too good an opportunity to miss. Plus, Wendy looks like she needs the company. Wendy pours two generous glasses, and Viola takes a sip. The wine is crisp, fruity and delicious, and she knows this large glass will slide down without any difficulty at all.

"Urgh."

Viola can't help but chuckle at the barely intelligible grunting noise that escapes from Wendy's lips.

Wendy laughs, too. "Sorry, but sometimes there are just no words, are there?"

Viola nods, and the two women clink glasses in solidarity. Wendy's smile drops, and she becomes serious and pensive. Viola senses Wendy is about to share, so she remains quiet and sips her wine.

"I know you must think that we're a fucking nightmare."

Viola is taken aback by the casual swearing. "No, of course not." But even to her own ears, her words sound insincere. But what is she supposed to say? "*Yes. I think you're all weird and, quite frankly, I'm a little afraid and more than a little concerned.*"

Wendy's voice softens, and it's clear she wants to get something off her chest. "We came here for a new start." Wendy's eyes fill up, and she takes a moment to steady herself and stave off the tears. "We've had our... problems." She sighs, and Viola gives her the space needed to find the words. "I'm not Mirabelle's birth mother. When she said I'm not her mummy, technically she's right." Viola can see how hard it was for Wendy to reveal this. "It's a horrible story, and Rhys would be furious if he knew I was telling you this."

"Then don't. Please don't feel like you have to. I'm here if you need someone to talk to, but don't share anything you're not happy about."

Wendy shakes her head, a little wine sloshing from the glass. As she does so, Viola observes that Wendy's glass is significantly emptier than hers.

"I feel like I'm going to fucking burst if I don't tell someone. Rhys is a very proud man, and sometimes I feel pulled along by him. I don't know how to explain it better than that."

Viola nods and Wendy smiles. Her eyes becoming glassier and more unfocused as the wine disappears from her glass.

"I've been a mother to Mirabelle since she was born. I can't have children. I had cancer when I was a teenager, and the treatment left me infertile. We used a surrogate for Mirabelle. Rhys was so determined to be a father. I'd made my peace knowing I'd never be a parent a long time ago. I was just happy to be alive. When we married, Rhys felt the same, but then..." Wendy swallows, and Viola can see that this conversation is both draining and cleansing. Getting things off your chest often has that effect.

"Then he changed his mind?" Viola offers up.

Wendy nods sadly. "Exactly. I wasn't keen to go through any medical procedures with eggs or implantation. Rhys never understood my aversion to it, but then he's never been through years of cancer treatment, so why would he?" Viola's heart breaks a little for this woman who's clearly been through so much. "Anyway, long story short. We found a woman, I won't go into how, who agreed to turkey-baste Rhys's sperm into her and have his baby." Viola can't hide her shock. Wendy sloshes more wine into her glass and drinks at least half in one go. "Rhys, in his infinite wisdom, recently decided to tell Mirabelle. Honesty is the best... blah, blah. Whatever. And since then, she's had him pretty much wrapped around her little finger. He'll do anything she wants. Gets her anything she asks for. And she treats me like I'm nothing. Nobody. And somehow, I'm just going along with everything day by day. Losing bits and pieces of my sanity and myself as I go. Fucking nightmare." Wendy tips back her head and knocks the remainder of her glass back. Viola moves the wine bottle away from her even though it's almost empty now. "Yep, good move. No more wine for me." Wendy puts her head in her hands, and Viola gets up and walks to stand behind her. Her head is bursting with questions, but Wendy needs comfort just now, not interrogation.

She puts her hands on Wendy's shoulders. "Thank you for sharing that with me. And honestly, whenever you need to talk, I'm here."

Wendy reaches backwards with one arm and slaps Viola's hands in a haphazard, uncoordinated manner. She's definitely drunk now.

"I'm serious. I think it's probably best that I come over when

Rhys is at work. We don't seem to..." Viola searches for an appropriate word, "...gel."

Wendy snorts. "Ha. Rhys doesn't gel with anyone except Mirabelle and his dad. He's like a prickly fox."

Viola laughs internally at the nonsensical comparison. "Indeed. So, the next time Rhys is at work, come over and we'll have a chat. Okay?"

Wendy sticks up her thumb in agreement, almost poking Viola in the eye. Viola realises she's the only fully functional adult in the room, and Rhys will be back any minute.

"Look, I think it's probably a good idea to get you to bed and me to be back home before Rhys returns from his run, don't you?"

Wendy's head flies up from the table, her mouth comically wide. "Shit!"

Viola quickly clears the glasses and pours the remainder of the wine down the sink before putting the bottle in the recycling. No need to give Rhys any further fuel to be annoyed

She helps Wendy to the bottom of the stairs. "Do you need help getting up to bed?" Wendy sways a little but still seems to have a modicum of control over her limbs. Enough to get upstairs, at least, Viola surmises.

"Nope. I'm good. Excellent. I'm a professional at stairs. Total professional."

Viola smiles warmly at Wendy and gives her a hug. "Make sure you go straight to bed, though."

Wendy salutes. "Aye, aye, captain." Wendy is adorable and hilarious, but Viola can't help thinking that Rhys won't see it that way. Viola lets herself out quietly and blows Wendy a kiss. Wendy waves before slowly closing the door and disappearing.

Viola stares up at the black, starless sky, listening as Wendy climbs the stairs and waits for calm and quiet to descend on the house before walking home.

CHAPTER TWELVE

Tucked up in bed away from all the madness, Viola takes a deep breath. She'd only been at home for ten minutes when she heard Rhys return from his run and let himself into the house. She truly hopes Wendy managed to get herself into bed and fast asleep in time. She mercifully hears no concerning noises from number 33.

Viola stretches out to reach her handbag from the bedroom floor, hooking the strap with her middle finger and dragging it towards her. Rooting inside, she finds Mirabelle's drawing, unfolds it, and smooths it out on her duvet. Viola smiles again at the happy picture of her and Mirabelle. Although, looking closer, she is sure there have been some alterations to the drawing since she last saw it at the dining table. Viola, Mirabelle, Rhys, and the house all appear the same. But the drawing of Wendy has had some alterations. Mirabelle has scribbled out her mother's face in black ink. Her previously blank, white face has been coloured in entirely. In contrast to the care and attention taken over the other figures, the pen marks are harsh and have creased and almost ripped the page.

At Wendy's feet is another black careless scribble that makes it appear as though Wendy is standing in thick tar or about to fall into a hole. It is such a horrible thing to see. So sad. For both mother and daughter. Of course, Mirabelle is only a child, but there is such anger towards Wendy evident in this picture. Too much anger to be living inside a small girl.

Viola's eyes are drawn away from Wendy's blacked-out face and towards the house, and she notices something else that wasn't there before. There is a small figure in one of the upstairs windows. The window of the locked room. Viola is sure she didn't see this figure in the drawing before. Did she simply not notice it, or is this something else Mirabelle has added? It is a drawing of a young woman or perhaps an older girl. Only her head and shoulders are visible, and she has blonde hair sitting up high on her head in a ponytail. Her face has been drawn very carefully. Rosy cheeks and a wide smile filled with teeth. What can be seen of her clothing is bright pink, and there is a yellow necklace around her neck, presumably to signify gold. Viola leans forward and pulls the picture closer, checking every part of it for any other possible additions or clues to who the woman in the window might be. There is nothing. So, who is it? What is Mirabelle trying to tell her?

Viola folds the piece of paper back up and places it in her bedside cabinet drawer. Whenever she thinks she is starting to understand what is happening at number 33, something else throws everything back up in the air. There is a message in this picture. Mirabelle wants to tell Viola something, and she needs to find out what for her own sanity and the safety and happiness of both Mirabelle and Wendy. Viola turns out her bedside light and closes her eyes, deciding she won't open them again until she falls asleep. She needs to rest. Eventually, exhaustion claims her, and she finds herself drifting off.

At some point in the night, Viola stirs and rolls over. She thinks she hears some commotion outside, perhaps a car or footsteps, but she's unsure. In fact, she's not even entirely sure she is awake.

Viola is back in a deep sleep before she can give it another thought.

CHAPTER THIRTEEN

MIRABELLE

I hope Viola likes my picture. She told me I'm really good at drawing and that made me so happy. I want Viola to know how bad Wendy is, and I got really cross when Viola came for dinner because she was being all smiley and nice to Wendy. I don't get it. Can't Viola see that she's horrible? So I drew her all black and messy.

All I want to do is go home. I want my family back. Daddy just keeps saying I have to be patient, but it's so hard. Anyway, Wendy managed to mess everything up all on her own. She drank a lot of wine and talked too much. She's so stupid, and Daddy was really mad, especially when I told him everything Wendy said to Viola.

I don't think I'll have to wait much longer now.

Daddy and I will be home soon.

CHAPTER FOURTEEN

The following day, Viola doesn't even try to convince herself to leave the goings-on at number 33 alone and get on with her life. She's invested now for various reasons, and she will either have to get to the bottom of it herself or call someone in. She's thought several times about calling the police. But she has no evidence of anything criminal occurring, no matter what she suspects. Rhys will simply give the police the same excuse he gave her – that his mother was locked in the room as a one-off for her own safety and with the agreement of her doctor. She's also decided she can't drag Nina or any of her old council colleagues into this. It wouldn't be fair. They're all retired now, and it would only upset them. If she feels there's a genuine case for involving children's social care, she'll have to take the formal route.

Still, her concerns seem nebulous, and every time Viola tries to pull everything together into a story that she could explain to a professional, she can't. It all comes across like the ramblings of a nosy neighbour and Viola is sure that's how they'll view her. So, that leaves it up to her. If there's anything concrete to find, she will find it, and then she can get outside help if needed.

Viola pulls on her dressing gown and makes her way downstairs for breakfast. There is no hiding away today. She opens the curtains and cracks open the living-room window to air the downstairs rooms. More dust than she would like covers the usually pristine surfaces, swirling unpleasantly in the air as a breeze circulates through the room.

She will clean everything thoroughly. She has always been house-proud, and cleaning is therapeutic for her, but all these distractions mean she has been letting things slide.

Feeling perked up by half a pot of tea and a couple of slices of toast and marmalade, Viola puts on her cleaning clothes. Dull, drab, and unattractive but entirely fit for purpose. She is a woman on a mission. She starts by opening all the windows widely and clearing the ornaments and plants from the windowsills. All the curtains at number 33 are closed and their car is missing from the drive. Viola purposefully looks away, shrugging her shoulders, refusing to be pulled away from the task at hand. On her way to the kitchen to collect some more cleaning supplies, she hears a knock at the door and, without overthinking, makes her way to answer it. If she wants to return to a normal existence, she needs to start behaving that way, and a knock at the door would never have been cause for concern before all of this nonsense.

Her smile falls as she stands face to face with the man she now knows to be Rhys's father. The man who drove the jeep on the day of the funeral. Up close, it is obvious that he and Rhys are related. They are incredibly similar, both in physical appearance and demeanour. Despite the man being rather attractive, Viola immediately detects an off-putting aura of self-importance about him.

Next to him stands a diminutive woman. She is standing very stiffly, feet together and shoulders slightly hunched.

Clasped in front of her is a box-shaped handbag that reminds Viola of something Queen Elizabeth II may have held.

Viola finds her smile again. "Good morning." The small woman doesn't move or react in any way, but the man responds with a smile and unexpectedly thrusts his hand out. Viola has to stop herself from jumping.

"Good morning, Viola. I'm Duke, and this is my wife, Christine."

Viola looks down at his hand and eventually reaches out to shake it. What is it with these men and shaking hands? Also, Duke? It sounds more like a name for a Labrador than a grown man. Besides a slight tremor that makes her soft cheeks tremble, Christine remains mute and unmoving. She has the typical powder fragrance that many mature ladies seem to favour. Viola wonders at what age society expects women to renounce their individuality and become invisible and powdery.

"We're Rhys's parents." Duke turns toward number 33 as he says this, as though Viola might have forgotten. The last thing Viola wants to do is let these people in. Even without the cleaning mission she has planned, she has no desire to become better acquainted with Rhys's parents. Why invite more bad energy into her house?

"Nice to meet you both. I'm sorry, but I'm just in the middle of something. Can I help you with anything?" Viola does her best to speak slowly and sound friendly.

Duke answers immediately, using a saccharine tone that turns Viola's stomach.

"No, we won't keep you. I just wanted to let you know that Rhys, Wendy, and Mirabelle have gone away for a few days." He smiles and fixes her with a challenging stare. Viola can almost hear his thoughts. *Go on. Go on, I dare you to question me.*

"Oh. I was round there just last night, and they never

mentioned anything." Viola's mouth feels dry, and a small bead of sweat breaks out between her shoulder blades and trickles all the way down her back.

"Yes. Rhys mentioned that you were invited over for dinner." Duke looks down at his hands and examines his pristine nails. "I think they realised they needed some family time. Moving is stressful, don't you agree?"

Viola nods, feeling herself shrink under this man's gaze and wishing she could be anywhere else. "Yes, of course. But–"

Duke holds out his hand and silences her. Viola can see where Rhys gets his atrociously entitled bad manners. "I just wanted to make you aware they'll be gone for a couple of days. That's all. Christine and I will be keeping an eye on the place, so you needn't worry about..." He waves his hand in the air looking for a way to finish the sentence, but it's clear what he means, and Viola wants to finish his sentence for him. Interfering? Butting in? Eventually, he speaks. "Checking on the house. I hope that puts your mind at rest. You seem like a very concerned and caring neighbour." He smiles out of one side of his mouth.

"Yes, well, thank you for that, Duke. I'd better be getting back to–"

He cuts her off again, and Viola promises herself that next time, she'll just keep right on talking. He doesn't get to stop and start her like this. She puts her hands on her hips and raises herself up as tall as she can. At the same time, Christine makes a barely noticeable movement towards her husband, tucking herself into his side. Viola looks into the woman's eyes, checking for any signs of fear, but there is nothing. Viola has seen this too many times in women of her generation. Her husband is her master. She's been brainwashed to feel inferior. It saddens her.

"Also, while we're putting your mind at rest, I wanted to echo Rhys's sentiments from yesterday. I do apologise that you were put in an unfortunate situation while we were at our friend's funeral the other day, but I can assure you that Christine was merely having a nap after taking an unfortunate turn." Viola doesn't say anything. She didn't buy this story the first time, and having it repeated won't change that. "Christine, tell Viola."

The way he speaks to his wife is instructional and rude, and Viola feels herself prickle all over.

Christine suddenly springs into life, her voice breathy, as though it's retreated beyond her throat through lack of use. "Yes, Viola. I wasn't feeling well, so I had a nap. I forget things. Duke and Rhys look after me ever so well." She gives Viola a small smile, looks up to Duke as though to check she has done well, and retreats back to her default position, handbag poised in front of her. The whole scene reminds Viola of a robot powering on and off. And Duke is clearly in charge of the controls. Duke claps his hand, and Viola flinches, as she suspects Duke hoped she would.

"Right then. Now that we've got that all ironed out, we'll let you get back to your day. Rhys and Wendy will be back in a few days, and I'm sure they'll be in touch."

Viola wants to ask so many things. Where have they gone? Why such a last-minute trip? What on earth is actually going on here? But something inside her deflates, and she nods, not even offering a goodbye.

There is something impenetrable about both Duke and Rhys. It doesn't seem to matter how much evidence there is to the contrary – they present their version of reality, and everyone just has to go with it. Plus, they are both obvious misogynists, and Viola really has no time for men like that.

Viola watches the couple as they walk down her path towards the large jeep parked outside number 33, which Viola hadn't noticed and is sure wasn't there moments earlier. Duke strolls slowly and confidently, and Christine takes four or five shuffling steps to each of his strides. Viola would love to think that she is witnessing a husband taking care of his wife who is experiencing deteriorating health. But instead all she sees is power and control. Dominance and submission.

Viola closes the door slowly and rests her back against it. What she wouldn't give for a day when the family next door didn't derail her plans and infect her mind with their unusual and downright odd behaviour. She looks around her living room. Dust motes still floating unattractively in the air. Duke said they'd be gone for a couple of days, and she has no idea where, so there is little she can do. She will clean today and return to her usual routine. Establish normalcy again. She hopes that Wendy, Rhys, and Mirabelle are simply enjoying a break together, an impromptu getaway to spend some quality time as a family and relax after the stresses of moving house.

However, a feeling deep in Viola's gut tells her that the reason for the family's sudden departure is something else altogether.

CHAPTER FIFTEEN

Two days pass, and Viola starts to feel more like herself again. She meets her friends, goes to the shops, and spends some quiet time reading and crocheting. She's grateful to once again feel happy and content. If Duke and Christine have been back to check on the house, she hasn't seen them. The curtains at number 33 remain closed, and there are no signs of activity of any kind. On the odd occasion that curiosity raised its head, she thought about peeking through the letter box for any signs of piled up mail, but what would that actually tell her? Nothing other than either someone has picked it up or they haven't received any.

Today, she is going to have a quick cuppa with Nina, pop into the florists, treat herself to some fresh flowers for the house and get some for Martin's grave. She'll visit his resting place this afternoon and do her usual spruce up of his plot. Viola has never felt that a visit to Martin's grave is required to feel connected or talk to him. They were together for so long that he will always be a part of her and this house. But maintaining his grave and headstone is a mark of respect, and she often worries who will keep it up and also tend to hers when she is gone.

Viola gets ready and leaves the house, but as she locks the door, she sees the imposing presence of the jeep on the drive of number 33. Talking with Duke will only put a dent in her mood, so she walks as quietly as possible down the front path, cursing herself for choosing to wear her sandals that make tip-tapping noises no matter how softly she places her feet. Her heart falls as she sees Duke's figure appear from the side of the jeep. He looks obnoxious in mirrored sunglasses far too large for his face.

"Ah, hello, Viola. Off out, are we?"

She'd love to reply that it's rather obvious she's going out given that she's just left her house and is, in fact, already outside but thinks better of it.

"Hi, yes, I'm going to meet some friends. Have a lovely day." She tries to end the conversation there and begins to walk away, but Duke clearly has other ideas.

"That's good. It's important to stay active and social, don't you think, Viola? Christine was quite the social animal before she became unwell."

Irritation fizzes inside her. This man is insufferable and patronising beyond belief.

Viola gives him a pinched smile. "Bye then."

"Bye, Viola." She really hates how he overuses her name. It's excessively familiar and gives her the heebie-jeebies. "And just to say that Rhys, Wendy, and Mirabelle will return on Saturday as planned."

Viola knows she should just keep walking. He's baiting her. Saturday is another three days away. That is not what he told her previously. He said a couple of days. If they return on Saturday, that will be more like a week.

"Oh, did they decide to stay on a little longer? I hope they're having a nice time."

Duke takes a few steps towards her, screws up his obnoxious face, and whips off his sunglasses.

"No. Whatever do you mean?" This man is a terrible actor, and she knows he is lying, but what does it matter. A couple of days, five days, six days – it's really not important.

"Oh, nothing. I just remember you saying they were going for a couple of days, that's all. But it doesn't matter, anyway. I'd best be off." Viola turns away but feels Duke move towards her, his oppressive presence suddenly behind her, far too close for comfort.

"I think you'll find I didn't say a couple of days, Viola."

She faces him. Why is he making such a big deal of this? "Okay. That's what I heard, but no harm done." Viola shrugs, trying to lighten the intense atmosphere. Duke tilts his head at her, and the corners of his mouth turn down in a theatrical sad smile. It's not a response she was expecting. It's the kind of look you'd give someone you felt sorry for.

"Well, these things happen as you get older, don't they?"

Frustration begins to build inside Viola, and her ability to keep her thoughts to herself and get on with her day is lessening with every word that falls out of his smug mouth.

"And what things would they be, Duke?"

Duke raises his hands in a placatory fashion. "Woah. Come on, Viola. Calm down."

If he says her name one more time, she thinks she might scream. "I am calm. I'm simply asking you what you meant."

Duke clasps his hands together and sighs as though he's being asked to explain something obvious to someone stupid. "It's just as we get older, we forget things, don't we? We misunderstand and misinterpret things."

Viola stands her ground. "Yes, I guess you must have forgotten that you said a couple of days. I understand. It's easily done when you get, as you say, older." She smiles, pleased with

THE FAMILY NEXT DOOR

the way she's managed to flip this around onto him. He's no spring chicken either and, when it comes to memory, Viola knows she is still in tip-top shape.

Duke's face suddenly darkens, and Viola feels her heart rate begin to pick up before his demeanour brightens again, and he laughs heartily. His change in mood does nothing to calm Viola's now racing heart and jangling nerves.

"All I am saying, Viola, is that it's important to be aware that forgetting or misremembering things is to be expected and that as a woman living on your own, you must ensure you are *safe*." He places extra emphasis on the word 'safe', enough to turn it from a statement of concern into something that feels like a threat. Both Rhys and Duke have the passive-aggressive approach down to a T.

Viola has undoubtedly spent enough time sharing air with this man. He has proven that, just like his son, there is no point trying to reason with him. In his eyes, his word is law.

"Well, you don't have to worry about me. Goodbye, Duke. I really have to go."

Duke replaces his sunglasses and makes no move to retreat or say goodbye, so Viola turns and walks away, promising herself that she will not turn back around this time, no matter what utter rubbish he tries to reel her back in with. She manages several steps before he shouts, "Take good care, Viola. Take very good care." His words are laced with bad intentions, and Viola feels a chill spread through her. For the first time since living on her own, she feels genuinely afraid for her safety.

———

Her encounter with Duke puts more than a dent in her mood. Despite her best efforts to hide it from Nina, she knows her dear friend spots her low spirits as soon as she joins her at their usual table in the café. They hug and air kiss as always, but Viola can feel a side eye from Nina as they embrace. Nina means the world to Viola, and she remembers her promise to herself not to reveal any of the goings-on at number 33 to her. Unloading onto Nina would only achieve one of two things: either she will end up worrying her closest friend unnecessarily, or Nina will encourage Viola to take action that she is not ready for, or worse, take the decision out of her hands. Working with families the way they did together for years is something that never leaves you. It was never just a job for either of them – it was a vocation, and Viola would be very surprised if Nina would be happy to leave this alone.

"What's up, Viola?" Nina looks at her with deep concern in her eyes, and Viola immediately knows that saying "nothing" is entirely out of the question. The waiter comes over, and they order coffee and a slice of carrot cake each. Nina raises an eyebrow in lieu of repeating herself, and Viola puffs out an exasperated breath.

"Honestly, it's just a bunch of things. I'm out of sorts, is all." Again, Nina doesn't speak – instead reaching her hand out and giving Viola's forearm a gentle squeeze. Viola continues. "It's my day to go to Martin's grave, and I've got new neighbours. I told you, it's not really anything. I'm just being a grumpy cow." Nina sits back and appraises Viola, tapping her index finger against her chin comically.

"Well, I'd say two out of the three explanations you've just given are utter rubbish." Viola can't help but laugh. Nina has a wicked sense of humour and knows just how to pull her out of the doldrums. "First off, nobody in living memory has ever described you as a grumpy cow. Me, on the other hand, I'm called that on an almost daily basis, but you, my friend, are anything but." Viola feels tears prick her eyes. Nina is, of course, right. Grumpiness is not a trait of Viola's at all. "Secondly, you love going to the florist, and I know your visits to Martin don't make you sad. So, unless something has changed there, which my Viola radar is telling me is not the case, I'm guessing your new neighbours are making you miserable. How am I doing? Ten out of ten? Nine?"

Viola rolls her eyes good-naturedly and smiles as the waiter comes over and delivers their drinks and food. The slices of cake are even larger and have more cream cheese frosting than usual. Viola can't wait to dig in, and when she looks up, Nina already has a forkful in her mouth and is making appreciative noises loud enough to alert the other customers.

"You're right. Of course, you're right." Viola thinks carefully before deciding what to share. "Kevin and Leo have moved out, and this new family have just moved in and they're..." Nina makes a winding motion with her hands, her mouth still full of cake, urging Viola to continue. "They're fine, I guess. There's a little girl who is very sweet, and I've kind of made friends with the mum, but the dad is... well, let's just say I've not warmed to him. He's like this old-fashioned misogynist, and he treats me like I'm some doddery old lady." Although there are glaring omissions in this story, it is essentially the bare bones of the truth.

Nina wipes her mouth with a napkin – the cake now demolished. "I hate men like that, and unfortunately, they're everywhere. You and I, we found ourselves two real men." Nina fixes Viola with a penetrating stare. "Now, I'm only going to ask this once because it's not like you to get so irritated by shitty human behaviour. After all, we've seen plenty of it." Viola nods, hoping that Nina is about to phrase her question in a way that won't force her to lie. "Are you actually okay? Has something happened with this family that you're worried about?"

Viola tries her hardest to hide her anxiety and fights the overwhelming urge to blurt out the whole bizarre story. "I am okay, and honestly, I just don't really like the whole dynamic, and more than that, I wish Martin was here. I'd feel better if I wasn't on my own." Viola shrugs her shoulders and takes a long drink of her Americano.

Nina studies her for a moment and then raises her own cup to her lips. "Okay. I get that. We've got a guy across the street a bit like that, and I guess I'd feel a bit weird if I didn't have Alistair around. But that's it – nothing else?"

"That's it. Plus, I miss having Kevin and Leo next door. I hadn't realised how safe they made me feel until they'd gone."

Nina nods, and Viola can sense that further interrogation will not follow. She can't decide whether she's relieved or disappointed.

Viola's mood picks up significantly after the combined hit of caffeine and sugar and the simple company of her closest friend. They talk and their time together seems to pass in a flash.

"I need to head back now, Viola, and I'm taking that smile on your face as a personal victory." They hug and walk towards the door together. "But call me anytime, remember, and if your neighbour starts acting like an arse, let me know, and I'll send Alistair over. Actually, scratch that, I'm tougher than him." They both laugh and wave their goodbyes, blowing kisses as they walk in opposite directions.

By the time Viola walks to the florist and makes her way to the graveyard, she is utterly exhausted. Thankfully, Martin's plot is in pretty good shape, and after disposing of the dead flowers and replacing them with the fresh bouquet she chose, she is able to close her eyes, stand in silence, and take a much-needed moment to be at peace with her husband's memory. It is not in Viola's nature to feel doom and gloom over Martin's death these days. His life was full and well-lived, and she finds it easy to celebrate him and call upon all their wonderful experiences together whenever sadness threatens to set in. But the family at number 33 has somehow sucked that ability out of her. What she wouldn't give to have Martin by her side, supporting her, taking away her fear, and comforting her. A tear falls down her cheek, and she rubs it away, annoyed with herself for letting all this overwhelm her. She has never once felt abandoned or self-pitying about Martin's death, and she recognises that she's dangerously close to this now. That's not a place she wants to be in.

Viola closes her eyes again and tries to summon Martin's energy. He wouldn't let any of this get in the way of their lives. He'd either act or leave it completely alone and certainly wouldn't tolerate any nasty behaviour from Rhys or Duke. He would fight fire with fire, unashamedly and without fear. Viola bids Martin farewell, blows him a kiss, and tells him she loves him before walking slowly home. Her mind is tired and sluggish, but she makes sure to lock and check every door and window before collapsing into bed.

Duke's parting words ring in her ears.

"Take good care, Viola. Take very good care."

CHAPTER SIXTEEN

Viola tries lots of things to lift her mood in the coming days. She gardens, visits the salon and has her hair and nails done, tends to her back garden, and sits in the sunshine reading. Determination mostly prevails, and although not completely free of the dark cloud that has become her unwelcome companion, she knows she has weathered the storm, and it will lift soon.

Viola credits her mum for her internal strength. She never felt anything but love and support growing up. Her mum told her she was strong and fierce – a force to be reckoned with – and this has been how Viola has tried to live her life.

She is in the kitchen preparing a salad to accompany the salmon she's roasted for dinner when she hears tyres pulling up outside. Immediately, she puts down the knife, wipes her hands on her apron, and moves to a spot in the living room where she can view the drive but not be seen herself. She wants to see that Wendy and Mirabelle are safe and well. She observes as Rhys opens the car door and helps an excited Mirabelle out. Mirabelle has a large purple teddy bear in her arms and runs into the house, waving it. Rhys comes in and out of the house several times, unloading bags and clearing out rubbish from the car. Viola watches intently as he fills a plastic bag with empty water bottles and food packets before returning indoors for the cordless vacuum cleaner Wendy used to clear up the glass Viola smashed during her visit. She is not surprised to see Rhys is intolerant of mess. It fits entirely with his controlling and obsessive nature.

Viola waits until Rhys has finished and the front door of their house is closed before returning to the kitchen. Seeing Mirabelle happy and full of life is such a relief, but she wishes she could have caught even the slightest glimpse of Wendy. Common sense would suggest Wendy had entered the house before Viola could see her. Whenever she and Martin returned from a trip, Viola would unpack indoors and Martin would empty the car. Still, she'd like to see Wendy with her own eyes. To achieve that, Viola needs an excuse to go outside. Knocking on their door is a definite no, but perhaps she might glimpse Wendy through the window if she gets a little closer to their house.

Deciding that watering the plants seems like as good an excuse as any, Viola goes to the back garden and retrieves the watering can from Martin's shed. She has kept everything in here just as it was, even though she has no idea what half of the tools and bits and pieces are for. She'll water all the plants that line the side of her path. If she doesn't see Wendy, she will go back inside and continue with her dinner as planned. No more interfering.

The watering can is heavy, and Viola struggles to carry it through the house with both hands without sloshing water around the living room. The evening is bright and crisp, and she breathes in the scent of freshly cut grass from the surrounding gardens. It's one of her favourite smells. She begins her task, accidentally drowning the first couple of plants before getting a better grip on her pouring speed. She can hear voices coming from Number 33, and she's almost sure Wendy's is mixed in there somewhere.

Hearing their door open, she does her best to stand up slowly and not look too eager to turn around and see who it is. But there is no need as Mirabelle comes bounding out of the house. Viola's worried she is going to crash right into her, but somehow, the sprinting girl skids to a halt barely an inch away from Viola's feet. The big soft purple toy is still in her hands, and Viola can see it is actually some sort of long-armed monkey, not a bear.

"Look at this!" Mirabelle grabs the long arms of the toy monkey and fastens them around her neck before running around again with her arms spread out wide. "Look, he goes round my neck!" Mirabelle's eyes are brimming with excitement, and Viola finds herself uplifted by the girl's natural exuberance.

"Wow, Mirabelle, that's amazing."

Mirabelle stops, panting, and a smile fills her flushed face. "Isn't he? He's called Tennis Ball."

Viola can't help but laugh at the utterly ludicrous name of the monkey. "Nice to meet you, Tennis Ball, and also, welcome back, Mirabelle. I hope you had a great trip."

Mirabelle is jumping up and down, barely containing her excitement. "Yep. The best. I'll go and get Mummy. She'll want to say hi." Mirabelle runs off, and Viola smiles to herself at Mirabelle using the word "Mummy" for the first time to describe Wendy. Clearly, their time away has had a positive impact on their mother-daughter relationship. Viola hopes she'll see the same level of contentment from Wendy. The poor woman has clearly had a difficult time with Mirabelle's reaction and subsequent upsetting behaviour after finding out that

Wendy is not her biological mother. This could be the new start she was hoping for.

Viola waits patiently. She can hear bits and pieces of the conversation from inside the house. Mirabelle sounds whiny, saying things like "Come on, Mummy" and "Just come outside." Viola can't make out any of the specifics of Wendy's response to her daughter. Still, it is clear that for whatever reason, Wendy doesn't want to come outside. Viola walks over to number 33 to let Wendy know there's no need for her to come out and talk.

She shouts through the open door. "Mirabelle, I'm afraid I have to go inside now. I'll see you and your mummy tomorrow." Viola begins to walk away, but a small hand grabs her arm. Viola looks down at Mirabelle. The girl's face is red and cross, and her hand squeezes Viola's forearm painfully, her fingers digging into her soft flesh, her nails making crescent moon indentations in her skin. Viola crumples her brow, not wanting to admonish the girl with her mother so close by, but silently letting her know that this behaviour is not okay. Mirabelle's face falls, and she lets go and lowers her eyes to the ground. Viola rubs her arm. Mirabelle still has the monkey around her neck. Her eyes are wet and glassy, and she's shuffling her feet. She's clearly sorry for what she's done but is not saying so.

Viola bends down so they are eye to eye. "It's okay, sweetheart. I know you didn't mean to hurt me. I can see how excited you are, and I am so looking forward to hearing all about your trip from you and your mummy." Viola looks inside the door, but there's still no sign of Wendy. "But I think Mummy is busy just now so why don't we all meet up some other time. What do you think?"

Mirabelle's eyes brighten a little, and she sniffs and nods. Viola suddenly turns as she sees a figure flash in her peripheral vision, blocking the doorway to the kitchen before closing it altogether.

"Do you have someone else staying with you, Mirabelle?"

"No, silly. That's just Mummy tidying up in the kitchen." Mirabelle blinks widely and innocently. "Daddy's upstairs. He's tired after driving. But I don't get why driving makes you tired. It's just sitting down and turning a wheel. How tiring can..."

Viola lets Mirabelle's words fade into the background, considering what she can say next.

"That didn't look like your mummy, your mummy's not–" Viola stops, not wanting to finish the sentence.

Mirabelle laughs and, for some reason, does a pirouette. "Oh, I know. Mummy looks different now because she's got a baby in her belly." Mirabelle beams at her. "I'm getting a baby brother." Mirabelle does another pirouette and announces, "Ta-da!"

Once again, Viola finds herself in an incomprehensible situation, with absolutely no idea how to respond or what to think. She had almost managed to convince herself that there must be a reason for all the disturbing goings-on. But there is simply no explanation for this. The woman in the kitchen doorway was definitely not Wendy. She had a similar build and hair colour, and yes, she only glimpsed her for the tiniest of moments, but that woman was most certainly not Wendy. And more than that, the woman Mirabelle is now calling Mummy is heavily pregnant. Viola has no words, and even if she did, her mouth is bone dry and unable to form them.

Mirabelle stands smiling at her. "Isn't it so exciting? I've wanted a baby brother for ages, and now they've got me one."

Viola stares at the girl. The words chill her to the bone. "*Got me one.*" You don't just get a baby. Something very wrong is going on here, and Viola has no idea what to do about it.

Where is Wendy? Who is this pregnant woman that has suddenly appeared? Surely Mirabelle must be mistaken. The woman she saw must be somebody else. What other explanation can there be?

"Are you okay, Viola? You look a bit funny. Shall I ask Mummy to get you a drink of water?"

"No!" Viola's aggressive response surprises even her, but the thought of meeting this woman feels like more than she can handle right now.

Mirabelle pouts. "Okay. No need to be mean and shouty." Mirabelle twists side to side, the monkey swinging in a weirdly hypnotic fashion as she moves.

Viola manages to shake her head. "Sorry. No, I think I'll go and lie down. I'm feeling very tired, Mirabelle."

Mirabelle seems placated. "Okay. Come over tomorrow, though. I didn't just get Tennis Ball, I got other stuff, too, that I want to show you."

Viola nods, dazed. "I will," she says while thinking that she most certainly will not.

Mirabelle waves and runs into the house, leaving the front door wide open. "Bye."

Viola forces her face into a smile and starts to slowly walk home. She simultaneously feels as though she's floating and also walking through quicksand. This is all far, far too much for her. Is she losing her mind? Somewhere, far off in the distance, Viola hears her name called. She doesn't respond and keeps trudging towards her house, but then it comes again, louder and more insistent.

"Viola." Rhys is standing in the doorway, arm raised and a sickening smile on his face. Viola gives no reaction. "Wendy wanted to come and say hello, but she's tired after the journey." Viola just stands there, watching him. "She's only got a few weeks left until the baby comes, so being in the car is pretty uncomfortable." He pats his own stomach.

Viola has nothing to say; nothing to give. So, she ignores him and prays she makes it to her front door before she faints. Her fingers and lips tingle, and she knows she needs to sit down very quickly or she'll fall.

"Goodnight, Viola. Take very good care."

Viola hears their door close and feels goose bumps rise up on her arms. She is cold. So cold. She stumbles into her house and collapses onto the sofa. Her head is pounding. She feels sick and utterly overwhelmed by what she has just seen. She knows she should be doing something, but she doesn't have the wherewithal to do anything but lie down at the moment.

Even as she lies there, unimaginable thoughts swirling and nausea building, she knows something terrible is happening. When her nerves settle and she rebuilds her strength, she will make sure she finds out what.

And when she does, she will make damn sure Rhys and Duke don't get away with it.

CHAPTER SEVENTEEN

Viola's usual plans have gone out of the window. Nothing else matters. Her sleep last night was filled with hideous nightmares. Wendy being tortured, Viola being chased, and Rhys laughing at her with a twisted and deformed face – demon-like and horrific.

More than once, she was startled awake, certain she could hear the sound of a baby crying, only for it to fade away into nothing. When morning finally came, she awoke drenched in sweat and had no choice but to strip her bed and take a shower to rid herself of the tortuous dreams. Anger is bubbling through her now. She has been far too passive, and she needs to act while she's still strong. She will not let Rhys and Duke make a fool of her. All of this is taking a toll on her physical and mental health, and she needs to take care of herself properly. Ensure she sleeps and eats well to keep her mind and body strong and rested. Nobody else will do it for her.

Viola recognises she has lived a life relatively free of traumatic events. Martin dying was easily the worst thing that has ever happened to her. She needs to handle her reactions better and build some resilience. She falls to pieces every time something unexpected happens with the family next door. Viola considers the word 'unexpected'. It doesn't even come close to describing the things that have occurred. Ludicrous, unbelievable, terrifying. These are better words, but still, they don't quite encompass it all. She wishes she had someone to talk to, someone she feels comfortable confiding and revealing this to. Someone she can trust to believe her and help her. Holding this on her own is too hard. But who would she tell, and what would she say? Her friends are wonderful, Nina in particular, but this feels too deep to involve them in. So, given the limited options available to her, Viola is back at her table making a list. She needs to do something, and that's all she can come up with right now. Try to organise her thoughts and write down what she needs to do. List the things that need to happen today, no matter what Rhys or Duke might try to bamboozle her with.

Only now does she understand why Duke was planting the seed of her being forgetful or misremembering things. But she is not some doddery old lady. She knows what she saw, she knows what she heard, and she knows something is very wrong. So far, her list looks like this:

1. *Visit number 33 and ask to see 'Wendy'.*

2. *If Wendy is not Wendy, call the police and report her missing.*

3. *If Wendy is not there or if Wendy is—*

Viola rips the page from the book, screws it into a ball, and throws it at the wall. It makes no sense anyway. All she can do is go next door and then work things out from there. No backtracking. No being fobbed off. So that's exactly what she does.

———

Rhys answers the door. He looks unsurprised and amused to see Viola standing there.

"Ah, good morning, Viola. I thought you might pay us a visit." *I bet you fucking did*, thinks Viola defiantly. "I do hope you slept well?" Viola is sure she sees him give her a wink, but she's not playing his games this morning. She has her own agenda, and if he knows what's good for him, he'll get out of her way.

"Is Wendy in?"

Rhys smiles with fake civility. "Yes."

Viola huffs and rolls her eyes when he doesn't say anything further. "Then may I see her, please?"

Rhys taps his index finger against his chin as though pondering her request. Viola has to ball her fists up tightly and bite her tongue to avoid exploding in a fit of rage. She hates this man so much. He steps back and to the side, allowing Viola to enter.

"Of course you may," he says before adding under his breath, "seeing as you asked so nicely."

Viola ignores him and walks through to the kitchen. The décor looks just the same: shiny and sterile. The only change is the woman sitting at the table, flicking through a magazine with a large mug of green-tinged hot water next to her. Herbal tea, most likely. The woman looks up and smiles at Viola before standing. She has blonde wavy hair. It is beautifully glossy and thick. Her frame is small, and Viola guesses she is usually petite with a slender waist. Viola's eyes fix on the enormous pregnancy bump straining against a nautical-style navy-blue-and-white-striped shirt. She takes a deep breath. This is when she would typically become overwhelmed and lose her ability to think and act rationally.

But not today. Today, she will maintain control. She will fight.

Viola watches as the pregnant woman waddles towards her, still maintaining an air of elegance despite her almost comical size. Viola fixes on her mouth as she speaks, looking for any speck of something she recognises, but there is nothing. She has never seen this woman before in her life.

"Hi, Viola! It's lovely to see you."

Viola thinks the woman might hug her, but instead, she stands a few feet away, rubbing her tummy as though trying to summon a genie from a lamp.

Viola maintains a steely calm. She can do this. These are only people, and there is nothing special about them. "Hi, I'm sorry, I don't think we've met."

Rhys walks over to the woman and puts his arm around her in precisely the same possessive way he did with Wendy the night of the dinner.

"Now, Viola, I know Wendy is blooming at a rate of knots, but surely that doesn't make her unrecognisable." He laughs and strokes the woman's pregnant belly. She looks up at him lovingly before turning back to Viola, her brow furrowed and blinking far too rapidly.

Viola knows that the further she gets into conversation with these people, the more confused and in danger of being pulled into their web of deceit and lies she will be.

Viola fixes her eyes on Rhys. "Where is Wendy?"

Rhys steps back from the woman pretending to be Wendy and points jokingly with both index fingers at her before shrugging his shoulders.

"Viola, are you feeling okay?"

She grits her teeth. "I'm completely fine, Rhys. But as we all know, this is not Wendy."

Rhys and 'pretend Wendy' look at each other with mock concern in their eyes. He strokes her on the face.

"You go lie down, sweetheart. This isn't good for the baby."

She smiles, and he kisses her on the forehead. Viola watches every inch of their movements, waiting for them to slip up or reveal something to prove that this is all a charade.

'Pretend Wendy' gives Viola a small, uncertain wave and says, "I hope you feel better soon, Viola," before leaving the room and ambling up the stairs.

Viola tries to control her shallow, ragged breathing and to stand tall.

Rhys takes a step towards her. "Maybe you should go home and lie down too."

Viola feels the shift in his behaviour like a physical force. The jovial air he possessed moments ago is gone, and what's left is threatening and frightening.

But Viola has been here before, and this time, she is prepared. "I'll give you one last chance, Rhys. Tell me where Wendy is. I don't care who that woman upstairs is, but I want to know that Wendy is safe." A horrible thought falls into Viola's mind. "And Mirabelle, too. As long as I know they are both safe, I'm more than happy to leave you to whatever sick and twisted game you think you're playing here."

Rhys turns his head slowly, and Viola follows his line of sight. Mirabelle is standing in the doorway. How on earth did she get there? Mirabelle's face is thunderous. Her eyes are dark and stormy pools. When she speaks, her voice sounds different. Throaty and sinister.

"I'm right here, Viola. Why don't you go home? I don't like you anymore." With that, Mirabelle turns on her heels and walks away. Viola is astonished and wounded by Mirabelle's words, and she pushes back the tears that are beginning to form behind her eyes. When she looks at Rhys, she sees pure delight on his face. He is enjoying every moment of this macabre performance.

"Go home, Viola. Go home and leave me, Wendy, and Mirabelle the fuck alone." He smiles sweetly as though he'd just spoken a completely different sentence. Viola gathers all her strength and nods her head. She can't stop her voice from shaking but manages to say her piece, nonetheless.

"Don't worry, I'm going. Expect a visit from the police."

Rhys follows her out of the kitchen, but she doesn't stop or look back despite the venomous tirade spewing from his mouth.

"Don't you fucking dare! Who the fuck do you think you are butting into our lives? You're senile. You're delusional. Who on earth will believe a mad old bat like you?" Rhys laughs, but there is a hint of nervousness in his voice, the only thing stopping Viola from bursting into tears. He's rattled by her threat of involving the police, which is the first thing she'll do when she gets home. She only hopes Mirabelle can't hear his foul language and vile insults.

Viola walks out of the front door with purpose and attempts to slam it behind her. Instead, it connects with some part of Rhys's body and she hears it thwack against him. Viola hopes it hurts. She hopes it hurts like hell. Viola rolls her ankle as she awkwardly steps from their garden path onto the street. A sharp stabbing pain that makes her shriek. It stalls her only briefly before she hunkers down and carries on through the pain. Nothing can stop her this time.

Rhys is still behind her, but she has tunnel vision now. He doesn't exist anymore. She is going home, and there is nothing Rhys can do about it. That is, until he says those words. Words so hideous she feels her heart shatter into a thousand tiny pieces. She whirls around, clutching her chest, and more than willing to kill this spiteful, disgraceful liar of a human being if she had the means.

Her jaw clenched and her eyes red hot with fury, she whispers, "What did you just say?"

Rhys swaggers towards her, hands in pockets, swinging his hips. He leans down and places his mouth close to her ear. Viola wants to scream in his face, but she listens because she needs to hear him say it one more time.

"I said, think twice before calling the police. You don't want to ruin Martin's memory."

Viola is trembling uncontrollably. Rhys's breath is brushing against her ear, making her want to vomit. She realises she's shaking her head rapidly from side to side.

Rhys speaks again, a little louder this time but no less malicious. "I suggest you do as I asked and mind your fucking business. Martin was a good friend of my father's, and I would hate for you to get yourself into something... unfortunate."

Viola is desperate to know what he is talking about and even more desperate not to hear something that would shatter everything she thought she ever knew. Martin was a good man. Of course he was. Rhys is just trying to find another despicable way to hurt her. He's evil and conniving, and dare she say it, he's very bloody good at it because her heart aches and her soul feels broken. She looks up at Rhys with watery, desperate eyes.

"Call the police if you must, Viola. It will be fruitless. The only person who will corroborate your story is you. Maybe they'll even think you're not safe to live on your own anymore, especially if your concerned neighbours suggest it." He places his thumbnail between his front teeth, creating a snarling expression. Viola flinches. "But don't say I didn't warn you, and perhaps have a good look through your husband's effects before you decide whether to make that call.

I think you'll find yourself seeing things completely differently."

Rhys leaves without saying another word, and Viola wishes that the ground would open up and swallow her whole right where she stands.

She is empty.

She is beaten.

She has absolutely nothing left.

CHAPTER EIGHTEEN

MIRABELLE

I thought Viola was my friend. Why isn't she happy about my new baby brother? She's being mean and horrible, and why would she care more about stupid old Wendy than me?

Daddy says she's jealous because she's old and lonely and can't remember things properly. That kind of makes me sad, but Daddy says I need to stay away from her because she'll try to spoil everything for me.

I didn't like Daddy being mean and sweary at Viola. That wasn't nice at all. But he said he did it for me. He told me Viola wants to ruin everything and that she doesn't want me to get a new baby brother.

I know Daddy would never let that happen.

He always makes sure I get what I want.

CHAPTER NINETEEN

Viola lies on her sofa, the remnants of her tears making her face feel cold and clammy. She hasn't called the police, nor will she. Not yet, anyway. She lets out a strangulated moan, hating everything about this situation and the vile man who has placed her in it. She sits up slowly and tries to tidy her hair, vaguely remembering pulling at it in frustration while crying earlier.

The last hour or so is cloudy. A cacophony of emotions pulling her every which way, leaving her utterly drained and with no clue as to what she believes. Viola knows deep in her heart that Martin was a good man. No, a wonderful man. He would never have been involved in anything sinister. He didn't have it in him to be unkind to anyone, and definitely not anything involving harming women or children. Martin was an old-fashioned gentleman. Rhys only knows his name because she had told him it when they were having dinner, and it's clear to anyone who hears her talking about Martin that she is proud of the man he was. Rhys is using this fact to hurt her. That's what he does. He's a snake in the grass, and when he saw her becoming stronger and less intimidated by him, he attacked her Achilles heel. The memory of her beloved husband.

Viola knows, though, that she will take a look through Martin's things, even if only to reminisce and raise herself up after her vile encounter with Rhys. She is now confident that the horrible man next door has a proclivity for violence. He's not simply domineering and arrogant. Once she has ensured that nothing in her house ties Martin to Duke or Rhys, she will call the police and tell them everything she knows. Intimidation won't stop her this time. She won't have blood on her hands.

Viola throws two large pillows onto the bedroom floor and lowers herself onto them, pulling her legs into a crossed position. Her knees crunch in rebellion, but she takes a moment and finds a vaguely comfortable position.

Martin's paperwork is in one of the drawers of her divan bed. She hasn't thrown any of it away, just in case she needed it at some point. Viola has no plans to move house, but she recognises there may come a day when a house with stairs isn't suitable for her. She smiles as she sees an array of envelopes and folders piled up neatly inside the drawer. Martin loved order and was brilliant at dealing with all the life admin that Viola found as dull as watching grass grow.

Flicking through the documents, Viola finds nothing to back up Rhys's claims, although she has no idea what that could even be. What is she looking for? Instead, she decides to look at every piece of paper in the drawer. She feels terribly guilty for doubting Martin, but Rhys is twisted and his manipulation is horribly convincing. Viola feels tears prick her eyes as she scans through an envelope full of every optician's prescription Martin received. They go back more than twenty years. She gave up telling him to throw it all out.

"You never know," was his usual response, and as Viola has discovered recently, you indeed never know what life will throw at you. A large white A4 envelope catches Viola's eye. The others have addresses and postmarks on them. But this one is blank apart from the words 'insurance policy' in tiny letters handwritten in the top right corner. And unlike every other envelope in here this one is sealed. Viola inspects the writing – it's definitely Martin's. She turns it over in her hands. It's light and must only have a page or two inside. Butterflies flutter in her tummy as her sixth sense kicks in. She knows there is something important in here. Something Martin was keeping from her. Sweat starts to break out on her brow, and she wipes it away before tearing it open. Whatever is inside will not change simply because she chooses not to look at it. Denial will only leave her vulnerable.

She closes her eyes and pulls out the contents, her heart rate escalating uncomfortably. The first thing she sees is a piece of paper that she recognises. It's the final payment on their mortgage. She relaxes and exhales slowly. Viola remembers raising a glass of bourbon with Martin the day this arrived. When Martin retired, five years earlier than planned, he got a much bigger lump sum payment than Viola was expecting. It was enough to pay off the remainder of their mortgage. She was not surprised to hear that Martin put a little extra in their pension pot each month. Planning ahead and being sensible with money were most definitely his strengths.

A smaller envelope is stapled to the back of their final mortgage statement. Small, white, and again sealed. The kind you'd expect to see with a thank-you card or a little Christmas card inside. She decides not to separate the two and instead manoeuvres the tiny envelope around until she can poke in a finger and prise it open. She wiggles her fingers inside and pulls out a small folded piece of paper. Viola sits back, her hands tremulous and a horrible sinking feeling in the pit of her stomach. Whatever Rhys was hinting at, this is it. She can feel it.

The innocuous piece of paper feels like an unexploded

bomb in her hands. But before she can bring herself to unfold it, there is a knock at the door. Viola looks at the paper. She knows she'll need time to digest whatever she discovers, so she needs to either ignore the door or wait until she has dealt with whoever the unwelcome visitor is. The decision is made for her as the knock comes again, more like a banging this time. Whoever it is will not be easily put off. She lifts her duvet and slides the papers underneath it, safe for when she returns. Viola's legs are partially asleep, but she forces herself up and down the stairs, pins and needles shooting through her feet. She doesn't care who is at the door as long as she can get rid of them quickly and get back to the task at hand. If it is Rhys or the woman pretending to be Wendy, they'll get the door closed in their face. Viola opens the door, and her stomach lurches. Her visitor is neither Rhys nor 'pretend Wendy', but they are most certainly unwelcome.

It is Duke. Alone this time, without his limpet of a wife. Viola chastises herself for thinking of the poor woman negatively. She's probably been through a lot with such an obnoxious and domineering husband. But emotions are not what they should be at this moment in time. So, limpet it is.

Viola stares at Duke, one hand on her hip, refusing to offer any kind of greeting. He doesn't bother with a sham smile this time. His face is still and businesslike.

"Hello, Viola. May I come in?"

She mirrors his cadence and intonation. "Hello, Duke. No, you may not."

His lips form a thin smile, a horizontal slit in his stony face. "I think you'd rather be sitting for what I have to say, but we can talk here if you wish."

Viola's stomach flips. People usually say that when they're going to tell you about a death or something equally traumatic. "I don't wish to talk with you here, there, or anywhere if I'm honest, Duke. So, I'll be closing the door now." Viola holds the door-frame, hoping that he will step backwards and avoid the need for her to shut it in his face. But something tugs inside her. Bloody curiosity again. If this man has something to say about her husband, she wants to hear it.

She huffs out a big breath. "Okay. Here is fine. You have two minutes, and then I'm gone."

Duke clasps his hands together in front of him and nods. "Very well." His expression changes, less cold now and somewhat pensive. This unnerves Viola even more. She doesn't want this man's pity.

"I wanted to correct something my son said earlier and to apologise for what I hear was a very heated and expletive-filled exchange." Two minutes isn't going to last long if he keeps on with the superfluous words. "I assure you he won't speak to you like that again. Please accept my apologies."

Viola tries not to focus on the absurdity of a father apologising for the behaviour of his fully grown son who has a child of his own, but instead simply accepts the apology.

"Okay. Thank you. What do you want to tell me?"

"Are you sure you wouldn't rather go inside?" Anger flares in Viola's eyes, avoiding the need for her to respond, and Duke holds his hands up. "Okay. Okay." Viola waits impatiently, tapping her foot rapidly for effect. "When Rhys said that Martin and I were friends, that wasn't entirely accurate." Viola hates the sound of Martin's name in his mouth but feels a slight sense of relief at what he just said. "Martin and I had a professional relationship, that is all. He handled the rental agreements for all of my properties, including number 33."

Viola feels as though the breath has been knocked out of her lungs. What Duke has said could be true, in the sense that that was what Martin did for a living. But wouldn't he have told her that he handled the lease for the house next door? Also, the timelines make no sense. Wendy and Rhys have just moved in, Martin couldn't have had anything to do with that. Her head spins, confusion clouding her thoughts.

"The other point my son was trying to make rather ineloquently is that my family requires a certain amount of privacy. We don't want neighbours interfering in our business. Martin understood that and assured us that you did, too."

Viola screws up her face. "That makes no sense. I'd never met your family until recently, and Martin died years ago." Grief strikes her unexpectedly as it often does, particularly when having to use Martin's name in the same sentence as the word 'died'.

Duke raises a finger. "Ah yes, well, I acquired number 33 some years ago. I've been renting it out privately using Martin's services. I only recently decided to take it off the rental market and I was planning to sell, but when Rhys mentioned that he and Wendy were looking to move and start afresh somewhere, this seemed like the perfect place." He smiles, and even though he has explained everything rather well, Viola still feels confused and as though he's not telling her everything there is to know.

"I pride myself on helping my family when I can. The property market isn't what it used to be. It's hard for young families these days, you know."

Viola is sure her face looks ridiculous. She had never set eyes on this man until recently. If he has indeed owned the house next door all of this time, surely she would have seen him, and she would definitely have noticed any appearance of his monstrous car. Plus, even though Martin never really discussed his job, forever telling her it was boring and he was quite happy to leave his work behind the second he left the office, wouldn't he at least once have mentioned that he was managing the rental of the house next door? He definitely would. So, either Duke is lying, or more disturbingly, Martin was hiding the fact from her for some reason.

Thoughts whirling around her head, she allows Duke to continue his explanation, one that hasn't even begun to broach the disappearance of Wendy and her replacement with a heavily pregnant woman.

"So, you see, number 33 belongs to me. Martin used to rent the property for me and now my son and his family live there. That is all."

Viola considers this. She wishes she had some way to sense-check this with Martin but realises she will have to accept the fact she will never know for sure. And anyway, Duke is completely ignoring the Wendy issue.

"But what about Wendy?" Duke's eyes narrow, and Viola swallows uncomfortably. She has to do this. She needs to know. "I'm not senile and can't be convinced that I am. That woman next door is not Wendy, and I need to know that she is safe, or I'm going to have to call the police. Can't you understand that?"

Duke's jaw twitches, and once again, Viola is reminded of the resemblance between father and son. No words are needed to express the threat and menace emanating from him.

When he finally speaks, his tone is icy cold. "Martin was compensated for his understanding that my family requires privacy. If that is required again, I'm sure we can come to some arrangement." Duke folds his arms and lifts one eyebrow. Viola can't help thinking he looks like a comedy villain.

"No, I don't need your money. I just want to know where Wendy is." She is incensed now. Does he think that just because he paid Martin well, he has some kind of hold over her? Is she trying to bribe her? Does he think she has no decency?

Duke is unmoved by her outburst. He leans his head closer to her and whispers conspiratorially, "Indeed. And as I said, the reason you don't need money is because of me."

He hisses the last word at her, and Viola feels momentarily frightened.

"I don't believe you." She tries to stand tall, but the weight of the possibility that he could be right pushes her shoulders down, and she knows that the key to the truth lies underneath her duvet cover upstairs.

Duke takes a step backwards, straightening up and smoothing down the front of his crisp black shirt. "Whether you believe me or not is of no consequence. But I urge you, and I won't say this again, to leave us alone and let us live our lives. I promise you that meddling in our affairs will not end well. That is not a threat, my dear, before you accuse me. I'm not in the habit of threatening people. It is a simple statement of fact."

Viola has nothing to say. She has no answers and wants to ask him more questions and demand an explanation. But the conviction with which he speaks is paralysing.

"Good day, Viola. Think about what I've said. Carefully."

Duke nods as a parting gesture, and with that, he is gone, leaving Viola dumbfounded and lost for words yet again.

CHAPTER TWENTY

Not wanting to sit uncomfortably on the floor for a second time, Viola pulls out the ticking time bomb from under her covers and sits on the bed.

Viola unfolds the small piece of paper and is unsurprised to see a banking receipt. She recognises the bank details as their own. When she sees the figure transferred, her mind explodes. One hundred thousand pounds. She feels faint. This is a lot of money, the kind of money that people go to jail for. The details on the transfer are from Mr Duke Awbry to Mr Martin and Mrs Viola Waterhouse. This means that a payment came from Duke not just to Martin, but to Martin and her.

She drops the piece of paper as though it is scalding hot. The dates fit with when Martin retired. No reason is given for the transfer. No other notes or explanations. Only the cold hard evidence that Martin accepted one hundred thousand pounds from Duke and never told her a thing about it. Viola starts to weep. It sickens her that somehow, Duke owns a piece of her life, her marriage. Duke and Martin knew this, and she didn't. Unwittingly, she has been spending money from that horrible man for years. Living in this house mortgage-free and all of the freedoms that afforded her and Martin are because of him.

This amount of money cannot simply be a part of Martin's job. Did her husband accept hush money? How could he have done such a thing? Viola can't find it within herself to correlate this deceitful act with the man she spent her entire life with. He was a man of honour.

Viola sits hunched over and deflated. All the fight sucked out of her. The bank receipt has landed face down on the bed, and she can see some writing scrawled on the back. She grabs for it ferociously and pulls it towards her, wiping away tears and blinking her swollen eyes. There are two small lines of text written in ink. Viola feels her heart break as she reads them. A message from the grave.

The first line states, *I'm sorry, Viola. I did it for us.* She can almost hear his voice in her head as she reads the words. Next, she takes in the second line: *I love you. Please be careful.*

She wants to screw the paper up and tear it into a thousand pieces. Rid her house of this horrible evidence of her husband's deception. How could he have left her with this? Yes, he died shortly after his diagnosis, but there was still time for him to reveal his secrets. To prepare her. Instead, he left her vulnerable and forced her to discover this all by herself. She feels lost and full of despair. She lets the note fall from her hand. She doesn't need to reread it. The words are ringing in her ears, and she's not sure she'll ever be able to think of anything else again.

Her husband betrayed her.

Whatever Duke and his family are embroiled in, she is complicit now, too. Martin has trapped her, silenced her, and left her with no hand to play. Her head is thumping from the deluge of tears that continue to pour from her eyes. She's amazed she has any left. She shuffles her legs across the bed and lets her feet fall with a thud to the floor. Her heart is empty, and she thinks it may stop working at any moment. She finds herself walking to the bathroom and she looks at her devastated face in the mirror. She looks haggard, and her face is blotchy and misshapen from crying. She's surprised that she still looks like herself because she feels like a completely different person now. One tiny piece of information has cracked her open and smashed her back together in an entirely different configuration. She is altered and will never think or feel in quite the same way again.

Viola reaches for the plastic tumbler she uses to rinse her mouth after brushing her teeth. She fills it with water, gulps down the entire thing, and then repeats. The two glasses of water sloshing around in her tummy will hopefully make their way to rehydrate her brain and quash this splitting headache.

She wipes her face with the back of her hand and shuffles back to bed. She won't move from there for the rest of the day, maybe never. What would be the point? She looks at the open drawer under her bed. She wishes she could return to the moment before she opened it and unlearn everything. Just be happy and ignore the weirdness next door. Martin was right. Curiosity does only bring trouble. And now she's in a whole load of fucking trouble.

She decides to put everything back where it was and never open that drawer again. As she reaches for the piece of paper with Martin's admission on it, she notices another small section of writing in the bottom right-hand corner. Tiny lettering, even smaller than the words printed above. She pulls her reading glasses down from her head and squints.

The first line is a postcode printed in capitals. All but the final letter matches the postcode of this house, so it must be a location somewhere nearby, and below it is one word: 'Querencia'. Viola reads the word out loud, unsure of how to pronounce it and with no idea of what it means. But if Martin wrote it here, he surely wanted her to see it. Is this a place, or a person that can help her? His way of protecting her if this came back to bite her after he was gone? Viola reaches for her phone, which is discarded at the bottom of the bed, and searches the internet for 'Querencia'.

She first sees something related to bullfighting. That can't be right. She inspects Martin's writing again, checking the spelling and comparing it with what she has typed into the search bar.

She scrolls down and finds a second definition: 'A place from which one's strength is drawn – where one feels at home. The place where you are your most authentic self'. Almost every other search result is a variation of one of these two meanings, with a couple of results related to people for whom Querencia is their surname. Is that it? Does Martin want her to seek someone out at this address? Someone who could help her? Viola yearns for more clarity. Martin is trying to tell her something, but she doesn't know if he is telling her to go to this place or to stay away. Viola types the postcode into her maps app and sees that the location is less than a mile away. It's a little further than she'd prefer to walk, but there is a bus stop nearby.

Viola sighs and curls up under the covers, blocking out everything. Tomorrow, she will do some investigating. She'll take the number 17 bus and find out what is at the location Martin has written down. Her expectations are low, and she may have to simply accept everything that has happened and become comfortable with this new normal.

Viola eventually falls asleep with her aching head a swirling mess of unpleasant thoughts.

CHAPTER TWENTY-ONE

When Viola wakes, she is achy and confused. Thankfully, her headache has abated, but having slept deeply, she has barely moved, and her joints feel stiff.

She slowly unfurls and checks the time on her phone, appalled to see it is almost midday. She rubs her dry eyes and tries to form a basic plan for the day in her mind. The number 17 bus comes every fifteen minutes, so there's no need to check the timetable, and she can get on at the top of her road. That part is easy. Other than that, she'll need to play it by ear. See what she finds when she gets there. She can't deny she's afraid of what she might discover, but that is far outweighed by the threat she feels from the family at number 33.

She can't believe Duke and Rhys will simply leave her alone if she decides to mind her business. She doesn't trust them. Plus, what is she allowing to happen if she remains silent? A woman is missing. She could be hurt or even dead. Plus, are 'pretend Wendy' and her unborn baby in danger, too? This is too much weight for her to carry on her shoulders, and currently, her hands are tied.

So, even though she is afraid, if the address and the name

'Querencia' offer any support or way through this, then she has to at least try.

———

It is a miserable day outside. Viola pulls the hood of her raincoat over her head and holds it tight. Fine rain swirls in the wind, hitting her from every angle. It's not exactly suitable weather for investigating, but at least it means the streets are quiet, and thankfully, there is no one to be seen next door.

She hurries to the bus stop and is relieved when the number 17 arrives after only a few minutes. After showing the driver her bus pass, she takes a seat near the back. The only other passengers are a harried-looking young woman and a squirmy baby on her lap. The baby has bright pink chubby cheeks and a trail of drool running from mouth to chin. Viola would usually make conversation, ask the mother if she's feeling okay, and perhaps enquire if the baby is teething. But today she sits quietly, her handbag in her lap, her eyes downcast.

Two stops later, she thanks the driver and disembarks. The rain has ceased but dark clouds threaten more, and Viola tucks in close to the hedgerows to avoid the wind. Checking her phone, she memorises the route to the destination. The app tells her she needs to walk for three minutes in the direction she is currently facing, then take a left, and at the end of the road, follow a small path. On the digital map, it looks like there is one large building surrounded by a smattering of smaller ones. There is lots of grassland surrounding it, a farm perhaps.

Viola begins her journey, walking quickly and making it to the path in less than two minutes without encountering a single soul. The path is wider than she expected and is more like a dirt road. The perimeter is lined by tall, bushy trees, and she is prevented from seeing anything other than the entrance. A large wooden gate is blocking her way, easily wide enough for a car to pass through. Looking down, she sees fresh tyre tracks in the dirt going both in and out. A large sign is fixed to the centre of the gate with cable ties. Printed in large white capital letters against a red background are the words – PRIVATE PROPERTY. VIOLATORS WILL BE PROSECUTED.

Viola looks for some kind of bell or intercom, but there is nothing. She has a little chuckle to herself at the appearance of her name in the word 'violators'. Far too close to her own name for comfort. Without any visible way to contact anyone inside, Viola checks the gate. It has a simple lever latch, and while stiff, it is not locked. She manages to pull it open, nipping her finger as she does so. She winces and sucks it, the metallic taste of blood filling her mouth. Examining her finger, she's relieved to find it's only a tiny cut and will heal on its own. Nothing to get excited about.

If she enters here, there is no way she can pretend she didn't see the sign. It's large, and its message is abundantly clear. But sometimes, being old and invisible does have its benefits. She hates to play the doddery old lady card, but if it keeps her from getting in trouble, she'll do just that.

The path takes a sharp left turn after about twenty paces, and suddenly, the main building comes into view. It's a large red-brick building with white shutters on every window; most of them closed. There is nowhere for her to hide now. If they have any type of security camera, she will already have been seen. Trying her best to look non-threatening and a little lost and unsure, she ambles towards the house. The front door is dark grey and double-fronted. Two long vertical silver handles make it look more like a giant kitchen cabinet than the front door of a dwelling. There is no knocker and, again, no doorbells or buttons to press.

Viola looks around her, searching for anything that might

help her alert someone to her presence. The walls on either side are metal, like the inside of an elevator, minus the buttons. Above her head, she spots a small camera, the same colour as the door and tucked into the corner. She definitely wouldn't have noticed it if she hadn't been scouring. The camera is pointed directly at her, so she does the only thing she can think of. She waves and smiles. The camera doesn't move, and no sounds indicate anyone approaching the door.

"Hello." Viola has no idea if the camera picks up sound, but she may as well try. Once again, there's no movement or noise. She is about to turn around and see if there is another more accessible entrance when she hears a faint crackle of static coming from her left. She turns and sees several small holes she hadn't noticed on the side of one of the shiny panels.

Tentatively, Viola puts her face close to them and speaks. "Hello." She can hear heavy breathing but no immediate answer. She waits, nerves beginning to creep up on her while she listens to the static.

Eventually, a voice answers her. It is distorted but sounds like a woman, and furthermore, she sounds furious.

"The sign clearly says no trespassers. Please leave."

Viola's immediate thought is that, in fact, the sign does not say that. It says PRIVATE PROPERTY. VIOLATORS WILL BE PROSECUTED. But she's not sure that would help with ingratiating herself.

"I'm looking for Querencia. Am I not in the right place?" She keeps her request vague, not knowing whether Querencia is a person, a place, or even anything at all. She thinks she hears whispering in the background, and when the woman speaks again, she is a little less angry, although far from cordial.

"Who sent you?"

Shit, what does she say to that? My dead husband? No, that

wouldn't do. She decides to try something risky and prepares herself to leave swiftly if it doesn't go as planned.

"I'm a friend of the Awbry family. I know Duke and Rhys." She leaves it there, and this time, there is a longer wait for a response with even more whispering.

"One minute, please." Viola tries not to show her glee that it works and maintains a calm and poised position, knowing that the camera is likely monitoring her every movement.

After significantly longer than the one minute advised, the large door makes a clicking sound followed by a hiss. It reminds Viola of when the professor with the crazy hair opened the door of the time-travelling car in *Back to the Future*. This place is odd.

Both doors open slowly inwards, and before her stands a painfully thin woman, dressed in a black shirt and pencil skirt with pinched lips. Her hair is scraped back so tightly into a bun that Viola wonders if the woman is able to blink. The entranceway is very grand, with high ceilings, but it has been decorated in a completely unsympathetic fashion. This is definitely a period home, but it is sleek and modern inside. In fact, it looks almost exactly like Wendy and Rhys's kitchen. A sense of unease unfolds within her, which only escalates when she hears the door close behind her with a hissing sound. The air feels too still, odourless and sterile. It's like she is inside a sealed box rather than a large Victorian building.

The woman, who hasn't yet introduced herself or even asked Viola her name, points to a plastic seat resting against the wall and, without moving anything on her face apart from her tiny lips, says, "Please take a seat. I'll be right with you."

Viola does as she asks, and the woman skitters away through another door that seems to unlock and seal in the same way as the front door. Viola casts her eyes around the large room, but there is nothing to look at. Just lots of empty space and plain silver walls. Weird. She knows she has taken a stupid risk by coming here alone. Even more so now she is essentially locked in with no idea of what is about to happen next and with no means of leaving.

Tension begins to build within her, but she has no time to ruminate further as the interior door opens suddenly, and the woman who greeted her appears at her side as though by magic. The woman roughly grabs Viola by the elbow and yanks her up from the seat. Viola's mouth falls open in surprise. Firstly, she's shocked by how strong the petite woman is. Viola must be twice her weight, and she lifted her up without breaking a sweat. The front door hisses open, and Viola is pushed unceremoniously towards it. She has to concentrate hard to stop herself from stumbling. Looking over her shoulder, she is greeted by a stare of undiluted rage in the woman's eyes. Everything happens so fast that there is no time for Viola to react or even form any thoughts about how she should respond. She is shoved outside.

The terrifying woman's parting words are delivered through snarling teeth. "Get out. You will regret this."

The door closes, and Viola finds herself standing exactly where she was mere minutes ago, with no idea of what just happened.

CHAPTER TWENTY-TWO

Viola wastes no time leaving the property and, thankfully, there is a bus waiting for her to get straight on.

Now, back home and feeling relatively safe, she considers what she has learned from her brief and unpleasant visit. Unfortunately, not a lot, and she has most likely gotten herself into more trouble with Duke and Rhys. She is fully expecting a knock on the door at any minute. Another warning, or perhaps something more severe this time. She considers going back upstairs and taking another look through Martin's papers. There could be something else, more information on that place and what it's for. Instead, she takes out her phone and does a bit more online sleuthing. The only thing she has looked up so far is the word 'Querencia'. This time, she types 'Querencia', 'Awbry', and the postcode of the building into the search bar, hoping it will provide the link to a business website or something that tells her what the place even is. But instead, numerous media articles appear. She clicks on the first one. It's a piece from a magazine from five years ago titled '*How I escaped Querencia*'.

As Viola reads, her chest tightens and her pulse thumps faster and harder. The picture accompanying the article shows a blacked-out figure of a man. The man the story is about has changed his name, choosing to go by 'James', and has since fled the country for his own safety. That in itself is worrying, and Viola knows that by reading further, her mind is not about to be put at ease. What James describes is horrifying, and if she was concerned about her safety before, she is now terrified. Duke and Rhys are undoubtedly dangerous individuals. James explains how he started a relationship with a young woman and was introduced to Querencia through her. He reveals she initially told him that Querencia was a charity organisation that provided support to the local community.

Social events and classes were available, as well as onsite training and support groups. James had found himself struggling to find work, somewhat adrift, and feeling lost with what he wanted to do with his life, so he initially found it a great place to spend time. He explains how Querencia gradually became more controlling and how he started discovering unusual beliefs from the family running the organisation.

Seemingly, the aim of Querencia is to build 'perfect families' and for members to live as a community away from the rest of society. James names Duke and describes him as initially very caring and kind, giving him opportunities to better himself and learn new skills, offering support and counsel. As James gained members' trust, he was allowed outside the training rooms at the front of the main building and shown the other parts of the property. He was astonished that many families, including children of all ages, lived onsite. At least a dozen families were housed in the main building alone. Bathroom and kitchen facilities were shared, but each family had their own living space. He became alarmed that everyone looked, acted, and sounded similar.

It was odd. The women looked a lot like my girlfriend, and the men looked a lot like me. But everyone was extremely friendly and welcoming, so I sort of ignored it. It was nice. I felt accepted and supported. It all happened so slowly, and when I look back, I feel really stupid. I didn't realise I was being indoctrinated.

Viola shivers at the word indoctrinated, and for the first time, she realises what she is dealing with here. This is a cult. Duke and Rhys are running a cult.

Viola continues to read. As the months passed, James was shown the onsite school, a fully staffed medical centre that was more or less a small hospital, and the 'factory' – a large building filled with desks, computers, and telephones where many of the Querencia members worked.

It had the appearance of a call centre, but at first, I couldn't work out what kind of work they were doing.

Viola skims the central portion of the article, which mainly details the daily lives of the people who lived and worked at Querencia. They are all surprisingly ordinary and mundane. The final few paragraphs detail how James decided to leave when Duke and other senior but unnamed members of Querencia were pushing James and his girlfriend into marriage.

She was up for it, but we'd been together less than a year. I wasn't ready for marriage in general, never mind knowing whether she was the one I wanted to marry. At first, it was simply a suggestion. Then it became more forceful. Saying how could I refuse after all they had done for me, and they'd make sure I wouldn't work again after how I'd treated them. Nobody else who lived there seemed to think it was weird, but they were all a part of it. They were brainwashed.

Viola stops reading for a moment. This is bigger than she could have ever imagined. She's not simply up against the two men from the family next door. She is up against an entire organisation of people devoted to them who will follow and do their bidding. She reads on.

I couldn't work out what any of them were getting out of it, although they had somewhere to stay and work to do. I later learnt that the main source of income for Querencia was a series of telephone scams. They tricked money out of people in various elaborate ways. They regularly changed what they were selling or asking people to pledge towards. It was seriously corrupt. I was appalled and refused to work there, so they gave me handyman-type work. I think I was starting to fall deeper into their trap because I felt grateful for that job, and although I briefly considered reporting them to the police, I never did it. I've since discovered they have many people in their pockets and iron-clad plans to get out of anyone reporting their activities. They have it all sewn up. They're bulletproof. And that's why I can't reveal my identity. I know people must think of me as cowardly. But, trust me, if you'd seen what these people are capable of, you'd feel the same.

Nausea builds in Viola's stomach as she begins to understand the enormity of what she is now embroiled in.

Initially, I told them I was planning to leave. I missed my family and the normal bits of my life that I'd taken for granted. Going for a pint with my mates, ordering a takeaway, or even just cooking and eating what I wanted rather than sitting down to the weird communal meals we had in the dining hall. They told me I had signed a contract and had to give three months' notice, but I was free to go after that. I couldn't remember signing any such thing, but they produced a document with my signature on it. To this day, I am sure I didn't sign that piece of paper. I couldn't face arguing with them, so I agreed to finish up my three months. They did everything during that time to suck me in. I was treated well and promised a higher level position with perks if I stayed. None of it worked. Their promises were tenuous, and while they sounded good, when you peeled it back, they weren't actually offering me anything. I longed to get out of there. Finally, when my three months were up, I asked to see Duke. I was planning to thank him and say goodbye, to try and leave on relatively good terms. He looked at me with fake confusion and tried to tell me that I hadn't given him notice at all, that I must be mistaken. He called in some other members who corroborated his story. They tried to make me feel like I was going mad, forgetting things. They suggested I should go to the medical centre for psychiatric evaluation, that I might need medication. I wanted to scream and yell at them. The look on Duke's face was what stopped me. I could see pure evil in him. I knew that he wasn't going to let me leave. The last thing he said to me before I reluctantly agreed with them that I must have been mistaken was that staying here was the best thing for me. Duke said I wouldn't last five minutes out there after experiencing the serenity and safety of Querencia. It was a threat, and I knew my life was in danger if I tried to go against his wishes. The only way out for me was to escape and then disappear as far away as possible.

The fact she is reading this account means that James escaped, but that doesn't stop Viola's heart from thumping along wildly with every word. What a horrible thing for him to go through, and by the sounds of it, he's one of the lucky ones. If what he is saying is true, then there are likely deaths attributed to the desertion of Querencia. The thought makes her blood run cold.

I didn't try to escape right away. I knew they'd be watching me, and I needed to take the heat off myself. Thankfully, a couple of other newish members started asking questions and showing dissent around the same time. They were a lot more vocal than me, and I learnt from others that they were being treated in the hospital to help their mental well-being. I don't know if that was true. A couple of people seemed to completely disappear, and seeing as I knew nobody was being allowed to leave, I have no idea what happened to them. Everything was always spoken of in a positive light, as though the things they did were for the greater

THE FAMILY NEXT DOOR

good. It got more and more unnerving, and the people who spewed the doctrine at me started to behave less like humans and more like robot soldiers.

I waited three weeks before I couldn't take it anymore. I'd been tasked with patching up a fence panel towards the back of the grounds that had blown over during a stormy night. We were not allowed outside alone, so another member, a young man in his early twenties who seemed to think he'd landed on his feet in this place, and I were sent to repair it together. When he wasn't looking, I threw our hammer into a nearby bush and told him I couldn't find it. I suggested that one of us run back to find another. He looked unsure, so devout to the rules and terrified of upsetting anyone more senior. Eventually, I convinced him to run back quickly. Once he was out of sight, I threw the panel to the ground and ran to the boundary. The whole place is surrounded by an iron fence, cemented into the ground around the perimeter, and hidden with tall, bushy trees. Wires and spikes made climbing it impossible, so I scaled a nearby tree, climbed out across a sturdy branch, and flung myself outwards and across the fence. I was lucky to escape with only a sprained ankle. I could easily have broken my leg from that height.

I don't want to talk too much about what I did next. I don't want the leaders at Querencia coming for anyone I love on the outside. I thank my lucky stars that I didn't share anything about myself despite being asked many personal questions. I'm sure they have plenty of ammunition to use against other members. So many of them bared their souls and told them everything. Those people can never leave without putting their family in danger. Every day, I think about the young man who went to fetch the hammer. It didn't occur to me then, but I'm sure he must have been punished for what I did. I hope he is okay, but I suspect not. I unwittingly sacrificed him, and I hate myself for it. Somebody needs to stop them. I've tried the police but never heard of *anything happening to Querencia. I'm speaking out as a warning. I urge people not to fall for their lies. They will get their claws into you and won't let you go. They are dangerous people, and I don't want anyone else to go through what I did.*

Viola closes the article. A quick scroll through the search results identifies a handful of similar stories, all anonymous, giving her nobody with whom to make contact. She considers reading them all in detail, but for now, she has learned more than she can handle.

What in the world is she going to do?

CHAPTER TWENTY-THREE

Number 33 appears quiet and benign. Peering through a gap in her bedroom curtains, nothing distinguishes it from the other houses on the street. Viola feels like a prisoner. It's only a matter of time before Duke or Rhys discover she visited Querencia. One of them will surely come for her, and she knows her actions won't go unpunished. Wild thoughts rush through her mind. What if they kill her and make it look like an accident? She's an older woman living on her own, would anyone really dig deep if it appeared as though she tripped and fell down the stairs? Before she knew how truly dangerous they are, the threat of Martin's involvement had been enough to deter her from contacting the police. But now, no matter the truth or how Martin would feel about everything coming out, she needs to make the call. Martin would not want her in danger. Of that, she is sure.

Although saddened by the thought, Viola believes he could have accepted money to mind his business and give them a better life together. And this realisation makes her wonder about her other neighbours. Are more people in the street accepting Duke's hush money? Does more than one house on this quiet, unassuming street belong to the leader of a dangerous cult? Is the community she loves and thinks of as home morally corrupt? Even if Martin's involvement was more than simply turning a blind eye, she can't protect him at the expense of her own safety. And not just because he is dead; she'd feel the same if he was alive. He made his choices, and there are consequences.

Viola needs a little Dutch courage before she calls the police. A smidgen of bourbon, just a capful. She doesn't want to be inebriated when they arrive, but she doesn't want to appear like a dithering wreck either. As she slowly trudges down the stairs, the realisation of what her life has become hits her, and she feels as though she might fall to her knees right there in the middle of the staircase. She feels desperately alone and totally unprepared to deal with something of this magnitude. But she has no choice, this will not go away on its own.

Things just keep getting worse, and she is scared. More scared than she can ever remember being. That is until she enters her living room and sees Duke sitting comfortably on her sofa. The grumbling fear she felt merely seconds ago now pales in comparison to the gut-wrenching horror that encircles her and threatens to knock her off her feet. Viola can't speak. Her legs start to shake.

Duke barely reacts to her appearance. He remains sitting, legs crossed, and one arm draped lazily over the back of the sofa. He looks completely relaxed and at home, and a new burst of fear licks at her insides. Before she has a chance to think, her body decides to run away. She finds herself turning in readiness to bolt up the stairs.

"Sit down, Viola." Duke sounds almost bored as he speaks, fed up and exasperated at dealing with her unruly behaviour. It's very much at odds with the situation they find themselves in. Viola turns to face him. He hasn't moved an inch. She can't make out anything in his expression. He doesn't look angry or upset. He looks blank. If he wasn't blinking, he could be a mannequin. The eeriness of it stops her in her tracks. Tears begin to form in her eyes.

Slowly and confidently, he uncrosses his legs and rests his hands on his knees. "I just want to talk. Can we do that?"

Viola is trembling uncontrollably now, and she knows if she tries to speak, she will scream. She shakes her head, tears rolling down her cheeks.

Duke sighs. "Look, I can see that you're upset, and there's really no need to be."

Viola wants to run at him, to scream and roar out all the fear that is currently paralysing her. How can he say there is no need to be upset? He has broken into her house. But she does nothing.

"I'm sorry to just turn up like this." He dangles a small bunch of keys from his fingers. "I have a key. I didn't break in."

Viola's mind whirls. Why does he have a key to her home? How many times has he been in her house? She is so annoyed with Martin.

"Look, Viola, we definitely need to talk. Come to some sort of arrangement. An understanding. Believe it or not, I'm not here to intimidate you or to cause you any harm. We need to find a way to get past this and live in harmony. That is all." He smiles briefly and tilts his head, scrutinising her reaction. Viola doesn't know how to react. All of her body's usual responses have been disabled. All her instincts are screaming at her to get away from this man. She doesn't believe a single word falling from his mouth. He is dangerous, and he is not here to talk. He is here to silence her, and the thought of what that might entail terrifies her.

Her eyes flick to the front door. It is closed, but is it locked? Her keys are upstairs in her handbag. If she tries to run for it and fails, she'll be in even more danger than she is now, if that is even possible. Plus, Duke is undoubtedly faster and stronger than she is. She scans the room for a weapon of any kind, something to hit him over the head with if he tries to attack her. Duke stands suddenly and begins to walk towards her. Viola shrieks, and he exhales loudly, clearly annoyed at his failed attempts to control the situation. His eyes flare, and his face contorts with anger. All the previous cordiality vanishes in an instant.

Viola starts up the stairs, her body moving faster than it has in a long time, her innate self-preservation kicking in. She is almost at the top. Safety is so tantalisingly close, and a glimmer of hope begins to blossom inside her chest. She's going to make it. She'll get to the bathroom, lock the door, and scream out of the window at the top of her lungs. Someone will hear her, and she'll be saved.

But she never makes it to the bathroom or even the top of the stairs. Duke is too quick and strong. Viola feels the last remnants of hope drain away, and a crashing despair rains down upon her. The last thing she remembers before everything goes black is a heavy presence behind her and an arm reaching over her shoulder.

She can't breathe.

This is it

She is going to die.

CHAPTER TWENTY-FOUR

MIRABELLE

I feel sad for Viola, but why did she have to be so stupid? She definitely shouldn't have gone to Querencia. Didn't she see the sign? I know old people need glasses for reading, but the letters are massive. If she wanted to go for a visit, she should have asked me. Daddy and Granddad wouldn't have liked it, but I could have made it happen. I always do.

Mummy, Daddy, and Granddad have been so stressed. Always whispering and acting like Viola is this massive problem. It's because they don't know how to talk to people and make friends like I do.

I watched out of the window when Granddad went to Viola's house. I didn't know he had a key. He should have told me that. Viola's my friend, not his. If anyone should have a key to her house, it's me.

He's promised me he won't hurt her, and he better not. If he does, I'll be so cross that I'll scream and scream and scream.

Sometimes, you have to hurt people because you don't have another choice. But Viola is different.

Viola is special.

Like me.

CHAPTER TWENTY-FIVE

Viola comes round and tries to speak, but something is covering her mouth. Her head is thumping, and her vision is blurry and swirling, making her feel nauseated. When she tries to move, she discovers that she can't. Her muscles scream as she tries to pull against whatever is trapping her but to no avail. Her body is aching and tender all over, and she has no knowledge of why. Is she in hospital?

She blinks her eyes rapidly and tries to bring the world back into focus. She has a strong urge to vomit but knows she mustn't with her mouth covered. She longs to wipe her eyes. As her body and mind wake up, she begins to recognise and understand the position she is in. She's sitting, and she can't move either her arms or legs. She tries to scream, but she sucks in whatever is covering her mouth and begins to retch painfully. Her consciousness waxes and wanes, and she thinks she either blacks out or drifts off to sleep several times. Time is elusive, and she cannot grasp how many minutes or even hours have passed since she first regained consciousness.

The next time Viola feels herself come around, she resolves to fight and stay that way. Yes, she's trapped, bound somehow, and her chances of escape are minuscule, but if she's unconscious, her chances are zero. She flexes her fingers in and out and focuses on the movement and the feeling. Anything to keep her mind from drifting into oblivion. Shapes begin to appear in the room, but they have no form or substance. Nausea engulfs her, and she is desperate to close her eyes. It's horribly bright, and her head is splitting. But she keeps blinking, homing in on the different objects and colours that are starting to emerge, pushing the sickness deep down and refusing to let it overcome her.

A large dark form in front of her shifts slightly. While she still has little to no ability to discern outlines or details, she suspects this is a person, and her worst fears are confirmed when she hears the familiar cadence of Duke's voice.

"Don't struggle, Viola. Just relax and you'll start to feel normal soon."

Viola has already decided against battling whatever binds her. Even if she had the strength to try and wrestle free, her restraints feel solid and secure. She'd only risk harming herself, and she needs to conserve what little energy she has left to remain lucid. Instead, she concentrates on her breathing and wiggling her fingers and toes. They are the only things on her body over which she currently has any autonomy.

Duke barks out a laugh. The inappropriateness jars Viola, and she has to focus extra hard on her breathing.

In. Out. In. Out.

"You gave me quite a run for my money there, Viola. You see, it's not like in the movies where you place a rag over someone's face, and they're unconscious in seconds. It takes minutes, and let me tell you, you fought like hell. I've got a serious black eye coming up. I have to give it to you – you caught me off guard."

He chuckles again. Viola continues to blink regularly and

breathe slowly and deliberately. Duke's body is beginning to become clearer. The outline of his head and limbs starting to take shape. How she wishes she could see his face. Hearing that she gave him a black eye gives her a small flicker of satisfaction. She rotates her head from left to right, scanning around the room and trying to focus on something else. Why is her vision so damn poor; has he done something to her eyes? Gradually and insufferably slowly, the room comes back into focus. Viola feels an intense thirst and desperately wants the gag removed from her mouth. Somehow, that feels like the most demeaning part of her current predicament. Her focus returns to Duke as he speaks again.

"You'll feel fine soon enough. Like I said before, people come round fast on TV and have all their faculties. It takes much longer in real life, but I guess nobody would want to watch that. Artistic licence, I suppose."

What on earth is he talking about? Why is he giving her a science lesson on the realities of knocking someone out and its poor portrayal on television? But evidently, he is right, and she starts to feel more and more like herself as time passes. Duke's face finally comes into focus and, as she looks around, Viola sees that she is tied to a chair in the kitchen of number 33. Not one of those stupid plastic ones, but a chunky wooden chair. She would imagine it's heavy. Behind Duke sits Rhys, 'pretend Wendy', and Mirabelle. Viola takes a sharp intake of breath at the sight of the little girl and then immediately regrets it as she starts to cough and splutter. She is being held prisoner and these people are letting a child watch. The depth of their depravity knows no bounds. Viola both does and doesn't want to look at Mirabelle. She doesn't want her to be more frightened than she already must be, but Viola needs to see that she is safe and unharmed.

Viola's eyes fill with tears as she takes in Mirabelle's

unblemished face. She is wearing a yellow gingham dress, and her hair falls loosely over her shoulders. They lock eyes, and Viola can see that she is not upset or perturbed by what she is witnessing. She's looking at her the way she always does, with curiosity and a hint of mischief. Viola's heart sinks as she suddenly understands that this mustn't be the first time Mirabelle has been part of a situation like this. The poor girl. Viola had worried that Mirabelle was suffering some kind of abuse, but she couldn't have ever imagined this. Who would? This is the type of thing, something so unusual and at odds with how an ordinary family should behave, that will screw a child up for life. This thought ignites the first iota of strength that Viola has felt since coming to. There is a vulnerable little girl here, and if the adults in her life are so messed up they deem it perfectly fine for her to be witnessing this, then she needs to do whatever she can to stop them.

Duke clicks his fingers and pats his leg as though summoning a pet dog. Mirabelle beams and runs to him, jumping onto his knee and throwing her arms around his neck. Viola watches, horrified. Her eyes wide, unable to look away.

"Can I take that off her mouth, Granddad? It looks like she's going to throw up and I don't want to see that." She blinks her long lashes at him.

Viola desperately wants the disgusting rag removed and makes a gagging motion, hoping to encourage Mirabelle to ask again. She clearly has some control over Duke and his actions.

Mirabelle jumps off his knee and stands in front of Viola. "Can I, Granddad? Please." Mirabelle is already reaching around the back of Viola's neck to find a way to undo the gag.

"Okay, but wait, honey."

Mirabelle stops and looks petulantly at her grandfather. "Why?"

He strokes her blonde curls, and Viola feels sickened by this action. Their relationship is disturbing in so many ways.

"Because I need Viola to promise to be quiet. We don't want her screaming, do we?"

Mirabelle's forehead crinkles before she nods and runs out of the room. Viola's heart begins to race. What will they do to her now Mirabelle has gone? Mirabelle returns seconds later and returns to her spot directly in front of Viola. Relief begins to flood through her body.

Until she sees what the girl has in her hands.

Mirabelle is holding the secateurs she was playing with the first time they met. And she is pointing them at Viola. Viola looks at the sharp blades and then at Mirabelle. The little girl's face is severe and stony, a look Viola can't reconcile with her age and appearance. She feels light-headed and the world starts to fall away before she passes out. The last thing she hears is Mirabelle's sweet, tinkling voice.

"Don't worry. I've got this, Granddad."

CHAPTER TWENTY-SIX

A light tapping on the side of her face rouses Viola. It takes her a minute to remember where she is, but then it all comes flooding back, and she lets out a yelp. Mirabelle has pulled up a chair and is sitting so their legs are touching. Her feet are at least a foot off the floor. She's just a child.

A quick scan of the room reveals that they are now alone. Viola looks at Mirabelle with watery, desperate eyes. The businesslike expression remains on the little girl's face, but there is a softness in her gaze now.

"I took the rag off your mouth."

Viola hadn't even noticed and, in the absence of the adults, finds she has no desire to scream. What would it achieve anyway? The gag may be gone but she is still powerless and tied to the chair.

"Thank you." Viola's voice is croaky, and there is a revolting medicinal taste in her mouth that fills her nostrils when she speaks.

"I like you, Viola. Well, I mean, I did until you were rude to Mummy, but I'd still like to be your friend." Mirabelle smiles expectantly, a gesture full of purity and innocence.

Viola's addled brain is a jumble of feelings and thoughts. She is tied to a chair, conversing with a little girl she's only just met about being friends. She has been drugged, pulled from her home, and is currently the prisoner of this family. This family who are the leaders of a dangerous cult. Has there ever been a situation more absurd and bewildering than this? However, Viola knows that to have any chance of getting free, she has to play along with Mirabelle. Get her on side. She licks her lips and swallows, grateful for the fresh air that she is now able to pull into her lungs.

"I like you too, Mirabelle. But I don't like being tied to this chair. It hurts. Would you help me?" Viola hears shuffling and footsteps, someone rushing towards the kitchen.

Mirabelle's eyes darken. "Leave us alone, Granddad! I told you."

Viola is astonished at the ferocity and dictatorial tone that the girl summons. The footsteps immediately halt, and she hears Duke slowly retreat. Viola puffs out a sigh of relief. Mirabelle she can handle, but Rhys and Duke are a different story altogether. Although perhaps she should reassess that. Mirabelle may be small, but she still holds all the power in the room at this moment.

Viola suddenly remembers the secateurs. She can't believe she forgot the reason she passed out again, and her eyes scan frantically to Mirabelle's thankfully empty hands before spotting them on the table, still very much within the girl's reach.

Mirabelle turns to see what Viola is looking at. "Oh, those. I only use them if I need to. But we're friends, so I can leave them over there."

Viola's eyes fill up. She mustn't scream or wail, but she feels any power she possesses over her own body ebbing away.

Mirabelle pulls her knees up to her chest. "I know you don't like Daddy or Granddad." It's not a question, and Viola doesn't want to say anything that might change the current calm mood between them, so she forces a small smile and stays quiet. "But you like me, right?" The hope in Mirabelle's eyes is heartbreaking and this time, there is no need to question what the expected response is.

"Yes, I like you."

Mirabelle beams. "See, that's what I told them. And you'll listen to me if I tell you our story?"

Viola feels like she might completely break down if she has to hear anything more traumatic than what she already knows. This whole situation has gone from bad to worse to indescribably horrific and insane. But she sticks with the plan and gives what she knows is the correct answer.

"Of course I will."

Viola's heart leaps as Mirabelle yells towards the door.

"I told you!" The dynamic between Mirabelle and the adults is confusing at best. She holds something over them, which may be the only thing keeping Viola alive.

"It's a big story, so you're going to have to listen real hard and not fall asleep, okay?" Mirabelle raises her eyebrows, and Viola almost laughs at how she is being addressed. But then it makes perfect sense that Mirabelle would feel superior. That's how they treat her.

"I won't fall asleep, I promise."

Mirabelle nods and starts her story.

"I know you've been to Querencia. You shouldn't have done that, you know?"

Viola forces her eyes down by way of apology. She has to maintain the subservience that the girl expects.

"That's our home. There are big signs saying people shouldn't go in. If you wanted to see it, I would have taken you." Viola looks up briefly, maintaining her regretful expression, and nods sombrely. "You see, the world is full of bad people, horrible families where the kids get hurt, and nobody looks after them properly." Viola's insides are starting to squirm, but she needs to keep her composure and just listen. "At Querencia, all the families are perfect. The children are the most important thing and they are loved. Children are the future, you know that, right?"

Viola feels a sudden urge to laugh hysterically. Mirabelle is speaking to her as if she were a child. But she can tell Mirabelle is expecting an answer. "Yes, I know." She manages a small smile, and Mirabelle nods perfunctorily before continuing.

"I think the reason you don't like Daddy or Granddad is because you don't really understand what they are doing. They are making everyone's life better. Querencia is a village full of happy people. Every day there is like a holiday. You would love it."

Viola feels this might be a good moment to interject. There is still much for her to know, and she doesn't want to spook the girl or shut down her story with a question she doesn't like. She must hold back on all of the queries that are burning inside of her. Where is Wendy? Are people being hurt at Querencia? Can they leave if they want to? And many, many more.

"Mirabelle, that sounds like a lovely place. Can you tell me what it's like there?"

Mirabelle smiles widely, and her eyes sparkle with excitement. Viola hears footsteps approaching behind her and Duke's calm but stern voice.

"Remember the rules, sweetheart."

Viola doesn't acknowledge Duke's appearance and looks down at her knees, avoiding eye contact. She fully expects Mirabelle to yell back like last time, but her response is sweet and soft.

"I know, Granddad. You taught me well."

Viola breathes out thankfully as she hears Duke walking away.

Mirabelle leans in and whispers conspiratorially. "I know the rules better than him." Then she rolls her eyes and giggles before sitting back and continuing. "Querencia is like a special club. It's only for good, kind people who want to live together nicely." *A cult*, Viola thinks. *It's a cult.* "We don't let just anyone live with us, and we kind of keep it a secret. My family is the main family, so we are sort of in charge of deciding who gets to come in. I'm the firstborn daughter of Querencia so I'm even more special than anyone there, even Granddad. I've got loads of nice friends, even grown-up friends. Daddy says I'm super grown up, so I'm good at being friends with everyone."

The little girl seems to swell with pride, and Viola has to stop her face from forming a grimace. The firstborn comment is troubling – is Mirabelle being treated as some kind of deity? Plus, she can only hope that the friendships Mirabelle speaks of are simply that and nothing more sinister. These horrible people have twisted this innocent child's version of reality. Indoctrinated her and placed her on some weird pedestal. But she's young, and there is time. Time for her to live a full and normal life if, somehow, Viola can get her away from all of this.

"We've got a school, and a telephone room where most of the adults work. There are loads of places to play, and I get to help with cooking and everything. It's honestly so cool. And when I'm older I'll be in charge of all of it." Mirabelle stops and ponders momentarily as though unsure how to say what she wants next.

Viola tries to encourage her. "Go on, dear. I'm listening."

"I know, but you don't live there, so I don't think you'll get it."

"I'll try. You're explaining everything so beautifully."

Mirabelle studies Viola for a moment, her eyes narrowing. "I'll know if you are lying."

Viola doesn't doubt that for a second, which is why she chooses her words carefully. "I know you will. I won't lie to you, Mirabelle."

The girl watches her, her eyes moving slowly, and Viola notices again that she is not blinking, just as she was the day they met.

"Okay. But don't butt in. This is the important bit, okay? The bit they didn't want me to tell you. But I said you would get it."

Viola nods, knowing they are now at the crux of everything.

"Everywhere has rules. Like you have the police and everything. But that doesn't work, and there are lots of bad people out there who are still committing crimes and stuff." Mirabelle stops and taps her chin with her index finger. It's a rather comical sight. "So, we have our own rules, better rules. Our families are perfect, and we have a special area for people who need a bit more help understanding."

Viola can read between the lines. She can see past the child-friendly explanation Duke has given to Mirabelle, which is now being parroted back to her.

Viola speaks softly, knowing she is taking a considerable risk in asking a question. "And how do they help them understand?"

Mirabelle shrugs. "I don't know. You'll have to ask Daddy or Granddad. I'll get to do all of that when I'm older. I don't go in there. I know they have special buildings, and once people get better, they come back and join us in the main bit. Well, most of them do. But I don't know what actually goes on in there."

All three adults suddenly come rushing into the room. Rhys stands behind Mirabelle, placing a protective hand on her shoulder. Duke stands in solidarity next to his son. Both men are glaring at Viola with matching vitriolic stares, their faces telling her in no uncertain terms that further questions from her will not be tolerated.

Mirabelle has clearly stepped over a line with her final revelations, and Viola is not inclined to ask for further details. She values her safety too much. Plus, these men are far from trustworthy. They will only lie to her.

In the background, Viola glimpses the woman pretending to be Wendy and she appears somewhat distressed. Her body is slumped over the kitchen counter, and she looks sweaty and uncomfortable. Viola's first thought is that they must have hurt her, but then she remembers the pregnancy, and panic sets in. The size of her bump is certainly suggestive of a full-term pregnancy. But nobody else in the room seems to have noticed. All eyes are on Viola, waiting to see what she'll do next. Not one of them has noticed the panting noises and anguished look on the pregnant woman's face.

Duke and Rhys's continual glowering begins to ignite a fire inside Viola. Who do these men think they are? How dare they think they have the right to subject her to this. The effects of whatever she was drugged with have now worn off, and her determination is returning with a vengeance. Is she really just going to sit here and let them do this to her? These are people who, by their own admission, live by their own rules. It would be extremely short-sighted to think that if she plays along, nods, smiles, and promises not to reveal their secrets, they will simply let her go. Viola takes a deep breath and stares right back at them, unflinching and ready.

"If you hadn't noticed, I think the woman you're pretending is Wendy is about to have her baby."

Rhys steps towards Viola, his arm raised and face thunderous and twisted. She closes her eyes, waiting in anticipation of the blow that's sure to land any minute and prays she manages to survive it.

Instead, Viola hears Duke's voice, rough and insistent. "Get a grip, Rhys. We can deal with her later."

Viola risks opening one eye and flinches when she sees Duke standing in front of her, his face barely inches from hers. He puts his hands on her shoulders and squeezes hard, just as Rhys did the night they had dinner together. Horrible shooting pains rip down both of her arms, and she stifles a scream. *That bloody hurt.*

"Don't you dare move, Viola. If anything happens to Wendy, I will make sure you pay." Duke stands up, wipes his brow, and quickly joins his son before shouting back at Mirabelle. "You watch her, sweetheart. Daddy and I are going to help Mummy. You keep an eye on Viola. There's a good girl."

Viola takes pleasure from the apparent dread and anxiety laced through Duke's words. He is clearly worried and unsure of how to deal with the possibility of a woman in labour.

Mirabelle does as she is asked and inches her chair closer to Viola, their legs now intersecting. The silence between them is uncomfortable. Mirabelle appears unnerved by the scene around her. Although Viola doesn't like to see the girl frightened, she's worried she'll only make things worse by talking to her. Instead, she mouths words of reassurance silently.

"It will be okay, sweetheart."

Mirabelle switches emotions from nervous to excited at an alarming speed. "Oh, I know. I just don't want to watch it. That would be yucky. I can't wait to meet my baby brother, though. We're going to call him Eli. I helped pick his name with Mummy and Daddy."

Viola glances over at the commotion in the kitchen. Duke

and Rhys appear to be arguing while 'pretend Wendy' sits, thankfully looking a little calmer and less pained. A chill runs through Viola when she realises they are not arguing about how to manage the impending arrival of a baby but rather what to do with her, their prisoner. She listens, tension building inside her as Rhys speaks next.

"We need to take her with us to Querencia. She can't be trusted."

Duke counteracts with, "If we take her, she'll see everything and then she'll have to stay permanently, and surely you can see that won't work."

The back and forth continues. "We don't even have to take her inside. We can get someone to watch her in the car or something. But if we leave her here–"

"No. That's final. I will talk to her and make sure she knows the consequences if she talks. You need to be with your wife. Your baby is coming. Take Wendy to Querencia and make sure she is taken care of."

Rhys looks as though a vein is going to burst in his temple, but there is a demonstrable hierarchy between the two men that Viola hasn't witnessed in person before. Rhys seems to understand his place and doesn't say anything further.

"Good, this is not the time for disagreements, son. Stay focused on our goal and maintain your strength and belief. The line of our family must be protected at all costs. Be a man. Your son is coming."

Rhys's eyes tear up at Duke's speech. Viola looks from one man to the other, marvelling at just how self-important they are. 'The line of their family' – what even is that? It sounds like something Henry VIII might have decreed. The men hug and Viola realises that while transfixed on the egotistical display, she has been ignoring Mirabelle. But the girl has been watching, too, and Viola notices a new sadness in her eyes.

"Are you okay, my love? I think your baby brother will be arriving very soon."

"I know I'm the first daughter and all that, but do you think they'll love him more than me?" Mirabelle's voice is small and tinged with sadness. She hugs herself, which is likely an unconscious reaction but clearly loaded with meaning for Viola as an observer. The unbearable truth is that, yes, even with whatever importance the cult might place on the firstborn daughter, she thinks that Duke and Rhys are the type of men who would love a son more than a daughter, even if they don't show it.

Viola stares deep into Mirabelle's melancholy eyes. "That's not possible. When parents have another baby, they grow more love in their hearts so that they can love you just as much as they always did. Didn't you know that?"

Mirabelle looks up, and Viola can't even guess how she will respond. The girl constantly surprises her with her unexpected reactions.

Mirabelle wipes her eyes. "Yes, of course. Silly me. I just forgot."

They share a moment of knowing, each playing their part in the charade to protect Mirabelle's heart. Feeling closer to Mirabelle than ever, Viola feels the words tumble out of her mouth.

"What happened to Wendy?" Mirabelle looks at her, opening and closing her mouth, but no words come out. The adults are distracted, and nobody is watching their conversation. This is her only chance to find out the truth. "Please, Mirabelle, I just want to know that she is safe. That's all I care about. That you are safe, and Wendy is safe. I know that lady over there isn't her. Please tell me. You can trust me, I promise."

Viola sees genuine fear in the girl's eyes for the first time.

Evidence that Mirabelle is perhaps not quite so sure of her position in this family and the protection it affords her.

"I'm not supposed to talk about it. It's in the rules. Remember what I said? Perfect families."

"Mirabelle, look at me. I understand. Is Wendy safe?"

Mirabelle looks down, her internal debate playing out across her face. "Yes. She's safe. She's at Querencia. She wasn't my mummy, that's my mummy over there, and I love her. Please don't be mad."

Viola feels herself crumple at the vulnerable, confused child in front of her. She has seen this girl be happy, angry, and downright menacing. She has heard from Mirabelle's own mouth that she has hurt people with the secateurs she was brandishing earlier. But this pitiful sadness must be the worst thing she has seen or heard from her. No child should ever have to feel like this. She desperately wants to tell Mirabelle that these people are not good or kind despite what she has been duped into believing. That she is not the most important thing in the world to them or the people who subscribe to their warped ideals. They are controlling, delusional, and dangerous. But at this moment in time, what Mirabelle needs is kindness and reassurance, and Viola will provide what her parents are clearly too selfish to.

"I would never be mad at you, Mirabelle. Thank you so much for telling me." Viola wants to reach out and touch the girl's face, but her hands remain bound, and they are beginning to lose all feeling. Mirabelle doesn't appear entirely placated, but the deep sadness seems to have lifted slightly.

Movement from across the room prevents further discussion between them, and Viola starts as Duke suddenly claps his hands. The room falls silent except for the heavy breathing of the woman in labour.

"Everyone listen! Mirabelle, you will stay with me and

Viola. We will take her home and make sure she is safe." Mirabelle's face brightens, and Viola wishes she could share her enthusiasm. Nothing about Duke accompanying her home suggests any kind of safety. Still, at least she will be set free from this chair, and Viola will have more at her disposal in her own environment. Perhaps a way to summon help or to plan an escape. Viola gives Duke no reaction.

"Your daddy and mummy will go to Querencia together, and we will all be able to celebrate Eli's arrival soon."

Mirabelle bounces up and down on her chair, once again joyful at the imminent arrival of her brother.

Duke and Rhys nod at each other, and Duke walks towards Viola with a knife. He quickly and adeptly removes the ties from her hands and feet before throwing the knife onto the table. Viola considers grabbing it before Duke turns back around and takes it with him. *Damn it*. She rubs her aching wrists and ankles. Her whole body is screaming, and as she tries to move, the injuries from her scuffle with Duke on the stairs reveal themselves one by horribly painful one. Nothing feels broken, but sharp shooting pains ricochet throughout her limbs against a background of dull agony.

Viola looks across at 'pretend Wendy' on the chair. Something has changed. Something about her doesn't look right. She is too pale, and a sheen of sweat covers her greying skin. It is evident that something is very wrong, and they need help immediately. Viola wants to run to her, but she knows that will likely result in her being restrained again.

"Duke!" He turns immediately, the volume and insistence of Viola's shout alarming him. She points, her arm trembling. "I think something is wrong."

Viola watches Duke's face pale at the sight of the woman, and he rushes to her side. Things are escalating quickly, and she now seems delirious, swaying, and barely holding her head up.

Duke shouts, "Rhys, get over here. You need to go. Now!"

Viola feels a small hand curl around hers and grip tightly. Mirabelle is afraid. Viola pulls her closer, wrapping both arms around the girl's quivering body. They watch as Rhys and Duke attempt to lift the limp woman from the chair, but she is not responding, and as they attempt to pull her to a standing position, the weight of her pregnant belly topples her forward onto the floor. She makes no attempt to stop herself, and her shoulder and head collide with the hard kitchen floor but, thankfully, sparing the baby receiving the full force of the impact.

Viola is sure the woman is unconscious and she pleads with Duke, "You need to call an ambulance."

Rhys is now on the floor, trying and failing to rouse the lifeless woman. He appears utterly terrified and looks desperately at Duke to provide guidance.

Duke whirls around and stares at Viola, his teeth bared. "Get out of here. Go home, and don't you dare do anything stupid. Stay there and do nothing. I mean it."

As Viola stands, horrific pains shoot around her traumatised body. She keeps Mirabelle close. The girl is now shuddering and weeping by her side. Viola is torn between taking her chance and fleeing the house immediately and her deep human need to protect the lives in this room. There is a woman, an unborn baby, and a little girl at risk. She doesn't trust these men to do the right thing. Their self-preservation will win out over the lives of anyone else here.

Viola feels tears running down her cheeks, and she squeezes Mirabelle tighter. "I will do exactly as you say. But I can't leave until you call an ambulance or let me call one. Please. I beg you." The tears are coming thick and fast now. The woman is still showing no signs of responding, but the shallow movements of her chest indicate she is at least still breathing. But her breathing looks ineffective and rapid. Too rapid. If someone doesn't do something soon, she is going to die.

Duke's face is scarlet, and Viola shrinks back involuntarily. She wouldn't be surprised if he tried to forcibly remove her.

"I said, get out! My family is none of your concern. Get out of my house." Viola has only ever seen Duke completely in control of a situation, and the fact that he is rattled and disordered somehow gives her strength.

She straightens her shoulders and stands her ground. "No. I will leave once an ambulance is called." Viola looks back towards the woman, who now seems to be drifting in and out of consciousness rather than appearing completely comatose. Which seems like an improvement of sorts. "I will not allow you to let this woman or her baby die. Now, get them an ambulance."

Duke's head looks like it might explode, but Viola doesn't move a muscle. She stares at him defiantly, letting him know there is no wiggle room here. She will not be intimidated, not when there are two innocent lives on the line. Viola feels Mirabelle unstick from her side. She looks down at the girl, who is clearly panic-stricken. Her mouth is wobbling, and tears have begun to flow down her cheeks. Viola reaches out her hand, but Mirabelle's face hardens and she pushes Viola's arm roughly away.

A strange stillness falls over the room at Mirabelle's reaction. Something needs to happen and fast, but it's as though everyone is waiting to see who makes a decisive move. Mirabelle suddenly runs out of the kitchen, wailing hysterically, and Viola is glad the girl is out of the way. This is likely to get even uglier, and it is no place for a child.

Duke turns to Rhys and barks instructions. "Help me lift her and put her in the car."

Rhys looks down at the woman carrying his child, who is

now even paler, her breaths fast and shallow like the wings of a hummingbird. Viola notices a flicker of something in Rhys's eyes. She can see conflict in there. He doesn't agree with his father, and Viola senses her opportunity.

"Rhys, no. Can't you see that she needs an ambulance now? We have no idea what is wrong. She might die. Your son could die. Come on, forget everything else. Surely their lives are the most important thing?"

Duke grabs Rhys's arm roughly. "Don't listen to her. We need to get her to Querencia. They'll both get the best care there. You know this, Rhys. Don't let her confuse you."

Confused is indeed the perfect word to describe Rhys. He looks like a little boy, faced with an impossible choice and afraid of the consequences no matter what he chooses.

"Fine. I'll call them myself." As Viola makes to take her first step towards the door to find a telephone, she hears a faint siren in the distance. Everyone in the room freezes and listens as the wailing sound increases in intensity. Viola puts her hand to her chest, new tears filling her eyes, this time of relief.

Duke lunges towards her, stopping only centimetres from her face. "What did you do? You'll pay for this, you meddling bitch."

But Viola doesn't care. The cavalry is on its way. There is nothing he can do to stop it now. Viola and Duke both turn as Mirabelle comes marching into the room.

"Don't call Viola horrible names, Granddad. And anyway, I called the ambulance, and I'm really cross at you and Daddy for not listening."

Viola wants to scoop the little girl up and cradle her. She has saved the day. Duke looks completely stunned, staring open-mouthed at his granddaughter. If he lays one hand on her, Viola knows she won't be able to control herself.

"Don't look at me like that, Granddad. Mummy needs help,

and my baby brother in her tummy needs help. You wouldn't get it for them, so I did it. You know you have to do as I say so stop pretending that you're in charge." Mirabelle plants her hands on her hips, and Viola can't help but enjoy the effect it has on Duke. His face alternates between fury and disbelief. Viola has no clue what he will do next.

The sound of the sirens peak, and Viola hears the ambulance screech to a halt outside. Rhys is now sitting on the floor, comforting his wife and stroking her hair while muttering to himself. A loud knocking at the front door echoes through the kitchen and without thinking, Viola moves as quickly as she can to answer it. She makes it barely two steps before she finds herself being pulled back. One arm wraps roughly around her middle and another around her neck. She fights hard. She will not let Duke knock her out again. She closes her eyes, kicking and punching in all directions with every ounce of strength she has. Viola digs deep and is sure she has made it when she feels cool, fresh air hit her cheeks. But when she opens her eyes, she finds herself outside the back door of number 33, the garden behind her. Duke shoves her hard in the chest, and she tumbles backwards onto the grass. She can still see through the house, and Rhys is at the front door letting the paramedics in.

Duke snarls and hisses at her, "Go home and stay there. Do it now, or I promise you, I will make sure Mirabelle suffers."

The door closes, and she hears the sound of the key turning in the lock. Viola tries to focus on the fact that the pregnant woman and her unborn baby are now in the best hands. Her heart is hammering, and her wrist is throbbing. She must have put it out to break her fall. But all she can focus on are Duke's final words and the horrific realisation that it was not an idle threat. Mirabelle is under the illusion that she is somehow in charge of this family, but they are clearly manipulating her young, fragile mind and using this 'chosen one' nonsense as a way to keep her on side. Rhys at least showed a modicum of integrity when he saw that lives were at stake, but not Duke. He is evil personified, and as soon as she knows mother and baby are safe and in the hospital, she will get Mirabelle away from him.

By any means necessary.

CHAPTER TWENTY-SEVEN

Viola pushes herself onto her knees and eventually to her feet. Her legs give way several times. Her body is exhausted, and the agony she feels in her muscles and joints is relentless. She needs to get home and take something for the pain. She sneaks through the side gate and shuffles her way towards her house. The ambulance remains outside number 33, but everyone is still inside. Nobody is around to see her as she opens her door, stumbles into the hallway, and locks the door behind her with her last ounce of strength before crumpling into a ball on the floor.

At this moment, all she wants is to give up. So much has been taken from her, and she feels physically and mentally empty. Her life is never going to be the same. She will never feel safe. The small but hugely important parts of her world, like visiting her friends or enjoying her garden, will always be tainted by the threat of Duke and Querencia. She has unwittingly made a dangerous enemy, and she knows this will haunt her to her dying day.

Viola doesn't know how much time has passed. The street seems quiet. Has she been asleep or simply dissociated from the world and retreated inside herself? She is still on the hallway floor, stiff and in pain. Rolling onto her back, she manages to plant a foot against the wall. After several failed attempts, she eventually pulls herself up using the banister for support. Making her way to the kitchen, she grabs two painkillers from the cupboard and washes them down with several large gulps of bourbon straight from the bottle. She is dehydrated and alcohol is probably the last thing her body needs, especially with the tablets she has just taken, but, quite frankly, she couldn't care less. The whole world, as she knows it, has been obliterated. Standard rules no longer apply. She closes all the curtains downstairs, shutting out the world. The ambulance has gone, and there are no other cars outside number 33. She can't find the energy to think or care about what might be happening to any of them – even Mirabelle. Her heart is too damaged to do anything other than beat and keep her alive.

An overwhelming need for sleep washes over her and she climbs the stairs, wincing with every step.

She falls into bed, fully clothed, and sleep consumes her.

CHAPTER TWENTY-EIGHT

MIRABELLE

That was such a weird night. Good things: I had a lovely chat with Viola. She actually listened, and I believed her when she said she wouldn't lie to me. I don't know what Daddy and Granddad's problem is with her. Plus, Viola was amazing when she thought my baby brother was in danger. She was like a proper superhero. So brave, telling Granddad what to do. Most people don't dare talk back to Granddad. I can, but that's because I'm the firstborn daughter. It's nice to be special.

And that brings me on to the other good thing. My brother. He must be here by now! When I called the ambulance, I knew they would take Mummy to the hospital, which made me a bit sad because I really, really wanted to see Eli before anyone else. But what were those grown-ups even doing? It was obvious Mummy needed an ambulance. Sometimes, adults can be so dumb.

I'm sure I'll get to meet Eli tomorrow, and then me, Daddy, Mummy, and Eli can have a big family hug. We'll be the best perfect family at Querencia. I can't wait.

But last night wasn't all good. I'm a bit worried about Viola. Granddad shoved her out into the garden, which made me want to cry. I yelled at Granddad really loud and ran up to my bedroom and slammed the door. Even though Viola is clever and sunshiny, she's actually really old. I hope she's okay. But I have to stay here at Querencia for now. Until Eli and Mummy are back. I hate waiting for them to come home as well as worrying about Viola. I mean, is she sad or hurt? Not knowing is making me feel all squirmy, which I don't like one bit.

Maybe I need to find a way to contact Viola. I bet she'd love that.

CHAPTER TWENTY-NINE

Days pass. Viola doesn't know how many. She sleeps a lot and eats just enough to keep her alive. She shuns the bourbon in favour of water and cleans and tends to the numerous scrapes and scratches that litter her skin. Her body is covered in bruises, but paracetamol is enough to take the edge off the pain. She is almost certain nothing is broken. The swelling in her wrist is improving and it has full range of movement. She avoids looking in any mirrors. She doesn't want to see the injuries on her face, but more than that, she doesn't want to see herself.

Thoughts of Mirabelle and Wendy try to invade her mind, but she banishes them. She is not strong enough to help anyone, and anything she has tried has ended in disaster.

Nobody has knocked at the door, and a small pile of mail sits behind it. She knows she should probably open it or at least check for anything urgent, but nothing feels important anymore. She has turned her phone off. There is nobody she wants to speak to. She mourns the loss of Martin more than ever. This grief is new and twisted, making her feel nauseated, angry, and bitterly sad. He was her everything, and she had decided she owed it to his memory to keep living and enjoying life after his death. Now she has discovered that he was a liar, an entirely different man than the one she loved, there seems little point to anything.

―――――――

Viola recognises she is falling into a pit of despair and letting melancholy take charge, but she is okay with that right now.

The curtains have remained closed, though she has taken the odd peek through her bedroom window. There hasn't been one single sign of life from next door. As her body heals, she starts to allow herself to think about what she is going to do next. She knows she should probably move house. Go far away and start again somewhere else, where they can't find her. But she is old and doesn't want to uproot her life. Plus, where would she even go?

The supply of fresh food in the house has begun to dwindle. The milk has long since expired and the fridge is almost bare, but she can last at least a few more weeks with what she has in the cupboards and freezer. She doesn't need much, and any enjoyment she used to get from food has evaporated. All of the paracetamol has gone, but she doesn't really need them anyway. The pain has almost disappeared, but she feels weak from lack of any activity. She has picked up her crocheting bag a few times but hasn't made a single thing. The television has remained off. She has done absolutely nothing, and she can feel her mind beginning to rot. Perhaps she will just waste away.

Viola stands in the kitchen, sipping a glass of water, when a movement catches her eye on the counter near the sink. She slaps her hand over her mouth and recoils at the sight. Ants. There are ants crawling all over the worktop. She watches them momentarily, and it's as though they are the first thing she has seen clearly since she left number 33, days or perhaps even weeks ago. She has been walking around in a haze, noticing nothing, only surviving, and an intense feeling of shame flows through her at the self-indulgence of her behaviour.

She takes a good look around her kitchen. Dirty plates and cups are scattered all over. The bin is overflowing, and there are crumbs and bits of leftover food everywhere. The whole place is disgusting. Looking at the glass in her hand, she is horrified to see it is covered in smudges and streaks of goodness knows what. She puts it down, retrieves the rubber gloves from under the sink, and sets to work.

The cleaning of the kitchen feels ceremonial. With every cup and plate Viola washes, she starts to see the world a little clearer. With every counter she wipes down, she begins to feel more like herself. Her mission extends into the living room, and she begins dusting down all the surfaces, hoovering and tidying up the clothes and debris scattered across the sofa and floor. Tiredness sets in, but it is a good sort of tiredness, the kind you get from hard work and exercise, not the soul-crushing tiredness you get from sadness and apathy.

Finally, she plugs her phone in to charge. As it comes back to life, she hears the ping of many messages and calls coming through. She will deal with those later once the house is sorted.

After many hours of hard labour, Viola walks through her house admiring every room. Her bedroom was the biggest shock to her. Bedsheets stained with food, plates and dirty underwear strewn everywhere. She has been living like a feral animal. Now, her home is back to how it should be. Everything is clean. The curtains and windows are open, and fresh clean air flows through the rooms, bringing them and her back to life. She has one final clean-up job to attend to before she tackles the mail and her phone calls and messages.

Herself.

Facing her reflection in the bathroom mirror, Viola turns her head from side to side, examining every aspect of her face. The bruises are less visible with her dark skin. While she can easily see the slightly discoloured patches, others are unlikely to notice. A little bit of make-up will sort that right out. She is horrified to see the state of her teeth. They are yellow and furry-looking, and she brushes them vigorously, spitting out blood mixed with toothpaste. She has always taken great care of her teeth. Something else her mother always impressed the importance of upon her.

Viola considers how easy it was to lose herself. She has been lucky to have had good mental health. She has watched friends suffer, and helped families through her work, not really understanding fully how it must feel, only knowing how debilitating and terrifying it would be. She looks at herself closely, recognising the spark reigniting in her eyes. This was a temporary moment in time for her, caused by something terrible that happened. She knows that isn't the case for a lot of people, and for that, she feels hugely grateful.

Clean, presentably dressed, and content with the state of her home, Viola sits on the sofa with her now fully charged phone and the stack of mail she collected from the mat behind the front door. There are a few numbers she doesn't recognise, spam or sales calls most likely, and no voicemails. Feelings of guilt rise within her as she reads the messages from her friends, and in particular the numerous messages from Nina. She has left a lot of people worried about her. However, in a way, this warms her heart. There is plenty in her life to fight for. She fires off a variation of the same message to all her friends. She is reluctant to lie, but the truth is definitely off-limits. Viola tells them she has been helping a neighbour through a family emergency and hasn't checked her phone. She apologises profusely and promises she will see them very soon. And she means it.

Messages immediately come back.

As long as you're okay.

Hello, stranger. Glad you're okay.

Looking forward to seeing you at the café.

And one from Nina that brings a tear to her eye and a realisation that she has acted at just the right time.

Thank bloody God. You were hours away from me calling the police to check on you. Never do that again. Love you xxx

Viola responds with another apology and promises that she will never go AWOL again without an explanation. She is so grateful for Nina and all her other wonderful friends and their caring and forgiving natures. She will make it up to them. Next time they meet, tea and cake will be on her.

As she rifles through the post, she sees nothing unusual. Flyers, junk mail, bills, all the things she was expecting. Nestled among them is a folded piece of lined paper with a handwritten message.

I knocked, but there was no answer. Call me and let me know you're okay, Nina x

Viola promises herself she will call Nina later to check in properly, she hates that she has worried her so much. Clearly, there must have been at least one knock at the door, but Viola can't remember hearing it.

The final item of mail is a plain white envelope. It does not have a name or address on it. Viola turns it over in her hands, looking for any identifying features, but there is nothing. Subsequently, she has no idea when this was delivered. She rips it open, and there is a handwritten letter inside. Her hands shake as she begins to read.

> *Dear Viola,*
> *I would be honoured if you would join me for afternoon tea.*
> *2pm on Friday 11th August at Querencia.*
> *I hope we can use this meeting to come to an understanding.*
> *Your presence is of utmost importance.*
> *Yours*
> *Duke*

The words have been written in a beautiful calligraphy style. The grandeur and pomposity of the invite do not surprise Viola. She can easily imagine Duke sitting with a feather quill and a pot of ink. She checks inside the envelope again, making sure there are no accompaniments to the invite. Yesterday, Viola wouldn't have had a clue what day it was, but now she has reorientated herself, she knows that Friday 11th August is tomorrow.

To anyone else, this invitation would seem cordial. A little too formal, perhaps, but certainly polite. But Viola can see the meaning beneath the words and feel what is inferred between the lines. She has to go. She is expected. Even in her slovenly state, the memory of Duke's parting words has never left her.

"Go home and stay there. Do it now, or I promise you, I will make sure Mirabelle suffers."

It shocks Viola that she could exist, no matter how insignificantly, while knowing what Duke had promised and doing nothing about it. That in itself shows her just how incapacitated she became. She barely maintained the will to live, and in doing so, she lost the will to do anything else. Viola reads the letter one final time. There is no internal debate to be had. No weighing up of options. She will go to Querencia tomorrow. She will go because she can't handle the potential consequences of not going. Undoubtedly, she is placing herself in the path of danger, and she is aware there is a chance she might not return unscathed or even return at all.

If Duke is the kind of man willing to harm his own granddaughter in pursuit of his beliefs and wants, then he would scarcely blink an eye at extinguishing Viola.

All she can do is try.

And try, she will.

CHAPTER THIRTY

Viola hasn't had anywhere near enough sleep for the day ahead. But then, she's probably slept way too much recently. With her new-found energy and purpose, it's unsurprising that her body won't yield and allow her to rest.

Although she made significant progress yesterday with getting her life back on track, one thing she failed to rectify was the lack of groceries in the house. Providing all goes well today, she must go to the shop for some kitchen staples on the way home. Viola sighs and rolls her eyes at the absurdity of planning to pop to the shops on the way back from Querencia. Who is she kidding? There is no chance today will go well. She is walking freely into a lion's den and will not emerge unharmed. She would be foolish to think that the invitation for afternoon tea and the request that they 'come to an understanding' is all this will be. At best, she will be subjected to bribery, offered money, or perhaps threatened with who knows what to keep quiet. At worst, well, she doesn't really want to think about that too much. Her days of descending into despair and anguish have taught her one thing at least. She values her life and the things and people in it. She doesn't want that taken away from her, and it saddens and frightens her that that choice could be so easily taken out of her hands.

She needs to make at least one person aware of where she is going and decides she will text Nina just before she goes into Querencia. That way there won't be time for Nina to talk her out of it, but someone will be able to find her if this all goes horribly wrong.

Viola does not dress the way she usually would for afternoon tea, far from it. Although she hasn't done any physical activity more strenuous than walking or gardening in years, she still has some exercise attire. She is relieved to find that it fits. She scrapes her hair back and secures it with pins. She can't help but laugh at herself when she looks in the mirror. She looks like a prison inmate in her grey tracksuit and white trainers. But how she looks is not important today. She needs to be as agile as possible. Prepared to fight or run away. Both things she has little skill in. Nevertheless, she needs to give herself the best possible chance, so sportswear it is.

Viola briefly considers taking some sort of weapon with her but can't think of anything that would be useful. Anything large, like a baseball bat, which she doesn't own anyway, would be immediately obvious and unlikely to ingratiate herself with Duke and his family. She considers slipping a small knife into her backpack but, in the end, decides to go sans weapon. Her bag will probably be searched or taken away from her anyway, plus she's not convinced she has it in her to stab someone. Even Duke.

As Viola walks to catch the bus, she looks around at the people living ordinary lives: the teenager with his hood pulled up, engrossed by his phone; the older man constantly sniffing and wiping his nose. Does she look just as ordinary to them? Is there anything about her appearance that tells the world what has happened to her life?

Viola follows the same route to Querencia as last time. She opens the large gate with the prominent warning sign and follows the path to the front door. Her heart flutters and her stomach swells with nerves, but she pays no heed. As soon as she set foot out of her front door, she decided there was no going back. And so, she keeps walking, through the fear, against her better judgement. Stalling or turning back will only make her nerves worse.

She focuses on the large red-brick building as she walks toward it, her head held high and footsteps never faltering. She stands at the shiny silver entrance and waits. From her previous visit, she knows there is no way to attract the attention of those inside, and she won't give them the satisfaction of watching her searching or peering around the entrance. She simply stands, trying to stop her body from trembling, and waits for someone to greet her.

As before, a female voice comes through the speaker to her left. It sounds like the woman who told her to leave last time, but thankfully, the greeting is much more welcoming now.

"Good afternoon, Viola. Please come in." The automatic doors open, and Viola takes several steps inside. As she thought, she is indeed greeted by the same woman with the tightly pulled back hair. The woman is smiling, which looks unnatural on her stretched face. Viola gives a small smile back and, despite expecting it, flinches when the doors hiss and begin to close behind her. She regains her composure quickly. Appearing skittish and nervy is not the impression she wants to give.

The woman extends her lithe arms towards the same plastic chair Viola was offered the last time she was here. "Do take a seat. Duke will be with you momentarily."

Once again, Viola is struck by the oddness of everything here. Who actually speaks like that? "No, thank you. I'm happy standing." The woman narrows her eyes, and her smile becomes a pinched line. Viola suspects she's used to having people do exactly what she tells them to do.

"Very well." The woman turns and walks robotically out of the room. Viola lets out a sharp breath of relief as the door hisses closed. That woman makes her feel uneasy. There's something too harsh and mechanical about her. Although she fits right in with this cold, sterile environment. Both of them are devoid of any character.

Viola hears footsteps approaching the door and braces herself for the woman's return. Instead, Duke walks through the door and stands with his back against it, allowing her to see into the long, straight corridor before her. Duke is sharply dressed in black as usual, but he looks a little thinner, his face drawn and a hint of shadow under each eye. He looks tired and stressed, and Viola finds this reassures her and boosts her confidence. Seemingly, he is human after all.

"Would you like to come through, Viola?"

Viola moves her eyes from Duke to the corridor and back again. She can't hide her trepidation. She is already locked in behind one door, and who knows what lies in store for her beyond this one.

"I have afternoon tea ready for us, as promised. I assume, given your arrival, that you'd like to join me?" He's right, of course. What would be the point of stopping here? Viola nods and clears her dry throat. The air in this place seems to lack any moisture, and the nerves aren't helping. She walks past Duke, trying not to touch him with any part of her body as she does. "It's the third door on the right."

Viola counts as she walks. There are doors on either side of the corridor, all exactly the same and equidistant. It's like a hospital or a very barren hotel corridor. The doors are all solid with no windows or signs, nothing to indicate what might be inside them. The only noise is the soft, slightly squeaky sound of her trainers and the tap of Duke's shoes as they walk. Standing outside the door in question, Viola waits for Duke to do or say something. She has a sudden horrible vision of Duke pushing her inside and locking it. Leaving her to rot in a cell where she can't speak of their secrets and terrible deeds. A fierce urge to run overwhelms her, but before she can react, Duke reaches around her, brushes her arm with his, and turns the handle.

The door swings open, and Viola takes in the room before her.

CHAPTER THIRTY-ONE

Rhys sits behind a large glass table, identical to the one in the kitchen of number 33. Do these people bulk-buy their furniture? In front of Rhys sits a silver cake stand filled with finger sandwiches, scones, and beautiful patisserie. The sweet, buttery aroma is exquisitely inviting, especially considering Viola's atrocious diet recently. Coffee and tea sit to the side. The afternoon tea that was promised is actually here. Surely, that has to be a good start.

Duke closes the door behind them and walks around the table to sit next to his son. Three plates with cups, saucers, cutlery, and napkins are on the table. The only place setting available to Viola is directly opposite Duke and Rhys, and the layout gives Viola the impression she is about to be interviewed. It is very much a show of them against her.

Viola sits, thinking this could definitely be worse. For one, she is glad that no one else is in the room. No new Querencia members to get to grips with. She fully expected both Duke and Rhys to be here, and the absence of extra bodies is comforting. No additional weight for their side if things go awry. Plus, she is closest to the door, and with a table between the men and her and her own cutlery, she has a decent weapon and a potential exit.

Viola looks expectantly at them. Rhys is a shell of his former well-put-together self. His eyes lack the confidence and steel she has experienced previously. He meets her eye briefly but looks down quickly before turning his head to Duke. Tension hangs in the air between father and son. Rhys's downtrodden manner and deference towards Duke give the impression that he has been chastised and told to behave. Viola is fascinated by their dynamic, particularly as Rhys could undoubtedly overpower his father. But brute force is not what makes Duke strong. His power is born of his abilities to manipulate and coerce, his lack of conscience and humanity. And to Viola's mind, that is infinitely more threatening.

Duke interrupts the silence. "Tea or coffee, Viola?"

"Tea, please, with just a splash of milk." Duke nods and turns to Rhys, who obeys the silent command and pours tea into Viola's cup, never lifting his eyes from the pot.

"Same for me, please, Rhys." Rhys nods at his father and pours tea for all three of them before sitting down. Viola can't help feeling a twinge of concern for Rhys. Something she thought she'd never experience. He looks utterly defeated, and while he could do with being taken down a peg or two, she doesn't like the extra dominance this grants Duke.

Before she can thank Rhys, Duke speaks again. "Help yourself to food, Viola. All freshly prepared this morning."

In the interest of making this go as well as possible and because the food display looks absolutely delicious, Viola places two finger sandwiches on her plate.

"Thank you. This looks lovely."

Duke smiles, adds sandwiches to his plate, and then to Rhys's as though he were a child.

"I think you'll enjoy it, and I also hope this shows my intentions are good today."

Viola takes a bite of a smoked salmon and cream cheese sandwich and almost moans at how amazing it is. She desperately wants to eat the rest but answers Duke instead.

"And what are your intentions, Duke?"

"As I said in my invitation, I want us to reach an understanding."

Viola nods. "And how do you propose we do that?"

Duke rests his elbows on the table and clasps his hands together. "I've thought a lot over the days since we last met. And if I could, I would go back in time and handle it differently."

This admission surprises Viola, and she pops the remaining piece of the sandwich into her open mouth. She wasn't expecting anything but denial from Duke. Perhaps there is a way this won't end badly for her.

"What you asked of me was not unreasonable, Viola. You wanted to know that Wendy is safe. I understand that now."

Viola can't hide her astonishment. Is this the same man who threatened his own granddaughter's safety?

"Yes, that's all I wanted. All I still want. Wendy disappeared to be replaced by another woman, a heavily pregnant woman at that. How could I possibly just ignore it? But you tried to make me feel like I was going mad, not to mention the whole tying me up thing."

Duke holds his hand out, but Viola can't work out whether it's a gesture of apology or his usual bid to silence her. Either way, it irks her.

"As I said, if I could go back and change things, I would. But we both know that can't happen. So, I have an offer for you." He raises his eyebrows, but Viola maintains her stony expression. "There is some room for negotiation, but I'd appreciate it if you'd hear me out first."

Viola takes a sip of her tea. "I'll listen. But what I said about Wendy won't change."

"I understand. And with that in mind, I think you'll be pleasantly surprised by what I have to say."

Viola leans forward, mirroring Duke's posture. It's as though Rhys isn't even in the room. He doesn't interact at all – he just sits and looks down at the table.

"First of all, I want to apologise to you, Viola. This place is my life's work. It is a sanctuary, and I assure you, the people who live here feel the same way." Viola strains to keep her face straight. She doubts that very much but wants to hear what Duke has to say. "The people here are like family, and if I feel my family is being threatened, I will do anything to keep them safe and well. Surely, you must at least understand that?"

Viola thinks for a moment. "In a way. I can definitely understand protecting your family. But what you did to me, the things you said, and the threats you made. You can't possibly think any of that is okay?"

"And that's exactly what I'm saying. I regret what I did and the things I said. In no way am I trying to justify my actions. I'm simply trying to tell you my motivations, to get you to understand that my only wish was to protect my family."

"Okay. I'm glad we agree on something, at least." Undoubtedly, Duke should pay for what he has done to her, but shoving that down his throat feels fruitless and will only stop her getting the answers she needs.

"There are a few things I need to say before we talk about Wendy. First of all, your husband, Martin." Viola feels her chest tighten. "There are some things I think you should know, and I'm afraid they might not be easy to hear. But Martin was a good man, of that I assure you. Anything Rhys may have said to the contrary was simply meant to derail you. And for that, I apologise."

Viola's heart is in her throat, and she wishes Duke would stop using quite so many words and just get on with it. She stares at Duke, and he seems to get the message.

"Martin and I rarely met. Once number 33 had a secure tenant, there was no need to." Viola chews her bottom lip and nods.

"If you and Martin weren't close and your relationship was purely professional, why did he give you a key to our house?"

"Ah, yes. I thought you might ask that."

Viola raises her eyebrows. "Well?"

"Martin didn't know I had a key. I took it."

"You did what?" Although stealing a key is a relatively minor offence compared to the other things Duke has done, she remains appalled.

"The reason for me taking the key is explained by the story I am about to tell you. So if you allow me to continue, it will make more sense." Viola nods, still seething. "Thank you. When the tenants prior to Rhys moved in–"

"Kevin and Leo."

Duke waves his hand in the air to show his total lack of care about who his tenants were.

"When we were at the stage of exchanging contracts, Martin turned up unexpectedly at Querencia with some papers for me to sign."

Viola gasps and looks around her. She can't believe that Martin has actually visited this place. He could have been in this exact room. Sat in this chair.

"It wasn't the usual protocol for us, but Martin, ever the perfectionist, decided to come here when he couldn't reach me on the phone. Seemingly, you were about to go on a short break together, and he didn't want to cause any delays with the rental agreement while he was away from work."

Viola drags her mind back. Yes, that all fits. Just before

Kevin and Leo moved in, she and Martin took a lovely break to Loch Lomond in Scotland. She remembers it well. It rained pretty much the entire time they were there, and they spent almost every second indoors eating beautiful food and just being together. It was lovely.

"Well, there was, let's say… an unfortunate incident."

Viola isn't sure her heart can take any more of this. "Duke, please, just tell me. I need to know."

Duke nods. "Very well. Martin ignored the signs at the gate and drove his car through it. Querencia wasn't quite as established as it is now, and we had a few 'bad eggs' living with us then."

Viola frowns. She can't work out where this story could possibly be going.

"Let me explain. Trust me, it is relevant to the story. The Querencia family all live here for free. There is no cost for accommodation or food, and whilst work is encouraged, it is not forced. It's not such a problem these days. We have learned from our previous mistakes, but in the past, we had several residents who abused what we offer here."

Viola nods. She can absolutely see how that could happen. But what does this have to do with Martin?

"Anyway, as Martin was driving up that day, one of our more volatile residents attacked him."

Viola's eyes widen with horror, but Duke continues before she can interject.

"They didn't assault him exactly. They ran over and started banging on his car. Shouting, carrying on, that sort of thing. The person in question was a known drug user and troublemaker, and we were doing everything we could at the time to get him to leave."

"Oh my goodness." Viola's voice is a whisper and once again, she can't believe what she is hearing. She honestly

185

thought that she and Martin knew everything about one another. She thinks back to their break in Scotland. Was Martin's behaviour unusual? Were there any signs that something like this had happened to him? No, she doesn't think so.

"Was he hurt? What happened?"

"Martin was just in the wrong place at the wrong time, and no, he left shortly after, completely unharmed and with signed rental papers in hand. He was shouted and screamed at somewhat, the deluded ramblings of a drug-addled mind, I'm afraid. And unfortunately, he was threatened and asked to hand over money."

Viola feels all the blood drain from her face.

"Please don't worry, Viola. I'm simply telling you everything because I think it will help you understand the money situation. Martin left intact, exactly as he arrived."

"What do you mean by threatened?"

"It was silly, really. Our resident was doing some gardening work, although describing it as work might be stretching it a bit. He was mostly just messing around with some of our other unruly members." Viola shakes her head. He sounds like a disgruntled headmaster talking about disobedient children. But she needs to hear what happens next, so she keeps her face impassive. "We were doing our best to keep him occupied and our other residents safe. Anyway, I'm getting off-topic – you don't need to know all that. When he saw Martin's car, he grabbed a large stick and ran over. Vehicles hardly ever just arrive at Querencia like that. He started banging it against the car, and to his credit, Martin got out and confronted him. He was a very brave man, your husband. I will always admire the way he behaved in that moment."

A feeling of warmth spreads through Viola. Finally, she

recognises something about her husband in Duke's words. He was certainly brave and never afraid of confrontation.

"It was a lot of back and forth. The man asking for money, Martin refusing – politely at first and then less so. Unfortunately, things escalated, and before either of us could disarm him, he stood behind Martin with the stick pointed into his neck."

Viola again tries to recall her memories, but she can't remember seeing any physical evidence of what Duke is describing. There were no marks or cuts on Martin's skin.

"So, I tasered him."

Viola's mouth falls open.

"No, not Martin. His attacker, I mean."

"I know full well what you meant, but I'm still shocked. So, what happened then? Did you call the police?"

Duke rubs his hands together, and his eyes drift skyward. "No, we used it as an opportune moment to remove the man from the premises."

"We?" Viola's heart rate begins to rise. Is this where she will discover the nefarious act that earned her husband one hundred thousand pounds?

"I must start expressing myself better. When I say 'we', I mean us here at Querencia."

Viola calms somewhat, but not completely.

"So, what did Martin do and why was he given the money?"

"Let's just say Martin wasn't entirely in agreement with our planned course of action."

Viola plants her palms on the table in front of her. "No, let's not. Let's just tell the entire bloody truth, shall we?"

Duke leans back and crosses his arms. Viola simmers with anger.

"Fine. I can't understand what knowing every little detail will achieve, but if you must."

"I must."

"Martin wanted me to call the police, and when I wouldn't, he wanted to call them himself."

"Well, that would have been the right thing to do!"

"On the surface, yes. But you need to understand – that man was completely delusional and was making wild accusations that would have seriously damaged me and my family. Not to mention the blossoming Querencia. All I wanted was to use the opportunity of him being incapacitated to escort him from the premises."

"And is that what happened?" A sickening dread is making Viola feel that what happened was likely to be considerably worse than that.

"Eventually. After much back and forth, Martin agreed to leave Querencia and let me deal with the situation."

"I don't believe you. Martin would never have walked away like that."

"Well, he did. What would be the point of me lying to you now? I promised him I would ensure the man came to no harm and pointed out the fact that he himself was trespassing. That was all that was needed."

"So, you threatened him?"

"Not at all. You've seen the signs at the gate yourself, Viola. Martin remained unhappy with my chosen course of action. Still, ever the professional, he agreed to file the papers I had just signed and then told me he never wanted to work with me again. I agreed that was probably best, and I never saw him again."

Even though the worst of the story appears to be over, Viola still can't seem to regulate her breathing. "Then why the hundred thousand pounds?"

Duke shrugs and examines his pristine nails. "Insurance, I suppose. He didn't ask for the money, but then he never tried to return it. It made me feel a bit better knowing I had that security. Belt and braces."

Viola can't decide if she feels better or worse now she has heard this story. Did Martin do something wrong? She doesn't think so. There are definitely some questionable choices in there, but nothing overtly terrible. What would she have done in the same situation? She can't honestly say. Would she have given the money back? In all honesty, probably not.

"And the key?" Duke appears to have finished his story and hasn't mentioned taking a key to her house.

"I knew you and Martin would be away in Scotland for a few days. He'd told me himself. I paid a little visit to your house, took your spare key from underneath the flowerpot by the back door, and made a copy. It never ceases to amaze me that sensible, well-educated people leave a key 'hidden' outside in case of emergencies. I wasn't expecting to find one – you must agree it is careless to leave a key outdoors when you've gone away. But low and behold, there it was. It took me all of two minutes to find it."

Viola sighs. That key has been there for decades – it still is. They've never needed to use it, nor have they ever had anyone steal it or use it to break in. Even after recent events, it never crossed her mind. Duke is right – it is completely careless, and if she ever gets home, she will move it straight away.

"Anyway, if it's okay with you, I'd like to move on. Martin's story is not the main thing I wanted to share with you, and I don't think it's what you came here for either."

Viola tries to refocus. Duke is right. There'll be time to come to terms with everything she's just heard about Martin if and when she gets out of here.

"Okay. Go on."

Duke takes a deep breath. "I know you know this already, but I feel I owe it to you to say it out loud. When Rhys and his family arrived, his wife, Wendy, was not the same woman who recently gave birth to Eli."

Viola hears Rhys choke back a sob, and she is suddenly terrified about what she is about to hear.

She tries in vain to get Rhys's attention. "What is it? What happened?" Viola looks desperately from Rhys to Duke. Rhys looks inconsolable, yet Duke appears unchanged. Still calm and ready to continue his story. "Mirabelle told me that Wendy was safe and well here at Querencia. Was she lying?"

"No, what Mirabelle said is true. Wendy is here and I will prove that to you shortly. But there is more to say first."

Viola feels her heart steady slightly. She points to Rhys. "Then why is he so upset? I've never seen him like this."

Duke sighs and puts a hand on Rhys's shoulder. "His wife died in childbirth and he blames me."

Viola's stomach lurches as she remembers the pale and barely responsive woman in labour. Why hadn't she even thought to ask?

Rhys suddenly comes to life, and his outburst shocks Viola to her core. "I don't blame you, Dad. I blame myself. I sat back... It's all my fault." Rhys's voice cracks at the last word, and he grinds his palms into his eyes.

Viola watches the heartbreaking display. This explains Rhys's solemn and withdrawn behaviour. He is grieving and broken.

Viola manages a whisper. "And the baby? Eli?"

Rhys now has his head in his hands. Duke leans in and whispers something in his son's ear. Viola can't make out any of the words, but Rhys suddenly stands up and leaves the room without saying anything further.

Duke strokes his chin and shakes his head resignedly. "Baby Eli is healthy and thriving. He's being looked after. But Rhys, this has hit him hard. He needs time."

"Well, of course it's hit him hard. As it should. The mother of his baby has died." A terrible thought suddenly occurs to Viola. Rhys hasn't only lost his wife – Mirabelle has lost her mother. "Mirabelle. Where is she?"

"All in good time, I promise you. You'll get the answers to everything, but I fear we've gone off track slightly. Let's take a minute, and then I'll explain everything to you."

Duke picks up his tea and takes a large drink. Viola does the same, but the tea is now tepid.

"What was her name? The woman who died. I know she wasn't Wendy. But I'd like to know her name." A deep, aching sadness fills Viola's heart. No matter the circumstances, a young woman losing her life and two young children left without a mother is undeniably tragic.

"At the time of her death, her name was Wendy." Viola opens her mouth to speak, enraged that he can't drop the act even for one second, but Duke continues regardless. "My family and our descendants are the bloodline of Querencia. Wendy will always be Rhys's wife."

Viola screws her face up. "That makes absolutely no sense. Are you saying that being 'Wendy' is like a job and the women in the position are interchangeable? That's just ludicrous and actually fucking disgusting."

Duke seems taken aback by Viola's swearing. But the way he describes the women as disposable boils her blood, and swearing is more than required.

"No, not... exactly." Rage is building inside Viola now, and she wants to swing the cake stand at his stupid head. "I wanted my son to marry for love. That's what we want for all our family members here."

"But?"

"But Wendy, whom you met when they first moved into number 33, couldn't have children. This was something we didn't know at first. As my only son and the only way for our bloodline to continue, Rhys needed to have his own children."

It feels as though hundreds of tiny explosions are going off inside Viola's brain. How can any of this be real? It's like something from medieval times. 'Bear me a child or off with your head.'

Duke carries on, unperturbed by Viola's reactions. "Rhys, Wendy, and I came to an understanding. They would remain together, and another member of the Querencia family would be their surrogate."

"And that's the pregnant woman. Mirabelle's birth mother?"

"Indeed. After Mirabelle's birth, it was all going rather well. They were happy. Living here, completely content. We wanted another child to complete their family, so we repeated the arrangement with the same surrogate."

Viola feels like her brain is falling apart trying to input this unbelievable information. She is speechless but does her best to take in Duke's words.

"And this is where the trouble started. I realise it was a mistake now, but as Mirabelle was a little older by the time Rhys and I felt ready for another child—"

Viola can't hold her tongue any longer, and words fly from her mouth unchecked and uncensored. "You and Rhys felt ready? What about the woman? No, the women involved. Don't they get any say in this at all? What on earth is this place? A fucking farm for you and your family? I honestly can't believe what I'm hearing." Viola is out of breath, and her vision is becoming a little blurry. She needs to try and calm herself down.

"No, of course not. Do you want to hear this or not? And please, can we avoid the shouting and hysterics? It's helping no one."

Viola wants to punch him or throw a cream cake right in his

obnoxious face, but unfortunately, he is right. She does need to collect herself if she wants to hear the end of this horrifying tale. She closes her eyes and takes two deep breaths.

Duke continues. "As I was saying, Mirabelle was too old not to notice that Wendy wouldn't be carrying the baby, so we told her that she'd grown in another lady's tummy, but that Wendy was still her mummy." Duke stops and wipes his brow, his eyes glazing over as though remembering that time. "Well, we couldn't have imagined the reaction we got. Mirabelle was furious. I've never seen rage like that in a child, and her behaviour, well, I can't begin to tell you the things she did."

Viola is grateful when Duke doesn't elaborate further. Mirabelle is only a little girl, but the behaviour Viola has seen from her has disturbed her to her core.

"Mirabelle immediately pulled away from Wendy and actively began to hate her. We tried everything, but she just wouldn't listen. Mirabelle demanded to meet her birth mother. She threatened us and tried to run away. It was terrible."

Nothing less than you deserve, thinks Viola, but merely replies with, "And what happened then?"

"So, this is where number 33 comes in. Wendy, Rhys, and Mirabelle moved in and the idea was to cement them as a family before the arrival of baby Eli. Except, Mirabelle is quite a force to be reckoned with, as I know you've experienced yourself."

"She's a little girl, Duke. A confused little girl growing up in an environment that can't be healthy for her. What do you expect?"

Duke's face hardens, and Viola senses she may have crossed a line. "I'll ignore that for now, Viola. But please do not speak disparagingly about my family. I'm treating you with nothing but respect here, and I'd be grateful to have the same from you."

Viola sits back. To be fair, he doesn't have to explain any of this to her, and he's doing it at her request. Maybe her opinions, although valid, are best kept to herself for now.

"Okay, agreed."

"Mirabelle started to threaten Wendy quite alarmingly. She threatened to cut off her fingers while she slept, and then even threatened to harm herself."

Viola recalls the bandaged hand incident outside her window and shudders. She absolutely believes Mirabelle to be capable of what Duke is describing.

"She wanted her birth mother to move in and promised she would behave if we allowed it. Obviously, we couldn't let the neighbours see two women living in the same house, and we knew that at least you, and probably others, had already seen Wendy and Rhys on that first day. So, we moved her in and she agreed not to go out."

The locked room, Viola realises. Not, in fact, Duke's mother at all, but... and then Viola realises how horrible it is that this woman, this woman who has now lost her life, remains nameless in this story. She deserves better than that.

"What was her name, Duke? Yes, I know that she was apparently 'Rhys's Wendy' when she died, but she was someone before that, and I think it's disrespectful to keep referring to this woman as 'she' or 'her'. It's undignified and downright wrong."

Duke nods solemnly, seeming to agree with Viola, "At that time, her name was Jillian."

Viola speaks the name out loud, "Jillian," and says a short internal prayer for all of Jillian's lost years and the potential she will never reach.

"At Querencia, our families are whole, and we don't support the idea of divorce or separation." Viola rolls her eyes. Yet another controlling archaic rule to the detriment of women. "And when Wendy became... problematic–"

Viola is incensed. "Problematic?"

Duke raises his voice. "Yes, absolutely problematic and further encouraged after an evening of too much poisonous alcohol with you, might I add. Rhys should never have allowed that; I'm still annoyed at him for leaving you two unsupervised."

Viola can't help but laugh. Duke has said and done many things that prove he believes men are superior to women. But unsupervised? Not only does he think women are inferior, he places them on the same level as children. Viola watches as Duke seems to bite back from saying something, something aggressive and rude, she would imagine.

"I know we will never see life the same way, Viola. And I take some responsibility for veering away from the facts and giving my opinions. But I'm giving you what you asked for, so take this as your last warning. Do not mock me, or I will abandon the remainder of my story, and we will have to approach this differently."

Viola's breathing quickens. Although polite, this is definitely a threat from Duke.

"Okay, Duke. I'm sorry. Will you tell me what happened when Wendy disappeared?"

"I will."

Viola holds her breath. Terrified of what she is about to discover.

CHAPTER THIRTY-TWO

"Jillian moved into number 33 the day of Helen's funeral. That part of the story is true, so don't be getting any strange ideas about what happened there. I assure you Helen died of natural causes, and we held a funeral for her here. Although Wendy never admitted to it, I believe she purposely left the front door open that day, hoping you would do exactly what you did. That you would not simply pull the door closed, but rather you would go snooping and discover the locked room upstairs."

Viola huffs. "I don't think it's unreasonable to check around a house when the door has been left open. Do you?"

Duke smirks and lifts one eyebrow. "So, you're telling me that everything you did that day was purely checking the safety and security of the house. There wasn't even a hint of curiosity or, dare I say it, nosiness?"

Viola feels her cheeks flush. "Curiosity, yes, but I am not nosy. I was planning to check all the rooms, but when I got upstairs and found the weird bedroom and then the locked room, I became curious. Who wouldn't?"

Duke shrugs. "Fair enough, I guess."

"And what was with the twin pink and blue beds? There's

something really odd about that room. Surely you can at least understand that?"

"We believe in order and synchronicity here. It helps everyone feel like they are part of the same family, living and working together for the same cause."

Viola sits back and folds her arms. The afternoon tea is so tempting, but somehow, eating more feels wrong, given the nature of their conversation.

She must have been staring at the remaining food longingly as Duke chimes in with, "You can eat, you know. That's what it's here for."

Viola shakes her head. "After we've finished talking."

Duke raises his arms, palms facing her. "Okay. But don't feel like you have to abstain on my behalf. If you thought the sandwiches were good, wait until you try the fruit scones. They're to die for."

A wicked spark flashes through Duke's eyes, and Viola immediately wishes she hadn't eaten or drank anything from this place. Is she about to fall on the floor, convulsing and writhing with poison cursing through her body? To die for, indeed.

Duke barks a laugh. "Oh, come on, Viola. I understand you being a little wary of me and my home, but I am not about to poison you." He laughs again, and the noise makes Viola's skin prickle with irritation. She remains stoic.

"The beds, Duke. I asked about the beds."

"Yes, well, as I was saying, we promote uniformity and consistency. The room you saw was set up for siblings. The pink bed was for Mirabelle, and the blue for Eli."

"But he wasn't even born. Nowhere near ready for a single bed."

"Indeed, we encourage infants to remain in a room with their parents until they are ready for a bed. It's safer for everyone and promotes bonding. The other room has a double bed and a cot."

Viola considers this. Okay, so she got the bedrooms the wrong way around. Although the room was barren and decorated in stereotypical colours, it's definitely less unusual that it was eventually intended for siblings.

"But I saw Mirabelle in the room with the white double bed. Plus, that's where you had Jillian locked away."

"Yes, that's right." Duke doesn't even seem to flinch at the mention of a pregnant woman being locked away in a room. As though it were a wholly expected and usual occurrence. And perhaps here, at Querencia, it is.

"But why?"

"Because when Mirabelle insisted that Jillian move in, we had to rearrange things quickly. Rhys and Wendy moved into the children's bedroom, and Mirabelle slept in the double bedroom with Jillian."

"And Wendy and Rhys were okay with that?"

Duke puffs out a breath. "If I can speak candidly, Viola, I don't think any of us were okay with it. What I'd say is at that moment in time, Mirabelle was like a coiled spring. She was an unexploded bomb, threatening to go off and cause untold damage. She's a force to be reckoned with, and while that can be tricky to handle at times, I'd rather foster that and have her be a strong woman who stands up for herself and defends her beliefs than try and tame her."

"So, you pandered to her."

Duke thinks for a moment. "Yes, I guess I did." He reaches for a large fruit scone and accompanying jam and cream. He thickly coats both halves of the scone, jam first, then cream, the way Viola prefers. He picks up one half and slides the plate with the remaining half towards Viola. "I insist. It's delicious and entirely non-toxic, I promise you."

Viola accepts the plate but doesn't eat. His continual protestations about the food are more unnerving than reassuring.

"Okay, so you've explained the situation with the locked door. You claim the funeral was genuine, but I don't understand why you had to lock Jillian in that room if she was on board with what was happening. Locking a heavily pregnant woman in a bedroom with no access to a toilet or food is not okay, Duke. I'd go as far as to say it's abusive."

Duke rolls his eyes, once again reminding Viola that they are working from a completely different set of social norms. Trying to convince him that his rules and actions are wrong is futile, and if she wants to get more information, she needs to remember that.

"I'm getting a little tired of having to justify every decision, Viola, and I'm not quite sure why you think I should be held accountable to you. What makes you so special?"

Viola bites her lip. "You're right, and if you'll continue with your story, I'll do my best to keep my opinions to myself." She almost chokes on the words, but they are a means to an end, she needs to stay focused on the long game.

"I'd appreciate that. And for your information, the door was locked at Jillian's request. She feels safe here at Querencia and was afraid of being left alone in an unfamiliar house. I assure you I was of the same opinion as you, but she was insistent."

Viola simply nods, unsure whether she believes him, but realises she needs to let it go. "Okay, so can you tell me what happened to Wendy after dinner that night? I haven't seen her since, and all I want to know is that she is well. If she is here, and this is where she wants to be, then I promise you, I will leave you alone." Viola tilts her head at Duke. "If you'll allow me to leave, that is."

Duke takes a large bite of his scone, chewing noisily before wiping his lips with his napkin. He's doing this on purpose, making her wait and controlling the conversation. "I've said it before, I am not a monster. Querencia is a happy place. Everyone here wants to be here. We are a supportive and loving community. I promise you that Wendy is safe and well." Viola nods, not trusting herself to speak and disrupt the flow of conversation. "I'm sure it isn't news to you that the night you joined Rhys and Wendy for dinner, she had far too much to drink."

Viola nods in agreement, remembering the adorably tipsy Wendy, slurring and confusing her words before heading to bed.

"There are things Wendy said to you that night that she shouldn't have." Viola raises her eyebrows, quickly picks up the scone from her plate, and takes a mouthful. An effective and delicious way to stop herself interrupting Duke and calling him out for being controlling. "She shouldn't have revealed to you that she didn't give birth to Mirabelle, and before you start, she completely agrees with this and wholeheartedly regrets her conversation with you that night." Viola takes another bite. Letting Duke spout off this nonsense without responding is excruciating. "She lied to you about paying for a surrogate. I'm not sure why she did that, but at least she didn't go the whole hog and break the trust of her Querencia family."

Viola feels her heart rate pick up, and the food suddenly feels heavy and uncomfortable in her stomach. She swallows and fixes Duke with what she hopes is a look of genuine care and concern.

"Please, Duke. I won't say another word. Just tell me what happened."

"Wendy and I have talked at length about that evening. I'm not here to admonish or chastise my Querencia family. I'm here to support them on their journey. The stress and emotional turmoil of the rejection Wendy felt from Mirabelle was very difficult for her. She thought she had lost her place in her family and felt understandably scared and alone, something we never want anyone in our community to feel."

Viola eyes him as he speaks. His care for Wendy does seem genuine, in complete opposition to almost everything else she has witnessed from him.

"Here at Querencia, we don't approach anything from a selfish perspective. The needs of the individual come second to the needs of us all collectively. It's the only way to have a harmonious and successful society. Wendy had become inwardly focused and, for want of better words, had begun to feel sorry for herself."

Viola nods, finding herself strangely intrigued by Duke's explanations. She doesn't agree with him but feels she is at least getting to understand the inner workings of his mind a little better.

"Wendy agreed that her place in the family with Rhys and Mirabelle was no longer tenable and it would be better for everyone if she returned to Querencia for a period of readjustment, and that Jillian, Rhys, Mirabelle and baby Eli, once born, would be a family unit. Jillian would replace Wendy. I do recognise that must be seen as unusual to outsiders. But it seemed natural to all of us and, given the exceptional circumstances we were dealing with, we were all treading into unfamiliar waters. As I've explained before, we do not support divorce and separation. However, we are allowed to make adjustments that benefit the Querencia family as a whole."

Viola doesn't know what to say. If Duke is to be believed, then Wendy is here, happy and safe, moving on with her life, and Jillian is dead, leaving Rhys without a partner and his children without a mother. This whole situation feels overwhelmingly sad. Viola looks up and sees that her own sadness is mirrored in Duke's face.

"Jillian died from an amniotic fluid embolism." Viola has no idea what that is. "It's extremely rare, and there was nothing any of us could have done. Eli was delivered safely, and they did everything they could for Jillian, but her lungs and heart failed. It was an unavoidable tragedy, and we are all devastated. Rhys will come around, but he's grieving and if, for now, he needs to blame me, then I'm willing to take that role in his healing journey."

Viola feels a tear escape. What a horrific and tragic thing to have happened to this family. Nobody deserves something like this, regardless of who they are and what they have done. Viola is jarred suddenly from her musings by the sound of Duke's chair scraping across the floor as he stands up.

"Now, as promised, I will take you to see Wendy."

CHAPTER THIRTY-THREE

MIRABELLE

Viola is here!

I'm so excited but also so cross with Granddad for not telling me.

She was walking along the path, and I was on a bug hunt with my friends and our teacher. Nobody else found a ladybird except me. All they had were stinky woodlice and a gross spider.

At first, I didn't recognise her, she was dressed so weird. Viola does not suit a grey tracksuit. I'll definitely tell her that when I see her.

I was worried she had sneaked in again, but I hid around the corner of Phase One, and I saw her go in with Granddad. They actually seemed pretty friendly, so I don't think I have to worry about her.

It would be so cool if she was allowed to come and visit sometimes, but I don't think Granddad would like that. He's quite strict and doesn't like visitors, even nice ones.

Granddad better have a good reason for not telling me Viola was coming. There'll be trouble otherwise.

CHAPTER THIRTY-FOUR

When Duke says the words Viola has longed to hear, she feels as though she is glued to her chair.

"Now, as promised, I will take you to see Wendy."

Viola desperately wants to stand and follow Duke. This is the crux of why she is here after all, but a stifling sense of dread keeps her where she is. Duke has told her so much and revealed things she's sure no one outside of this place knows. No one alive anyway. Why would he simply let her go? Duke has freely admitted that his priority above everything else is the community here at Querencia and that the happiness and rights of the individual come second. If that is true, why would he allow her to see Wendy and then let her go?

But then, why hasn't she been harmed so far? Is she being lulled into a false sense of security before being attacked? In any case, there is no going back now, so Viola reluctantly forces herself onto shaking legs, takes a deep breath, and finds her voice.

"Let's go."

They re-enter the corridor, and Viola is surprised that they continue down it rather than going back towards the reception area. The corridor is a dead end, and unless Wendy is in another of these small rooms flanking the walkway, they will soon have nowhere else to go.

Duke doesn't look back, so Viola obediently follows him, holding her arms across her stomach and keeping herself contained and as protected as she can. As they approach the end of the corridor, Viola can see that there is, in fact, another door, identical in colour and completely flush with the wall. Duke pushes several buttons on a keypad off to the side, shielding it with his body as he does so, and the door clicks. He opens it and steps to the side.

A welcome fresh breeze flows in, cooling Viola's flushed skin. Unexpectedly, the door leads to the outside world. Viola fights a sudden urge to make a run for it. If she runs around the side of this building, surely she will end up at the same place she entered, back at the gate with the warning sign.

"Look, Viola. I'm only doing this at your request. Do you want to come or not?" Duke shrugs his shoulders as though he couldn't care less either way. Viola petulantly stomps past him, irked by his indifference and her own indecisiveness.

Once outside, she scans the view in front of her. The grounds of this place are enormous, and from here she can see just how many large buildings there are. A dozen, at least. The track in front of her forks into three separate paths, and at the end of each is an identical, almost entirely cuboid construction. Their appearance is very different from the building through which she entered. Not a red brick in sight. These buildings are grey, sleek, and unwelcoming.

The door clicks shut behind Viola, and Duke comes to stand at her shoulder. "These are our rehabilitation suites." Viola turns to look at him. "Come, I'll show you." She keeps pace with Duke, and he continues to talk as they walk. "The one on the left, where Wendy is staying, is our Phase One suite." He points as he speaks. "The centre building is Phase Two, and we have Phase Three on the right."

"Okay, but what does that mean?"

Duke stops at the fork in the path and turns to face her. "Everyone has problems sometimes. I know that and you know that. In the world you live in, people are expected to just get on with it. They go to work, pay their bills, and tend to their families. At Querencia, we give people the time, support, and space they need to truly heal." Viola nods despite the fact Duke hasn't answered her question at all. "The Phase suites are a programme of rehabilitation. A comprehensive, individually tailored package of care to allow that person to heal and grow holistically. After someone completes all three Phases successfully, they are deemed ready and equipped to enter or re-enter our wider Querencia community." He gestures at the remaining buildings behind the three in front of them. "Now, I won't be taking you out there. This is not a tour, and you are not a member of our family. I will take you to see Wendy, and then, as promised, you will leave here and return home."

Viola sighs. "You expect me to believe that?"

"I do. I expect you to believe it because it is true." He smiles and takes the left path towards Phase One. "This is a new situation for me, Viola, and I will admit that various ways of dealing with your intrusion into our life have crossed my mind. Some are more palatable than others. But this is what I have settled on. To try and reason with you, and then for us to go back to our lives. I can see you value yours, and while I know you disagree with what we do here, I hope I have demonstrated that both I and others here value our way of life, too."

A thought leaps into Viola's mind, and she only realises she has verbalised it after the words have left her mouth. "You threatened to hurt Mirabelle." She wishes she could rewind ten seconds, but the words are out, and they hang in the air between them like a bitter, acrid smell. Duke is very persuasive, and his behaviour is confusingly changeable. He has proven that he can be genial, particularly today. But how can the same man who threatened to hurt a little girl, his own flesh and blood, simply allow Viola to leave unharmed out of the goodness of his heart?

Duke's face is tight, his jaw clenched. "I would never hurt Mirabelle. I shouldn't have said that, and if I could take it back, I would. As Mirabelle has told you, the firstborn daughter of the bloodline family holds great importance for us here at Querencia. Rhys is an only child. I wasn't blessed with a daughter." Viola sees a sadness in Duke's face. "Mirabelle will never be anything other than safe here. She is revered and loved, and we will do nothing but nurture her until she is ready to take the helm. Mirabelle has a key role to play at Querencia. One that she isn't yet old enough to understand."

Viola feels her skin prickle. If there was even the slightest uncertainty about this place being a cult before, there can be no mistaking it now. And whilst her concerns for Mirabelle's physical safety are somewhat abated, her worries for the girl's mental and spiritual well-being have amped up significantly. She is desperate to explore this 'firstborn' notion with Duke further and find out what it actually means in reality, but they are at the entrance now. It's make-or-break time.

Duke reaches his hand out to yet another keypad lock and stares deep into Viola's eyes.

"Shall we?"

CHAPTER THIRTY-FIVE

Viola is getting used to the bleak, clinical appearance of the interiors of the buildings, and the Phase One suite continues that theme. She enters behind Duke into a small entranceway. There is barely enough room for them both to stand. Duke pulls a white plastic card out of his pocket and taps it against a small screen on the door before them. A small blinking red light switches to solid green, and she follows him through the door and up a steep set of stairs.

Duke waves the pass card at her. "You'll need to stay close to me. All of our interior doors require a staff key card. You don't want to end up locked in, do you?" He winks at her, and she feels the hairs on the back of her neck stand up.

The silence is eerie. There are no windows, and not a single sound from outside penetrates the walls. As she climbs, Viola finds it more and more difficult to breathe. She doesn't usually get out of breath going up stairs, and despite her apprehension about being here, she's certain she's not anxious enough to be feeling this breathless.

Duke must pick up on her laboured breathing. "All of our

Phase suites are air controlled. You'll get used to it. Just try and breathe normally."

Viola has no idea what air control even means, but she does as he suggests and takes deep, purposeful breaths.

Duke chuckles. "Granted, it's not exactly ideal to start with a huge flight of stairs."

Viola doesn't answer. Instead, she focuses on her breathing and discovers that Duke is indeed right. She is starting to feel much better – calmer and more serene somehow.

At the top of the stairs, Duke uses his card again, and they are greeted by another identical corridor with equidistant rooms. Again, everything is silent and still. She imagines this is what being in a vacuum must feel like. The air doesn't move, and there are absolutely no sensations: no smells, no noises, and no sign of another person. Absolutely nothing.

"You weren't lying when you said you like uniformity. How do you tell any of these places apart?"

Duke looks at her quizzically and completely ignores her question. "Behind each of these doors is the quarters of a Phase One resident. We can speak freely as every room is soundproofed."

Viola's eyes widen as horrible visions of people screaming and banging on the doors and walls spring into her mind. It's at this moment Viola realises she completely forgot her intended text message to Nina. Her plan to make sure that at least one person knew where she was. She shudders as it dawns on her that she is completely alone, and nobody will ever know to come looking for her here.

"We do it for them, you understand, so they feel they have freedom."

Viola puts her hands to her mouth, holding back the scoffing sound that threatens to erupt from her lips. This place is the exact opposite of freedom. If Duke notices, he doesn't show any sign of it.

"Wendy's room is the second door on the left. She is expecting you." They both come to a stop outside Wendy's room, and Viola looks up at Duke expectantly, waiting for instructions. "Every door requires a card for entry. I will let you in, and I will wait here. Take as long as you like. I will give you both total privacy."

Viola highly doubts this. Alongside the locked doors and controlled air, there must be cameras or microphones.

"When you are ready to leave, don't knock. I won't hear you. Wendy will show you how to call for me."

Viola looks at the door and then back to Duke, her mouth suddenly dry. "So, you're locking me in?"

Duke lets out a frustrated sigh. "Do you want to see Wendy or not? Frankly, I've had quite enough of your–"

Viola cuts him off. "Yes, and I'm sorry. I'm just nervous."

Duke's face softens. "And I understand that. But at some point, you'll have to either trust what I'm telling you or go home and forget about being able to see Wendy."

Viola closes her eyes and nods, as much to herself as to Duke. "I want to see Wendy." Before she can open her eyes, Viola hears the door beep as Duke unlocks it with his card.

"Very well. Push the door when you are ready." Viola puts her hand on the door but doesn't push. She is trembling and has a sudden urge to cry. Is this the last room she will ever enter? Is Wendy even behind this door? She feels Duke's hand on her shoulder. She wants to push him away, but his touch somehow grounds her.

"I hope you get what you need from this visit, Viola. Truly, I do." Duke's hand falls from her shoulder, and Viola finds herself pushing against the door and stepping inside.

CHAPTER THIRTY-SIX

The air inside this room feels even closer and calmer. It's such an odd sensation. Viola's fingers tingle, and she rubs her hands together in an attempt to feel more normal. Checking behind her, she discovers that Duke is gone, and the door is closed, both things that she doesn't remember happening.

She looks at the room before her, her brain is slow to take in and compute everything. She recalls Duke's instructions and focuses on her breathing.

In. Out. In. Out.

Wendy is sitting on the bed. She is dressed in a floaty black top and trousers, starkly contrasting the overwhelmingly white décor surrounding her. The room itself is sparsely furnished but somehow has a tranquillity about it. Accompanying the single bed is a small desk with a swivel chair and a single-door wardrobe. Viola knows she is scanning the room in an attempt to avoid looking directly into Wendy's eyes, and she has no idea why.

"Hi, Viola." Wendy's voice is soft, dreamy, and filled with warmth, giving Viola the nudge she needs to finally acknowledge the woman she went through all of this to see.

Viola walks cautiously towards the bed, taking in the sight of Wendy. She looks astonishingly well. Her make-up-free skin is glowing and her fair hair is shiny, falling around her shoulders in effortless waves.

"Hi, Wendy. You look... well, you look amazing."

Wendy smiles, and her eyes glisten with tears of happiness. Viola feels her own eyes well up, and her heart swells with relief. This is not the downtrodden, maltreated prisoner she was expecting to find.

"I only have one chair in here. Do you want to pull it over, and we can chat?" Wendy gestures at the desk, and Viola retrieves the chair and wheels it over before sitting down directly in front of Wendy. Everything feels utterly surreal in a way that Viola can't quite put her finger on.

Wendy looks Viola up and down and grins. "You don't look like yourself. I've never seen you look quite so sporty."

Viola flushes and gives a nervous laugh. "I wasn't sure what to expect, so I decided on function over fashion. And I agree, that's not like me at all."

Both women laugh together and stare into each other's watery eyes.

Wendy reaches out a hand and takes hold of Viola's. "Thank you so much for coming to see me. I'm sorry I've caused you so much trouble and pain. You can't imagine how terrible I feel."

Viola strokes the back of Wendy's soft hand with her thumb. "You have nothing to apologise for. None of what happened to me was because of you. You know that, don't you?"

"That's very kind, Viola. But I know my part in all of this. I knew I was starting to struggle. I should have come back here sooner. If I had, then maybe..."

Her voice trails off, and she looks down, her shoulders slumping.

"I take it you know what happened with Jillian?"

Wendy sobs, pulling her hand away from Viola and to her mouth. Wendy's voice is barely a whisper. "Isn't it just the most horrific news? And no matter what anyone says to me, I can't help but think that the stress of the situation I created by not leaving sooner definitely had an effect. It must have, don't you think?"

Viola shakes her head. She has no idea. Duke told her that Jillian's death was unavoidable, but is that the same as preventable? Would she have lived under different circumstances?

"Nothing you did made this happen, Wendy." Viola feels that's as much as she can say and remain completely honest. They sit in contemplative silence for a moment.

"So, has Duke explained everything to you? He told me he would."

"Yes, at least I think so, and honestly, I have no idea what to say to you. All of this has completely blown my mind."

"I get that. And again, I'm so sorry you got dragged into it all."

Viola smiles. "Well, I think I definitely had a hand in it. Next time I get new neighbours, if there is a next time, I'll be leaving well alone."

Wendy sniffs and tries to smile. "You will get to go back home. And you will get new neighbours." Alarm crosses Viola's face at the thought of another Querencia family moving in. "No, I should have said, Duke is selling the house next to you. Honestly, I never understood why he decided we should move there in the first place. It was a disaster waiting to happen." Viola nods in agreement. "But I can assure you that after you leave here today, that will be it. Your life can go back to normal."

Viola snorts. "Normal. You think?"

Wendy's face hardens slightly, and her eyes fill with

determination. "That's up to you, Viola. I know what has happened to you, and it must have been horrible and deeply traumatic. But you are safe now. You are alive and well, and you can either grasp that with both hands and make the most of it, or you can let it haunt you. I know what I would do."

Viola knows Wendy is right. There will be nothing to compensate for what has happened, and she has already seen the effects of letting things overwhelm her on her emotional well-being.

"Can I ask you something, Wendy?"

"Of course. Consider me an open book. I promise you, no more lies or secrets."

"Are you happy here? Is what I'm seeing in front of me real? Or are you being held against your will? Is this a cult? Are you a prisoner?"

Viola stops and takes a breath, realising that her questions came out far too quickly and all at once.

"That's quite a lot of somethings, Viola, but yes, I am more than happy to answer each and every one."

Viola examines Wendy's face intently as she speaks, searching for any hint of deception.

"Firstly, no, Querencia is not a cult. It is a community, a way of life, and I don't want you to think that how you saw me at number 33 is in any way a reflection of my life here or how I feel about Querencia. I have always been happy here. I love the Querencia family, and I'm eternally grateful they have continued to support me, even when I doubted them and turned my back. I, and everyone else here, can leave at any time. Anything you have heard to the contrary is a lie. People trying to make money with a sensationalist story. I promise you I am happy, and when I'm ready and strong enough – when my rehabilitation is complete – I will return to the community. I cannot wait to see everyone again."

Wendy beams a bright smile and tears once again prick her eyes. Not once during that entire answer did Viola doubt a single word Wendy was saying. If nothing else, Viola is sure that Wendy believes the things she is saying. Whether they are reality or not, is something that Viola will likely never know.

"But Duke has done some terrible things, Wendy. I'm sure you're aware. The way he has treated you, and his behaviour towards me. If he is in charge here, I can't understand how everything you tell me can be true." Wendy's mouth becomes pinched, and her eyes narrow. "I'm not saying for one second that you're lying, and I can quite clearly see that you are well and happy. But Duke told me lots of things that worry me, and he's been violent. He drugged me and tied me up, for goodness' sake. He locked Jillian, a heavily pregnant woman, in a room! I'm sure you understand why I thought you weren't safe."

Wendy's eyes soften, and she leans towards Viola. "Have you ever loved and cared for something or someone so much that you would do anything for them? That you would do things others can't even comprehend because of how vital that thing is to your life."

Viola's mind is immediately drawn to Martin and his keeping of Duke's money. She knows undoubtedly he did that for her, and if Wendy was asking this question of Martin, she knows what his answer would be. He would say yes without a second thought. Martin would have done anything for her, and she always thought she felt the same about him. But would she have done any of the things that Duke has done? No. She knows she wouldn't. Not for anyone or anything. She would find another way. A better way, where nobody needed to be hurt.

Viola considers lying to Wendy. It is clear Wendy is happy here, and she doesn't want to hamper her recovery in any way. If this is where she truly wants to be, then as a grown adult, that is her choice. But she can't lie. Wendy needs to hear what someone outside of Querencia thinks about Duke and the things he has done.

"Yes. I loved my husband, Martin, more than anything in the world. And I think he would agree with you." A solitary tear falls onto Wendy's cheek, and she looks overjoyed by Viola's admission. "But, for me, there has to be limits. I would have done almost anything for Martin. But, no, not anything. He was the love of my life, my everything, but that doesn't give me the right to hurt somebody else. We are all equal. I could never have done the things that Duke did to me, no matter what the reason."

Viola takes a deep breath, knowing this is not what Wendy wants to hear. Although Wendy is no longer beaming with joy, she doesn't appear angry or upset either. She is more pensive or reflective, and Viola feels a tiny flicker of hope that she may yet be able to talk some sense into her.

Wendy holds her hands together as though in prayer. "That makes me so sad for you."

Irritated, Viola retorts, "Why on earth would me not being willing to harm someone to protect the things I love make you sad for me? That's absurd. And I think how I feel is how most people do. Can't you see that?"

A sympathetic smile graces Wendy's face. "Of course, I see that. And that is why most people in the world are out there, and we are in here. We choose to live away from those who can't find it in themselves to love with the ferocity and deepness we are supposed to." Viola wants to bite back but worries she'll find herself in a pointless argument. "At Querencia, we are committed to one another. We are one, and that means we protect and support each other with the same intensity as we would ourselves. You can't deny that you would fight or cause harm to protect yourself if you were in danger. In fact, I know you have."

Viola senses a sinking feeling deep inside her chest. It is painfully clear that Wendy is wholly under the influence of this place. She has been indoctrinated.

"But protecting your own life isn't the same–"

"It is!" Wendy cuts Viola off abruptly. Her eyes are now filled with tears, and the calmness and serenity of earlier have vanished. Viola reaches out a hand, but Wendy doesn't take it.

"Wendy, it is okay for us to disagree. To think and feel different things. You don't have to cut me off like that just because I'm saying something that doesn't match what you think."

This seems to placate and calm Wendy, and she returns to her contemplative state before speaking. "Not at Querencia, it isn't. As I said, we are one. We all think and feel the same, and that protects us from harm. From the dangers of the outside world."

Viola stops herself from continuing with the obvious counter-argument. It will likely only end in another upsetting outburst from Wendy, and distressing her is not Viola's intention.

"And you are happy here?" Viola looks at Wendy pleadingly, praying for a crack in her programmed façade, but there is none.

"I'm better than happy here. I am loved. I am whole. I am part of something meaningful and important. One day, the world will catch up. The Querencia family will make it so."

Now they are back on safer footing, Viola admits to herself it is time to leave. Is Wendy truly happy? She doesn't know, but there is obviously no room for manoeuvre with her beliefs. Physically, Wendy is safe and well. Mentally, spiritually, holistically – well that is debatable. Viola stands, and she sees genuine disappointment cross Wendy's face.

"Are you going now?"

Viola reaches out and caresses Wendy's cheek. "I am. You look well, and you tell me you are happy, so my work is done."

Both women stare at each other, knowing their paths are unlikely to cross again.

"Thank you for coming, Viola. I'm exactly where I need to be, and I hope you can see that. I know you have reservations, but I promise you don't need to worry about me anymore. I have everything I need right here."

Viola nods, more misgivings than she can count still rushing through her mind. But she needs to take her own advice. Wendy is free to feel differently and believe in something that Viola does not. She needs to go home and leave all of this behind her, once and for all.

"Duke said you had a way of letting him know when I wanted to leave?"

Wendy reaches towards the wall and presses a tiny white button by the side of her bed. "Goodbye, Viola. Take good care of yourself, and although I'm sure you don't feel the same, I'm glad we met, and I will always remember you."

Viola doesn't know what to say. This family has brought considerable pain and anguish into her usually tranquil life. But one thing she's sure of is that she will never forget Wendy.

"I'll remember you fondly, Wendy. Look after yourself."

When Viola turns around, Duke is standing by the open door.

"I hope your meeting went well?"

Viola isn't sure which of the two of them he is asking, but after Wendy responds with, "Yes, thank you, Duke. We had a lovely time," Viola lowers her gaze and exits the room without a word.

CHAPTER THIRTY-SEVEN

Viola does something she never expected she would – she walks out of Querencia's front door without a scratch on her. She looks around the glorious green countryside and inhales deeply. Viola still can't quite believe she is being allowed to leave and knows she won't fully relax until she sets foot back inside her own front door.

Everything that Duke promised would happen has happened. She has had afternoon tea, he has answered her questions, and not once did she feel under threat from physical harm. He allowed her to see Wendy and immediately let her out of the room when she asked. He walked her promptly to the front door, wished her well, and opened it for her. Maybe, just maybe, his intentions are exactly as stated. Perhaps all he wants is to be left alone to continue with his life, and she can continue with hers.

Although she still has huge concerns about what she witnessed at number 33, she hasn't seen any evidence of harm at Querencia. Wendy looks healthy and well, better than Viola has ever seen her, and she speaks with warmth and positivity about living here and the people she considers family. Does

Viola agree with their beliefs and the way they live? No. Is there anything actually harmful or illegal going on here? She doesn't know, but she truly hopes there isn't, because that would mean Wendy and Mirabelle are safe and Viola can leave with a clear conscience and continue with her life.

Viola realises she has been standing silently in the doorway for too long and turns to look at Duke.

"You seemed lost in thought. I didn't want to disturb you." He gives Viola a big smile, and she laughs.

"This place has certainly given me a lot to think about! But I'm ready to go home now. Thank you for letting me see Wendy, and I wish you and your family the best of luck. Please give my love to Mirabelle and tell her I'll miss her."

Duke nods, and Viola can't believe she is having a pleasant conversation with this man, let alone thanking him.

"I've learned a lot from you, Viola." Viola's eyes widen. "Honestly, I have. I've learned not to react so aggressively and defensively when I feel like the Querencia family is under threat. I know I have acted appallingly at times. I don't even recognise myself in some of the things I did or said. I'm ashamed."

He looks down, and Viola has an urge to comfort him. Hugging or touching him is out of the question, so she tries with words.

"If you act like there is something to hide here, then people will think that. If you are aggressive and violent, then people will assume that's what you subject people at Querencia to. But if you act like you are with me now, it will be clear that this is a safe place and you care deeply about it and your family here."

Duke smiles at her. "That's exactly it, isn't it? I've been so intent on protecting Querencia that I have ended up hurting it. Well, no more. You have my word."

Viola and Duke exchange a quiet nod of understanding.

"Come, Viola. I will walk you to the gate."

They walk in sync, a companionable silence.

"And maybe change that awful sign you put up. If you're going for the non-aggressive approach, maybe something a little gentler in tone might be better."

Duke laughs, and Viola is glad he took her comment in the light spirit with which it was intended.

Viola turns as she hears her name being shouted. The high-pitched voice is far away and mostly lost in the air between them. But even so, she recognises it right away. It's Mirabelle, and she is running across the grass towards them, a whirlwind of excitedly flailing arms and legs.

Viola flits her eyes to Duke, expecting to see irritation or darkness back on his face, but instead, he lifts his hand and waves at the sprinting girl.

"I knew she'd never let you leave without saying goodbye." He laughs good-naturedly and shakes his head. Mirabelle's speed slows as she nears them, the long run sapping strength from her little legs.

She reaches them, red-faced and panting, forcing out words between breaths. "Hi... Viola. Are you... leaving now?"

Viola reaches out her arm to Mirabelle, inviting her to come closer for a hug. Mirabelle's warm body presses against Viola's hip, and the girl's hands wrap around her, squeezing tightly.

"Yes, I'm leaving now, my dear." She looks up at Duke with sincerity as she continues to speak. "And I've had such a lovely time here with your granddad."

Mirabelle looks up and they share a smile. "I'm happy about that. Will you still be my friend, Viola?"

Viola caresses the girl's fly-away hair and, not wanting to upset her, gives her a vague but not completely untrue answer. "I'll always be your friend."

Of course, Viola knows she will never come back here and

will most likely never see Mirabelle again. But she will always think of her tenderly and perhaps try to forget the secateurs and the toilet-roll hand bandage.

"I'm in the middle of a football game, so I better go. I'm my team's best player, and they'll lose if I'm away too long."

Viola looks down at Mirabelle's checked black and white summer dress. It is very chic but definitely an unusual choice for football. "I bet you're the fastest, too. I can't believe how quickly you ran towards us, Speedy Gonzales!"

Mirabelle wrinkles her nose. "Speedy who?"

Viola laughs and pulls her in for another hug. "You get back to your football. I hope you score a hat trick. Your granddad will see me out."

Mirabelle looks up, smiles, and wrestles her little fists into Viola's hands. They stand holding hands for a serene moment, and Viola thinks she might cry if she doesn't leave soon.

Suddenly, Mirabelle runs away just as chaotically as she arrived. She is full of life and energy, exactly as she should be.

"I'm glad you got to see Mirabelle before you go. For one, she'd have been very cross with me if you didn't, and I think it will do her good to have seen you and hear that you enjoyed your time with us. So, thank you for saying that. It means a lot."

"You're welcome."

Duke signals towards the path with an open palm, and they walk the remaining distance to the gate. Viola feels like she doesn't have much more to say, and evidently, Duke must feel the same. When they reach the gate, Duke simply opens it, and Viola exits.

"Goodbye, Viola. I wish you well."

Viola nods and returns his sentiments. "I wish you well, too."

She walks quickly down the street towards the main road and doesn't look back until she reaches the corner junction. The gate is closed, and Duke is gone: back to his community, back to Querencia.

Waiting at the bus stop, Viola slowly unfurls her left hand. She has kept it curled into a fist since Mirabelle pulled away and ran back to her football game. Inside is a small folded piece of paper. A parting gift from Mirabelle, a letter or a drawing, most likely.

Viola doesn't know how she managed to maintain a straight face and not give away the covert passing of the piece of paper. If Mirabelle had wanted to give her the gift in front of Duke, she would have done so. She slowly unfolds the paper, noticing that it is a handwritten note rather than a drawing. Viola reads Mirabelle's words.

Any feelings of relief or reassurance from her visit to Querencia disappear instantly, and a deep dark dread seeps into her every pore. She rereads the note to make absolutely sure she isn't mistaken. Viola is barely able to comprehend the hideousness of the words.

> Meet me at the gate.
> 9pm.
> They hurt me.
> Please.
> Mirabelle.

CHAPTER THIRTY-EIGHT

Viola is still shaking as the bus pulls up, and she gapes at the bus driver as the doors open.

"You getting on, love?"

Is she getting on? She has no idea what she is doing at this exact moment. She pulls out her phone and checks the time. It is just after 6.30pm. She looks up to see the driver tapping the face of his watch, and for want of a better option, she gets on and sits down. She's scared to look at the note again and doesn't need to. It is etched into her brain, and her world is again thrown into turmoil and confusion.

Viola knows that Mirabelle can be deceptive. But would she really play a trick this cruel? She's only a little girl, and she's been living in... Viola's thoughts trail off. If Duke and Wendy are to be believed, Mirabelle has been living in a kind and nurturing environment. Different from most people's, but supportive and encouraging, nonetheless. On the other hand, what if everything she has read online is true? Viola wants to scream. She was sure she had it all sewn up this time.

The vital question, the only question that matters is, "Is

Mirabelle in danger?" And honestly, Viola has no clue. Feeling more confused than ever, she focuses on the one thing she knows for sure – she can't take the risk that Mirabelle is being harmed. She would never forgive herself, and as she and Duke had agreed to part ways after today, she would never know if the girl was okay. If ensuring Wendy's safety brought her to Querencia, then ensuring Mirabelle's will elicit the same response from her.

Unsurprisingly, the relief she had hoped to feel when walking into her beloved home did not materialise. It is almost 7pm, and Viola knows she will be leaving her house again in a little over an hour.

She pours a large glass of water and gulps it furiously, the liquid sloshing around in her nervous stomach. She has to go back. One small saving grace is that Mirabelle's instructions were to meet her at the gate, so she needn't enter the grounds of Querencia. If this is simply an ill-thought-out prank by a confused and troubled little girl, she can return home. And if Mirabelle is there, she can whisk her away to safety. She can't take any chances waiting at the bus stop with Mirabelle. But Nina's house is only a five-minute walk from Querencia. She will take Mirabelle there and then call the police.

In the short time she has at her disposal, this feels like as good a plan as any. Although she absolutely dreads her return to Querencia, time is dragging, and waiting is only ramping up her already raging nerves. She's had to pee about a hundred times, and sitting still is a total impossibility.

Unfolding Mirabelle's note again, Viola examines it closely.

Meet me at the gate.
9pm.
They hurt me.
Please.
Mirabelle.

It certainly looks like a child's writing, and Mirabelle seems very bright and more than able to write a sentence like this. Still, she can't shake the mistrust she has for the girl. Her behaviour towards Viola has ranged from delightful and sweet as pie to downright malicious. She pushes her apprehension away. It will have no effect on what she does tonight. She will be outside Querencia at 9pm, no matter what.

Viola focuses on the centre line of Mirabelle's letter.

They hurt me.

The very idea makes Viola's blood boil. How anyone could hurt a child is beyond her. If this is true, these monsters will have to pay for their disgusting deeds.

They hurt me.

The question is, have they hurt Mirabelle already, or are they planning to hurt her sometime after tonight? Both options are horrific and sickening, but Viola prays it is the latter and she can somehow get Mirabelle to safety before whatever Duke and his followers have planned befalls her.

The same bus driver greets Viola at the bus stop and gives her a wry smile.

"Forget something?" Viola's cheeks flush, her hopes of

remaining inconspicuous tonight scuppered by this overly friendly man. He laughs and beckons her onto the bus. "Just kidding, darling."

Viola gives an embarrassed laugh, taps her bus pass to pay, almost dropping it in the process, and sits where she hopes the driver can't see her. She doesn't want to give him any further reason to remember her. Viola's nervousness is obvious. A sheen of sweat coats her brow, no matter how many times she wipes it, and she can't keep her breathing under control.

She looks at her reflection in the window as they trundle past trees and buildings, the landscape becoming sparser as they approach the stop closest to Querencia.

Offering a perfunctory "Thank you" as she alights, the driver, luckily, seems disinterested in any further conversation and eager to be on his way. Viola's feet are like lead.

Checking her phone once more, her stomach churns. It is 8.56pm. It's now or never.

She pushes the phone into her pocket, knowing she can't recheck it until either Mirabelle arrives and they are both far away from here or until she returns home alone. The light from her phone would immediately alert anyone watching to her presence, and if this is all a cruel ruse, she'll be in trouble with Duke for breaking her promise. That's the last thing she wants.

Viola reaches the gated entrance to Querencia and tucks in behind a large tree. She can see the gate clearly but is reasonably sure nobody can see her. Her heart is galloping painfully against her ribcage, and she would give her right arm to be anywhere else in the world just now.

Time has lost all meaning. Viola has no idea if she's been

standing here for ten minutes or an hour, but she is as sure as she can be that it's now after 9pm, and as such, Mirabelle is not coming. She shakes her head, not sure how to feel. Somewhat relieved, yes. Mirabelle is safe, and whatever the reason for her mean little note, nothing really matters but the young girl's well-being.

Nobody will ever know Viola was here. Duke will continue to believe they parted on good terms and life can go on. All she needs to do now is make it home undetected. Viola chuckles at the thought of seeing the same bus driver again. Instead, she decides to walk a short way towards home and then call a taxi. She's sure a few local taxi numbers are programmed into her phone.

Although locals would consider this a relatively safe place to be out at night alone, Viola wants to be home as quickly as possible. She's had enough of taking risks with her own safety. Taking a cautious step out from behind the tree, thoughts of being greeted by Duke's looming form make her sick with fear. But there is nobody there. Tilting her head skyward in a silent prayer of thanks, Viola takes her first tentative steps. The world remains quiet and still. Mirabelle is surely tucked up safely in bed, precisely where Viola plans to be very shortly.

Weary but relieved, Viola begins her journey home. She repeatedly glances over her shoulder, convinced she can hear footsteps, but remains hopeful it's her overactive imagination. And who could blame her for being hypervigilant? She is far too old to be creeping around at night playing amateur sleuth. It's time to get back to her home and her garden, her crocheting and close-knit circle of friends.

But something is niggling at her conscience, and whatever it is, it won't let her walk away freely. Something is clawing at her, drawing her back towards Querencia. Could there be something more to this? She ponders for a while to no avail, her steps so slow and short that she is barely making any headway.

Unbidden, a horrific image jumps into her mind. The most dreadful vision of Mirabelle attempting to sneak out and getting caught. Viola plays the hideous scene in her thoughts. Mirabelle kicking and screaming; Duke grabbing Mirabelle and dragging her back into the bowels of Querencia. Locking her away, alone and scared. Restraining her. Hurting her and maybe even… Viola stops still and turns to face Querencia, continuing her horrifying train of thought. Could Mirabelle's life actually be in danger? Although he swore he didn't mean it, Duke once promised he would make Mirabelle suffer.

Why had she not considered this before? She had been solely focused on two potential outcomes tonight – either Mirabelle arrives at 9pm, and they flee to safety, or Mirabelle doesn't arrive, was cruelly tricking Viola and is, therefore, safe and sound inside Querencia. How could she be so short-sighted as to ignore the third and most terrifying possibility? That Mirabelle was telling the truth, that she had planned to be at the gate at 9pm, and someone has stopped her.

Viola shudders, fear gripping her throat. Selfishly and desperately, she wishes this thought had not occurred to her. After all, Mirabelle could still be safe and well, and Viola might be about to stir up a hornets' nest. Realising she needs time to think and is no longer protected from view, she scuttles back to her hiding place and leans against the thick tree trunk for support. Is entering and trying to find Mirabelle worth the risk? What would happen to her if she was caught? Duke's good nature will likely not continue if she blatantly goes against their agreement only hours after they made it.

Viola stands, panting in the shadow of the tree. She has only seen the entrance building and the three rehabilitation suites inside Querencia. If she sneaked in to try and find Mirabelle, where would she even start? There were so many buildings behind the rehabilitation suites, and they all looked exactly the same. Mirabelle could be in any of them or somewhere else entirely. Every door is either protected by a key code or needs a pass to enter. There is literally no way for her to get inside. But despite the abysmal chances of success, she knows she has to try.

It's the situation with Wendy all over again, but this time, it's not a grown adult who's at risk – it's an innocent little girl. Viola feels the heat of indignation beginning to build inside her. Any adult who harms a child is beyond despicable, and if she has an opportunity to prevent it, no matter how slight, she has to take it.

Realising she is bursting for the toilet, Viola does something she hasn't since she was a carefree young woman and empties her full bladder behind a bush. Her cheeks flush even though nobody can see or hear her. But needs must. As she stands and pulls up her bottoms, she is convinced she can hear voices somewhere in the distance.

Heading back towards the gate, she carefully places every step, terrified she will stand on a branch and alert a potential attacker to her whereabouts. Not for the first time, Viola feels like she's in a movie. And if she were at home in front of her TV watching herself, she'd be screaming, "Run, you stupid woman, run!"

Viola makes it back to her hiding place in relative silence and listens. Nothing. She waits, feeling half mad with terror, but the voices do not resume. She's sure there were at least two people talking. They were far away, but it's difficult to confuse the distinct sound of voices with anything else.

Another noise breaks the stillness, and Viola expels the beginnings of a scream before clamping both hands over her mouth, forcing herself to remain still and quiet. Suddenly, she freezes. Fresh terror rears up and trickles down her spine. There is no mistaking it this time. That was definitely the sound of voices. But not solely voices this time. Accompanying what sounded like two male voices was an ear-splitting scream.

And Viola is absolutely certain that the scream she heard came from Mirabelle.

CHAPTER THIRTY-NINE

Viola fights through the fog of fear engulfing her and propels her body forwards. The remaining daylight is beginning to ebb away, and Viola is struggling to see details through the grey haze of dusk.

Undeniably, she is placing herself directly in the path of danger, but none of that matters anymore.

Mirabelle just screamed. A little girl is in trouble, and Viola has to do everything she can to help her.

The number of times Viola should have stopped, taken a breath, and called the police are too many to contemplate. But she has never done so, and she won't call them now. There isn't the time. Anything could happen to Mirabelle before the police arrive.

Feeling numb and her fear mounting with every step, Viola enters the gate to Querencia. Her whole body is trembling and fizzing with adrenaline, but she no longer cares if her presence is discovered.

Undoubtedly, she won't be capable of fending off Rhys and Duke. But if her presence can create enough distraction for

Mirabelle to get to safety, then it will all be worth it. It is a sacrifice she is willing to make.

The hairs on the back of her neck stand up. The sound of footsteps are getting closer, but it is impossible to pinpoint which direction they are coming from.

Viola stops. Twilight has evolved into night. Darkness surrounds her. Her eyes dart from left to right, but she sees nothing of substance in the gloom. She has absolutely no plan of action, and whilst wandering aimlessly is unlikely to help Mirabelle, what else can she do? Viola's head whips round as she hears a sudden burst of footsteps. Panic takes hold of her, sealing her throat and leaving her gasping for breath.

Someone is running, and they are coming towards her. The muffled male voices are still far from Viola. Terrifyingly, they no longer sound conversational and are now furious shouts and enraged roars. A small figure appears around the corner like a beacon in the night. They whimper and sob as they hurtle towards her. Viola's chest tightens, and her heart rate rockets as she takes in the blonde hair whipping around the sprinting figure's head.

It is Mirabelle, and she is clearly running for her life.

Viola emits a strangled cry. "Mirabelle!"

Viola's legs turn to jelly as two large dark shapes appear behind Mirabelle. The girl must hear them because she glances behind her before letting out a horror-stricken scream. Viola watches, drowning in terror. She wants to run to Mirabelle, but the only way to safety is to go back towards the gate. So, she stands in a haze of fear – helpless and defenceless.

The two enormous men begin to gain ground, the distance between them and Mirabelle now alarmingly small. They aren't Rhys and Duke. They look like bodyguards. Formidable and colossal.

"Keep running, Mirabelle." Viola's voice is shrill with panic.

When she senses the time is right, she turns and begins her own escape, knowing Mirabelle is not far behind her. She is certainly slower than Mirabelle and significantly more so than the girl's pursuers. Viola needs a decent head start if she has even the slightest chance of making it out of here intact.

Every joint and muscle in Viola's body throbs, and her chest heaves as she attempts to run. There are numerous stories of people unlocking superhuman strength and speed when their lives or the lives of their children are at risk, but it doesn't seem to be happening, and Viola isn't moving much faster than if she were walking. She grits her teeth and fixates on moving forward.

A squeak escapes from Viola's throat. The gate is almost within touching distance, and she feels the first spark of hope ignite inside her. Mirabelle crashes violently into the back of her legs and simultaneously grabs her arm. No words of greeting are uttered. Mirabelle tugs and pulls at Viola's arm as they continue to scramble towards the gate. The booming footsteps chasing them are moving ever closer, and Viola emits a terrified yelp when she thinks she feels hot breath on her neck. The gate is so tantalisingly close, and for a split second, she allows herself to believe they might actually make it. She hopes to God these men won't risk continuing their pursuit outside of the Querencia grounds.

Mirabelle suddenly breaks free from Viola and hisses breathlessly, "I'll get the gate." Viola watches, panic seizing her thoughts, as the girl fumbles with the gate latch.

Viola struggles to find enough air in her lungs to speak. "I left it open."

Mirabelle halts and whirls around to face Viola, her back pressed against the gate, her tiny chest heaving and her eyes wide and wild. Viola nearly clatters into her before rummaging around for the latch herself. In her haste, Mirabelle must have jammed it or something. After all this, surely not being able to exit through an already open gate won't be their downfall. They are here. They have made it. Failing now because of a stupid latch would be soul-destroying.

Mirabelle steps back as Viola yanks and pulls at the gate fastening in desperation. It's immovable and tears at the skin on her hands. But no matter what she does, it won't budge. She rattles it, but it doesn't give. Why on earth did this have to happen now?

And then Viola stops, her mouth falling open in a silent scream as she notices a tiny padlock looped through one of the holes in the latch. Viola opens and closes her eyes, shaking her head in disbelief. The padlock wasn't there before. She is sure of it. Did someone lock the gate behind her after she entered?

She turns to look at Mirabelle, her voice stolen by shock and devastation. The two hulking men stand on either side of the girl, dwarfing her. Viola doesn't recognise them. They are both enormous beasts: tall, broad, mean, and terrifying. They each have a hand resting on Mirabelle's little shoulders. All of the fight leaches out of Viola, and her body wants to fall to the ground.

But then she sees something: a spark of light, a glimmer in the darkness.

Mirabelle has something in her hand, and she is twirling it around her finger. The shiny object glints as it rotates.

It is a key.

The key to the padlock on the gate.

CHAPTER FORTY

Viola's mouth falls open, confusion clouding her thoughts. She looks from the key to the little girl's face and sees that she is smiling – no, not smiling – smirking.

Viola can't think. She tries to speak but can only manage one word before her ability to say anything else deserts her.

"What...?"

Mirabelle grins maniacally and looks up at the two massive men beside her before shrugging their hands off her shoulders. They stand like two sentries at her command. A sickening sense of understanding begins to dawn on Viola, and Mirabelle lets out a contemptuous giggle as she sees the realisation across Viola's face.

Viola's body begins to tremble. "You. What did you..." But at that moment, Viola knows further efforts will be futile, and she stops speaking. She stops moving. She just stops altogether. Viola's world falls still.

Mirabelle appears beside herself with delight. Utterly gleeful at Viola's discernible shock and distress. Mirabelle has won. Viola has been beaten at a game she didn't even know she was playing.

"When I saw you here with Granddad, I knew I couldn't just let you go." Viola stares at her, fighting the overwhelming urge to curse and shout at the little girl. Battling her desire to burst into tears. "I know Granddad told you about our lives here. Our perfect families." Viola nods and swallows uncomfortably, feeling like a shell of a human being, every ounce of her destroyed by Mirabelle and her unbearable deception. "It's rude not to answer when someone speaks to you, you know, Viola."

Mirabelle is taunting her, goading her.

Barely maintaining her composure, Viola responds through gritted teeth. "You haven't asked me a question."

Mirabelle raises an eyebrow and gives a small tinkling laugh, a laugh that would be utterly sweet and adorable under any other circumstances. Viola is aghast as Mirabelle steps towards her, almost skipping as she does so. The two thugs make to follow her, but Mirabelle holds both her hands up, and they stop immediately. Viola gapes, stunned at both men, who are somehow at the beck and call of this diminutive child.

"Very well, if that's how you want to play it, Viola." Mirabelle twirls the key around her finger again and rests one hand on her hip. There is something hideously provocative in her stance.

Viola knows she could reach out and grab Mirabelle from this distance. She could quickly disarm the girl and take the key from her. But the two human guard dogs would be on her in seconds. She would love to lunge forward and take her chances. However, even after everything Mirabelle has done – all the pain and hurt she has put Viola through – the facts remain the same. No matter what Mirabelle does or says, Viola will never be able to shake the fact that she is only a little girl. Something entrenched within her won't allow her to fight back. Even standing here now, Viola still believes that children of this age should not be judged or blamed for their actions. They should be helped, supported, and guided towards better choices.

"So, what happens now?" Viola keeps her tone flat and her face emotionless, knowing Mirabelle will thrive on dramatics and refusing to add any fuel to the fire. Viola flinches and staggers backwards as Mirabelle suddenly jumps in the air, her feet and legs fluttering rapidly as though trying to emulate some kind of ballet move. She watches in astonishment as the girl lands and then begins to clap her hands excitedly, her face a hysterical smile, her eyes squeezed shut with pleasure.

"Well, that's the best part. You're going to be a part of my perfect family!" Mirabelle lets out a little animated squeak that sounds more like it came from a small animal than a human. Viola finds herself shaking her head, a deep despair crawling over her. "Oh, don't be a spoilsport." Mirabelle pouts briefly before continuing. "I hated almost everything about that stupid, small house, except–" Mirabelle stops and gestures for Viola to complete the sentence, looking annoyed when all Viola can manage to do is open and close her mouth as though gasping for air. "Except you, silly!" Mirabelle does a pirouette and bows. "Viola, I hereby welcome you into my Querencia family."

Viola can only observe in stunned silence as Mirabelle mimes playing a trumpet salute before holding out her arm and performing a pretend knighting ceremony, tapping an imaginary sword onto each of Viola's shoulders in turn.

Mirabelle slips seamlessly back into her train of thought as though that whole ridiculous performance hadn't occurred. "You can't really be my grandma because, well, I've already got one of those, although hopefully not for too much longer." She crosses her fingers before she feigns falling asleep. "Ugh, she's such a bore. It's like she's already dead. A walking corpse." Mirabelle demonstrates a rather impressive zombie impersonation. "But then we've got the whole skin colour thing too, and no matter how many times I've wished before I go to bed, my skin is still this boring white colour. Soooo..."

Mirabelle drags out her final word before becoming pensive and still. Viola will never get over the speed and magnitude at which Mirabelle can change her emotions. It's alarming, like watching somebody with a split personality. The punctuating actions accompanying almost everything she says only add to the perverseness of the whole scene.

"So?" asks Viola, not at all sure she wants to hear the answer.

Mirabelle's face becomes serious. "I know, it's tricky, right? But then I think I came up with something that would work. You're going to be my nanny." Her eyes sparkle.

Viola knows she is expected to respond with excitement or joy at this news, not the terror and panic that are currently churning through her. Viola smiles, holding back tears as she considers what she can say next. If she can keep Mirabelle talking, that will at least give her some time to try and come up with something, anything, that can get her out of this.

"Okay... but what do your dad and granddad have to say about all of this?" Viola feels a hot flash of anger at the thought that everything Duke told her was utter lies. She trusted him and believed that, although misguided, he at least had good intentions mixed in amongst his strange beliefs.

Mirabelle shrugs her shoulders and sighs theatrically. "Oh them, they don't know yet."

Viola can't stop her mouth from falling open. "Then how did...?" She trails off and looks up at the two men. They are staring straight ahead, unmoving, like two cyborgs who have powered down.

"Oh, these are mine." Mirabelle smiles sweetly. "I know you

think Granddad is in charge here, and he pretends he is too. But he's not really. Everything at Querencia is for me. I get anything I want." Her sweet smile falls, and a dark, thunderous expression replaces it. "And so I should."

Viola's heart is pounding against her ribcage. She has no idea how she is maintaining her composure when inside she is screaming and falling apart.

"And what do you want, Mirabelle?"

The question was clearly unexpected as she stalls briefly before saying, "I wanted my mummy and my daddy. But they tricked me and gave me a horrible fake mummy."

Viola's heart breaks at Mirabelle's mournful expression. For the first time tonight, she looks exactly what she is: a confused and sad young girl.

"That wasn't kind of them, and you have every right to be upset."

Mirabelle wipes her hand across her nose and sniffs. "But then I got my mummy back and was so excited about Eli." Mirabelle's eyes glisten. "I can't wait for you to meet him. He's the cutest, squishiest thing ever."

Viola smiles, a choked-up feeling in her throat. What this girl has been through is heartbreaking.

"We were going to be the perfect family: me, Eli, Daddy, and my real mummy." Mirabelle is fidgeting now, picking at her fingers and wringing her small hands together.

"But?" Viola doesn't want to steer Mirabelle off course. This is the heart of everything.

"What do you mean, but? You know what happened. You were there. They killed her." Anger returns to Mirabelle's eyes. A burning, ferocious rage.

Viola tries in vain to calm things down. "No. What happened to your mummy was a terrible thing. But nobody killed her. It was just something awful that happened, and I'm so sorry that you and Eli lost your mummy. I can't imagine how that made you feel."

There is an eerie silence in the air as Mirabelle quietly seethes. Viola has no idea what reaction she is going to get.

Mirabelle eventually looks up, her eyes vacant. "I don't know how I feel. I know my mummy is dead, and I know I will never be a normal girl. You think I don't see it, but I do. You think I'm too young to understand, but I'm not."

Viola feels tears running down her face, her heart wrenching every which way as she listens to these desperate words.

"I know life is different out there, Viola. I'm not stupid. I know other children don't live like me."

Viola senses her chance. "Then come with me, Mirabelle. I will take you home and keep you safe. I promise you. I can make it so you never have to come back here again. I can help you. That's why I came here tonight. That's what I thought you wanted."

Mirabelle looks down, her head shaking slowly from side to side. "It's too late for that."

Viola steps forward and bends down, placing her hands on either side of Mirabelle's face. She lifts the girl's bowed head gently until their eyes lock.

Viola whispers, ploughing every ounce of feeling she has into her words. "It is never too late. Come with me, Mirabelle. Come and live a wonderful life outside of this prison. I promise you – I can make that happen." Viola pulls Mirabelle into a hug and squeezes her fiercely. She can feel her little body shivering against her chest.

Viola almost yelps with joy as she hears the girl speak. The words are small and smothered by their embrace. "Do you promise?"

"I promise. A thousand times, I promise."

Mirabelle pulls away and turns to her two companions. "You can go back now." Both men nod, turn and walk away without question. Viola can't believe what she is seeing. As Mirabelle stated, those two men really are hers.

"They weren't really chasing me before. I kind of did that on purpose. Make it look real, and then I could get the gate locked." Mirabelle avoids Viola's gaze, looking suddenly embarrassed.

"None of that matters anymore. Now, let's get out of here before anyone else realises you're gone."

They hold hands and leave Querencia behind.

"Can I really stay with you? Can I go to a proper school and have proper friends? Will you make sure they don't come and take me away?" Mirabelle's questions are rushed and fired in quick succession. Viola knows she can't answer any of them honestly and not leave the girl terrified.

"First things first. Let's get you safe. That's the most important thing." Viola squeezes Mirabelle's hand and feels the same reciprocated.

They walk swiftly and silently away. Viola doesn't know what the future holds, but she did what she came here to do tonight. Mirabelle is out of that horrible place.

She should feel stunned by the sudden shift from Mirabelle. The switch from planning to trap Viola inside Querencia as her nanny to leaving by her side occurring within minutes. But Viola is not surprised in the slightest. To say Mirabelle is complicated would be an understatement, but Viola feels connected to her. Although ill-equipped to comprehend many of the girl's behaviours, she can understand why Mirabelle is the way she is.

They did this to her. Duke, Rhys, and, to a lesser extent, Wendy, are all complicit. They were supposed to be her loving, nurturing family. But instead, they exposed her to a corrupt and conditioned environment.

There will be a long road of healing ahead, filled with many ups and downs for both of them.

But Mirabelle is finally free, and whatever happens next, Viola will be there for her.

CHAPTER FORTY-ONE

3 MONTHS LATER

Viola beams as Mirabelle runs into the room and sits beside her. The last few months haven't been easy for either of them, but as time passes, everything starts to feel more settled.

"How are you today, my lovely?" Mirabelle has brought Viola a beautiful drawing, as she often does when she visits. "Ooh, let me see what you've done this time."

Mirabelle flashes a beautiful, toothy smile. "It's me and you. Look."

And indeed, it is. It's a picture of the two of them hugging. "I love it. What a clever girl you are."

Viola never has to exaggerate when Mirabelle brings her artistic creations. The girl's talent only continues to blossom, and once again, she has produced a very accomplished drawing.

The figures are carefully drawn and neatly coloured in, and the surrounding trees are surprisingly lifelike. Inspecting it, Viola is taken back to the exact moment in time Mirabelle has depicted. Their heartfelt embrace before they held hands and walked through the Querencia gates together. That pivotal moment when their lives changed.

Viola doesn't comment on this, not wanting to take Mirabelle's mind back to what was a very emotional and traumatic night, especially not when she looks so wonderfully happy today.

"I will put this on the wall with the others. Thank you, Mirabelle." They smile at each other warmly. "So, tell me, have you just finished school?"

Viola watches with awe as Mirabelle waves her arms and jumps around, recounting her day.

"I got ten out of ten on my spelling test. I was the only person in the whole class to get 'disappear' right. Everyone thinks it's 'ss' but there's only one 's' in disappear. Did you know that?"

Viola laughs, her heart singing as she revels in the amount of love and life there is inside Mirabelle's little body.

"I'm not sure I did know that. Spelling is not my strong point."

Mirabelle gives Viola a stern look. "Well, then you need to practice. I'll help you. Next time I come visit, I'll bring you some tricky words to learn. We have this big, long list of what my teacher calls tricky words. But I don't think they're tricky at all. If I had named the list, I'd call it easy words."

Viola laughs heartily, bursting with joy. Mirabelle comes to visit Viola at least once a week now. She is thriving with the love and support of a caring family, and they are happy for Mirabelle and Viola to have time to themselves. And Viola is genuinely grateful. Time with Mirabelle is cathartic, never failing to raise her spirits and fill her with sunshine.

Although she tries not to ruminate too much, she knows things could have gone very wrong that night. Yet somehow, life feels better than it ever has. Mirabelle has taught Viola so much. She had been content with her life before the family at number 33 moved in and upended her whole world. Without a doubt, she missed and grieved for Martin, but she was grateful for what she had: her friends and her home.

But Mirabelle's arrival highlighted a gaping hole in Viola's existence. Deep, powerful connections and relationships. The kind of meaningful bond that she had for decades with Martin. Something more substantial and more profound than friendship. Mirabelle and Viola are forever bonded by their shared experiences, and Viola couldn't care for the girl more if she were her own flesh and blood.

Today, they spend their precious time together as they often do, with Mirabelle doing most of the talking. Viola is more than happy to listen and soak in all the new stories Mirabelle has to tell. Time always flies during her visits, and before they know it, their time is almost over.

Trying to hide her disappointment, Viola stands and opens her arms, welcoming Mirabelle in for a hug.

"I'll be back next week, and I won't forget that spelling list. You could always try picking out some long words in your books and testing yourself if you like. Just a thought."

Mirabelle shrugs, and Viola has to stifle a giggle at the hilarity of her grown-up behaviour. She is just adorable. They look at each other with watery eyes. Leaving is always sad for both of them, but Viola knows it has to be this way, and she must remember to be grateful to have Mirabelle in her life at all.

Halfway towards the door, Mirabelle turns, a thoughtful look on her face.

"Can I ask you something, Viola?"

"Of course. You can ask me anything, you know that."

"Do you like it here?"

Viola scans the room. The plain white sterile walls; the sleek, clean-lined furniture. They are so different from what she has always been used to, but now, they are her home.

"Of course I do, sweetheart. I love it here."

Mirabelle flashes Viola the most beautiful, genuine smile. "Good. And I'm so happy you're in Phase Two now, but if you try really hard, you'll be in Phase Three soon, and then we'll be able to see each other every day. Wouldn't that be brilliant?"

Viola grins and wipes away an escaped tear. "That would be amazing. And I promise you, I'm going to try really hard."

Mirabelle stands at the door to Viola's quarters and waves and blows a kiss. Viola pretends to catch it and presses it to her lips, treasuring their last moment together for today.

The door opens, and Mirabelle skips out. Viola catches sight of Duke in the corridor but turns away and returns to sit on her bed before he can make eye contact with her. She knows it is essential to remain civil with him to complete her rehabilitation successfully, and although she knows she must, she hasn't found it within herself to forgive him yet.

Duke didn't want her here, and she's pretty sure he still doesn't.

All of his thoughtfulness – inviting her to Querencia, allowing her to visit Wendy – was purely a means to an end. He didn't want to share this wonderful place with her.

Mirabelle has opened Viola's eyes and shown her that she wasn't in Duke's plan for Mirabelle's perfect family. And if it wasn't for his granddaughter's insistence, she would never have been welcomed into this extraordinary community. Mirabelle has helped Viola see the error of her ways, and once she has progressed through each Phase, she will become a permanent resident of Querencia.

Viola can now see how wrong she was. She was naïve and closed-minded. Fully taken in by the nonsense she had read online and allowing it to fuel her misunderstanding about what this place really is. Querencia is not a cult. It is precisely what Duke said it was. It is a loving, supportive community.

Martin would have loved it here, and Viola wishes he'd had

the chance to experience it for himself. She welcomed the opportunity to hand over her house and belongings to Querencia. They are building something groundbreaking and vital, but they can't do it alone. They need support, and she was more than happy to give to their worthy cause.

This is her home now, and as such, she has no need for her old house. If she ever decides to leave, and she can't imagine ever wanting to, she still has all her savings and her and Martin's pension pots. But she's positive she won't need it.

Having this time to heal herself has been so therapeutic. Ridding herself of her superfluous possessions was a wonderfully freeing experience. She has everything she needs here. She feels completely safe and protected.

That night, when she tried to take Mirabelle away from Querencia, is now a dim and distant memory. One that Viola has no desire to revisit. She knows that in the days that followed, she had some sort of breakdown. She remembers little of that time except how she felt: afraid, alone, and bewildered. Given what she had attempted to do, the Querencia community could have easily turned their back on her, kicked her out and left her to suffer. Instead, they welcomed her with open arms, cared for her, and nursed her back to health. For that, she will be forever grateful.

In the coming months, she hopes to build and strengthen her relationship with Duke, prove her worth, and help him understand that she deserves her place here. And the best part of it all, is that she will get to see Mirabelle every day.

Pulled from her daydream by a knock at the door, Viola sits up straight on the edge of her bed. This is what is expected when staff members enter a resident's quarters.

A petite young woman enters with a cup of tea balanced on a silver tray. Viola recognises her but can't recall her name. Diane or Diana, perhaps?

"A cup of tea for you, Viola. How are you feeling today?"

"I'm feeling good, thank you... Dana." The name pops into Viola's head at just the right time.

"Good. Do you mind if I sit with you for a few moments? I could use a wee break." The woman has a beautiful soft Scottish lilt to her voice.

"No, of course not." Viola picks up her tea and cradles it in her hands before taking a long drink.

Dana is watching her intently. Viola has come to expect and understand this. The drinks here are always more lukewarm than hot. Some of the residents, particularly in Phase One, are healing from terrible events or detoxing from drugs or alcohol, and they can be unruly or violent. Viola has never been any of those things, but she appreciates why this rule is in place. Everything here is to protect the Querencia family and keep them safe.

Viola yawns, a wave of tiredness coming over her.

"You look like you could use some rest, Viola. Why don't you finish your drink and I'll leave you in peace."

Viola rubs her eyes. "Yes, I think that might be a good idea. I think Mirabelle's visit must have tired me out."

Viola's words slur and she doesn't just feel tired – she feels spaced out, drunk even. And is that drool coming out of the corner of her mouth? She wipes her chin on her sleeve and tries to look at Dana, but her eyes can't focus. She thinks she hears the woman stand and walk to the door, but the room is spinning and tilting now, and Viola feels an overwhelming urge to lie down and sleep.

Viola can hear two voices now. Dana and another person. A man. Duke, yes, Duke is here.

"We better be quick. For goodness' sake, Dana, how much did you give her? We can't do this if she's comatose."

"I gave her the exact same amount I always do. She must

have an empty stomach or something. I don't know, I'm sorry. I'll hold and prop her up from the back while you speak to her."

Viola feels Dana's presence behind her and leans into her gratefully.

"Take some deep breaths, Viola. You seem a little out of it." Viola does as she is asked and starts to feel a little more alert, enough to see Duke is crouching in front of her.

"Duke. Hi." She finds herself smiling at him, all thoughts of him not wanting her here no longer mattering.

"Hello, Viola. I hope you enjoyed your time with Mirabelle this morning?"

Viola smiles and then snorts unattractively. Where did that come from? She really must get a grip of herself.

"I've come with some good news, Viola, but I can see you're a little out of sorts. Are you okay to have a little chat?" Viola reaches out towards Duke. Her hands feel tingly and look ethereal as she raises them up in front of her face. She wiggles her fingers, watching them dance and blur. This is all very weird.

"Viola!" Dana's voice is sharp and feels as though it pierces through Viola's brain.

She winces as she feels a painful squeezing sensation in her shoulders. "Ow!"

Viola hears unintelligible muttering coming from behind her. Dana seems upset with her, but she can't recall why.

Duke speaks to her again. He is all out of focus, and nausea roils in Viola's stomach.

"I'm delighted to tell you that you have completed your Phase Two rehabilitation, and we feel you are ready to progress to Phase Three."

Viola feels a flush of happiness and pride before the horrible nausea returns with a vengeance. "That's... good. I'm so..." Viola finishes her sentence internally. Happy, she's so happy. Her mouth doesn't seem to receive the instructions to move and speak. But never mind, she's sure everything is fine. She's going to Phase Three, and she'll be able to see Mirabelle every day.

"To move to Phase Three, I need you to sign a couple of forms. Just about your new accommodation – all routine, I assure you."

Viola looks down and is surprised to see a pen in her hand. Did she pick it up? "I'm not feeling so good, Duke. I'm not sure I should be signing right now. Can I have a sleep first?"

She's sure she hears Duke sigh, but she must have been mistaken because he answers her so kindly.

"Of course not. I completely understand."

"Good. Great. I think I'll sleep now." Viola tries to lie down, but Dana holds her rigidly. What is wrong with this woman?

Duke continues. "That's absolutely fine, Viola. But if you aren't able to sign today, I will have to give your room to another resident, and you'll get the chance to move again in another month. Mirabelle will be so disappointed. But don't you worry about that. I'm sure she'll get over it eventually."

Viola's heart starts to race, intensifying the nausea. "No. No, I want to go to Phase Three. I want Mirabelle."

"Well, only if you're sure you can."

"Yes. I can. Give me... pen. I'll do... now." Viola reaches out her hand before realising she is already holding a pen. Did she pick it up? She doesn't remember doing that.

Duke holds out a clipboard and points to where Viola needs to sign. She can't read it, but if she tells him that, maybe he won't let her sign. She'll have to wait another whole month, and she doesn't want that. She wants to see Mirabelle every day. She wants to be Mirabelle's nanny. It's all she wants.

Viola signs and Duke pulls the clipboard away and swaps the paper she just signed with another one.

"What's this one?" Viola tries to bring the document into

focus, but she can't make out a single word. There's a dark blob on the top right-hand corner of the page. Is that the logo for her bank? That's weird. She prods her finger at the blob, which is confusingly moving in and out of focus.

"Why's this here?"

Duke leans in and talks quietly into Viola's ear. "If you want to move to Phase Three, sign the form. If you don't, give me back the pen, and I will leave you to sleep."

He jabs his thumb at the page, and without a second thought, Viola scribbles what she thinks is her signature next to it.

"Good. Thank you, Viola. Dana, could you please help Viola into bed and come back and check on her in a few hours."

"Of course, Duke."

Viola feels herself being guided onto the mattress, her head sinking into the soft pillow.

"Ah, Viola. I know you're uncomfortable around me because Mirabelle convinced you I didn't want you here." Viola wants to answer Duke back, but the pull of sleep is too tempting. "I wanted to let you go. I thought you had earned it. I was going to give you your freedom. I made a deal with you and planned to stick to it."

Viola lets the words wash over her.

She hears Dana pipe up briefly, "Duke, I hate to question you, but should you really be saying this to her?"

"She won't remember a thing when she wakes, my dear. Think about how easy it was to convince her she'd had a breakdown. I could say anything right now, and she wouldn't recall a single word."

Viola feels a hand stroking her hair. It's such a wonderful, comforting feeling, and she finds herself drifting further and further away.

"It was Mirabelle who wanted you to stay initially – that

much is true. Once she decided she wanted you in her life, I'm afraid your fate was sealed. I've no idea what she has planned for you. I love that girl with all my heart, but my word, she can be wicked. You missed your chance to escape, Viola. I've never granted that before, and I don't think I ever will again. Nobody has ever been allowed to visit Querencia and then leave. You're one of us now, Viola, and unfortunately for you, that means you no longer have any of your freedoms or a single penny to your name."

Viola hears the words, but they mean nothing to her, and they fall out of her brain just as quickly as they enter.

"See, Dana, she can hear me and respond, but nothing is making its way in properly. She's not making memories. That's the absolute beauty of it."

Viola hears Dana mumble something. What did Duke just say? Something about her memory, she thinks.

"Let me prove it to you." Duke leans in close to Viola's ear and whispers. His breath tickles, and Viola laughs, but then she forgets why and covers her mouth with her hand. "I sent that ambulance away, Viola. Mirabelle was upstairs sulking, and I just sent them away and told them it was the actions of a bored, naughty little girl. A few apologies, and they were on their way to the next emergency."

Viola notices tears wetting her cheeks and wonders what on earth is happening.

"Eli was born healthy, and Jillian, well, sadly, she didn't make it. But that's neither here nor there. She was simply a vessel for my bloodline. Completely disposable."

Nausea hits Viola violently, and all she wants is for the world to stop. For everything to be quiet and calm.

"Don't tell Mirabelle, though. She'd be furious." Viola hears Duke laugh and wonders who has said something funny.

"Mirabelle seems to have formed a special bond with you,

Viola, and I've learned the hard way that if you don't give her what she wants, she will find a way to take it."

Sleep is dragging Viola away now, and she wishes Duke would just stop talking and leave her alone. Before she falls into the blackness, Viola can just make out Duke's final words.

"Good luck, Viola. I think you're going to need it."

CHAPTER FORTY-TWO

MIRABELLE

I knew Viola would love it here. I can't believe Granddad was going to make her leave. He said he wouldn't even let her visit. How mean is that? Plus, he tried to do all of this behind my back. He's been getting really bad at remembering his place recently. I've definitely got to do something to get him back in line.

I tried to tell Daddy about it, but he didn't listen. After Mummy died, he got so weird. He couldn't even be excited about baby Eli, which I thought was terrible. I don't think he understood why I wasn't really sad about Mummy. But she hadn't been my mummy for very long, and to me, the best thing about her was that she had my baby brother in her tummy. Granddad definitely gets that at least, and I wish Daddy would catch up.

I'm not totally sure Granddad is telling me the truth about Mummy dying. I won't say anything yet, though. I'll keep that inside my brain for now. It could be useful in the future.

I'm just happy that Eli is okay. Actually, he's better than okay – he's fantastic. He can't do much yet, but I love the way he looks at me. I'm going to be the best big sister ever, and I know he'll love me more than anyone else in the whole wide world. And that's saying something!

All of this has made me really angry with Daddy and Granddad. They were upset when I stopped being nice to Wendy. But they'd all lied to me, so why should I be nice? And Daddy was upset again when I wasn't super sad about my new mummy dying. I wish they'd stop telling me how to feel about everything and just listen to me. I'll give them another chance, but if they keep being like this, I'll have to do something about it.

Anyway, Daddy is in Phase One now. He's kind of stopped talking and just cries a lot. I heard him say to Granddad that he wanted to leave, and he was saying loads of mean things about Querencia. I told Granddad that if Daddy didn't want to live with us anymore, he should just leave. Granddad didn't seem happy with that idea, but it makes perfect sense to me.

Eli and I are living with a new family now. They seem nice. They are younger than Mummy, Daddy, and Wendy, and sometimes they don't seem to know what they're doing, especially with Eli. But that's okay because I do. They seem really stressed when Eli cries or wakes up at night. I've heard them arguing about it, but as long as they give Eli everything he needs, I won't get angry. I'm keeping a really close eye on them.

Something else brilliant that has happened is the new school here. I told Granddad that the old one was absolute rubbish, and I wanted to go to a real school where I could make lots of friends so badly that I almost left Querencia to live with Viola. That definitely got Granddad's attention. And I wasn't lying, either. We were almost at the end of the street when I realised I couldn't do it. What if Eli and I ended up getting split up from each other? That would be the worst thing ever. I wasn't sure what to do, so I yelled for Saul and Ezekiel. They're like my bodyguards, and even though they don't say very much,

I like having them around. They never argue with me or lie to me, at least.

Viola went completely nuts, though. She tried to drag me down the street. I feel bad, but I had to trip her up. Then Saul jabbed her with that stuff that makes people go all sleepy. I didn't want them to knock her out, but she wasn't listening to anything I was saying. It was like she was throwing a tantrum. It was embarrassing.

Viola is doing so much better now. I love how excited she is whenever I go and visit her. It makes me feel really important. Soon, she'll be allowed to see me every day, which will be brilliant as long as she doesn't start being weird again.

When Eli is a bit bigger, maybe when he's able to walk, I've decided I'd like a little sister. I'm not sure how that will work now that my and Eli's mummy is dead, but I will always find a way to have my perfect family.

Granddad knows how important it is to keep me happy, and if he forgets, I have lots of ways to remind him.

THE END

ALSO BY CHARLOTTE STEVENSON

The Serial Killer's Son

———————

The Guests

ACKNOWLEDGEMENTS

This book is dedicated to my daughter, Hannah. Thank you for listening while I told you the entire plot and for helping me brainstorm titles. This one is for you, beautiful girl.

Firstly, thank you for reading *The Family Next Door*. It means the world to me that you took the time to read something I wrote, and I appreciate every single one of my readers. Thank you from the bottom of my heart.

I remain overwhelmed by the care and support from the entire team at Bloodhound Books.

Thank you to Betsy and Fred for their continued belief in my books and my writing. You have made my dreams come true, and I am so incredibly grateful.

To the wonderful Abbie, you are the most fabulous and supportive editor, and I feel very fortunate to have been able to work with you again. What you do is akin to magic, and I am in awe of your talent.

To Tara, for not only making the inside of my book look amazing, but also for being only a message away throughout my entire writing journey. You are an absolute star, and I hope you know how much I value you.

To Patricia Dixon, who read this story first and helped me craft it into what it is today. Your guidance and friendship mean the world to me, not to mention your talent. If I ever become half the writer you are, I will be delighted.

To Hannah and Lexi for all your hard work in getting my

books out into the world and answering my many, many daft questions. You are fabulous at what you do.

To my amazing husband, who continues to listen to me talk incessantly about writing and supports me every step of the way. And to our three amazing children, I love you all more than I could ever say.

A NOTE FROM THE PUBLISHER

Thank you for reading this book. If you enjoyed it please do consider leaving a review on Amazon to help others find it too.

We hate typos. All of our books have been rigorously edited and proofread, but sometimes mistakes do slip through. If you have spotted a typo, please do let us know and we can get it amended within hours.

info@bloodhoundbooks.com